The citizens of Washington, DC, were lucky the bank robbers' escape truck didn't explode at the Federal Triangle Station.

FBI agents Hayes and Montagna take over the investigation, convinced the robbers will strike again and become more ruthless with every successful assault.

While Agent Hayes tries to keep pace with his lover's kinky bedroom fantasies, Agent Montagna has trouble dealing with his ex-wife's past and his immediate future, booze and bullets alike.

Blind Trust

ISBN: 978-1-4874-2340-7
Cover art by Martine Jardin

Published by eXtasy Books Inc or
Devine Destinies, an imprint of eXtasy Books Inc

Look for us online at:
www.eXtasybooks.com or www.devinedestinies.com

Blind Trust
Nick and Jacklyn Book 3

By

Ann Raina

Dedication

Muse, there isn't a time I'm not amazed at your insight, understanding, and unconditional dedication to the course of writing.

Chapter One

Nicolas Hayes glanced at his friend and partner, Jason Beckham, as he drove them back toward their office. "Tell me, Jason, why do you read your girlfriend's books even though you don't like them? That's . . . ridiculous. It's like going to a karaoke bar when you don't like singing."

"Oh, I do like it, but Elaine gets goosebumps every time I miss the note. I'm restricted to bathroom operas."

Nicolas snorted and rolled his eyes when Jason smirked. "Come on! It'd be like me taking a trip to the Caribbean even though I don't like swimming."

"You don't like swimming? You? The personification of a classic athlete—*can't* . . . or *won't* swim?"

Nicolas growled. "I can swim. I just don't like it. But that's not the point, right?"

Jason squirmed on the passenger seat and made a face. "I thought it'd please her if I showed interest in her interests. And since she's a bookworm, I thought reading her favorite authors would be the right thing." He lifted his gaze to the roof. "I didn't know what I was in for. After four books, I still don't know what to say to her. The stories are awful . . . tear-jerkers. Dripping honey right between the pages."

"But then you're cheating, right? You don't like to read. You hardly make it through the manuals of our training courses."

"They're so damn long."

"*You* read the summaries and leave the long versions to me."

Jason grunted and looked out the side window. "Do you like to take your lovely Mrs. France bowling?"

"Yes! And she wants to join us, if that was your next question."

"She's a terrible bowler, and she doesn't seem to improve."

"So what?" He shrugged. "We have fun together."

"Do you also take her to football games?"

"No." Nicolas huffed at Jason's grumpy tone. "I go with my friends. She says football's not a game she even wants to understand." He glanced at Jason. "If you don't want to read Elaine's books, just don't. She'll understand."

Jason's voice dropped. "I don't wanna blow this relationship."

"You won't. Honesty never ruins a relationship. Look, Jacklyn and I don't lie to each other. That's what makes our relationship—"

The squawk of the police radio echoed through the car, and Jason reached over to turn up the volume to hear the voice of a young officer.

"Dispatch, armed robbery at the Sun Savings Bank, twelve-hundred New York Avenue Northwest. Shots fired. We're—"

A crackling of static interrupted, and the officer added urgently, "Need support!"

"We're close by and could assist," Jason said.

Nicolas nodded, and Jason grabbed the mic. Before he could respond, the police officer was talking again.

"We're under fire! We have to retreat! Suspects are on the move in a black Nissan van, no logos, driving east!"

Jason pressed the button. "This is FBI Agent Beckham. We're giving chase at Thirteenth Street Northwest. How many suspects?"

"Three. At least two armed with *Beretta 93R* 9mm Machine Pistols. Proceed with caution."

"Roger that."

Nicolas hit the gas to take the corner, and Jason needed two attempts to put the mic back in its cradle.

"*Beretta 93Rs*, really? Is someone overreacting? Those are counter-terrorism guns." Jason turned on the siren and the blue lights.

A small *VW* hit the brakes and swerved to the right lane, blocking a white postal service truck. Honking followed. The black van with the suspects was speeding two cars ahead.

"They won't get far in the traffic," Nicolas murmured. "Unless they know a detour I don't."

"Fly? You appear to be trying to lift off." Jason clung to the door handle like his life depended on it.

Nicolas had both hands on the wheel and his focus fixed on the lanes ahead.

Five minutes earlier, Jason had laughed and called the day *freakily relaxing* with just one case report left to write in the afternoon. They had quipped about their boss, Sullivan, and whether he'd drop a pile of files on their desks just to quash their grins. Jason had voted to finish the report as soon as possible and sneak off without their superior noticing. Their plans had consisted of pizza and beer at a bar close to the Potomac and talking about their girlfriends.

Nicolas was gaining on the fugitives when the escaping van switched lanes and took a sharp left turn onto Pennsylvania Avenue at high speed. A truck in front of him came to a skittering halt, hitting the fender of the car ahead of them. The sound of crashing metal was deafening. The radio announced all units of the Metropolitan Police were ordered to answer the call for assistance. Nicolas slammed on his brakes for a driver who had lost control of his motorcycle and was skidding across the pavement throwing off sparks. While he steered the car around the bike, the van was gaining distance down the avenue.

"Damn it! What're they doing?" Nicolas hit the gas pedal again.

Jason reported their position to police headquarters.

The fishtailing van sped toward the next intersection and took a right turn on Twelfth Street at the last moment, cutting off a small Mazda and causing it to crash into a parked Mercedes. The car's alarm went off, but the sound was swallowed by other cars honking and coming to a skidding halt.

Nicolas changed lanes and turned right at a red light while the rest of the traffic came to a full stop.

Jason cursed. "They'll try Ninth Street to get on the Three-Ninety-Five!"

"We'll get to them before they make it." Nicolas swerved the car around a parked van. "What about support?"

"We've got two demonstrations going on as we speak. Police forces are thin but coming."

The radio announced messages about police cars being redirected to assist the FBI agents while Nicolas used the gap between two trucks to change lanes and got the van back into view. It passed an old Lincoln Town Car and swerved right onto the curb at the Federal Triangle, then stopped diagonally behind a sedan, blocking a lane. Honking started as the cars accumulated in the clogged lane.

Nicolas cursed under his breath while he raced in the second lane. The doors of the van opened, and three men with small backpacks jumped out and ran across the sidewalk toward the metro entrance, nimbly avoiding crashing into pedestrians. They were tall and looked like heavyweights, but they were also agile and fast. None of them turned around, as if they knew they were still ahead of the police.

"Fuck them!" Jason was out of the car first. "We gotta catch 'em before they reach the metro!"

Nicolas killed the engine, grabbed the key, and followed Jason through a throng of pedestrians toward the semi-darkness of the stairs. Jason was right in front of him and pushed a young man out of his way. To his left, a white Pomeranian was yapping and jumping. The old lady on his other side called to the dog while Jason was trying to step around it but tripped over the leash.

"What the hell!" Jason accidentally kicked the dog, and it flew against the handrail as he tried to grab the rail for balance. He missed and fell downstairs, bumping against more passengers emerging from the tunnel, finally coming to a stop three yards down the steps. Jason cried out. Someone cursed, one woman stopped to assist him, but Jason waved her away.

"Dadgummit! You stupid moron," the old woman yelled as she shuffled forward. "You hurt my dog. Now, *you* get out of my way," she demanded of a young woman with a large backpack. She bent to disentangle her whining dog. Two passengers helped her check whether the small Pomeranian was all right.

Nicolas moved around them and leaped down three steps to crouch beside his partner. "Are you okay?"

Jason grimaced holding his left knee. "Yeah. Go, get 'em. I'll call for assistance."

"Okay." Nicolas was back on his feet and jumped to the end of the stairs. He had the image of the three bank robbers in his mind as he scanned the tunnel and the people coming and going. He was tall enough to have a good view over the heads of the crowd but couldn't find the group he was looking for. He hastened on, trying to look in every direction until he spotted a man with black curly hair, a light brown jacket, and a brown backpack heading toward the platform of the blue line.

Nicolas ran as fast as he could, never taking his focus off the suspect. He was getting closer when the man vanished into a tunnel to his left. Nicolas pushed through a group of foreigners studying the map of metro stations and turned the corner. The man with black curly hair was nowhere in sight.

Nicolas kept searching, not believing he could've lost the guy. People stared at him, and someone complained about his rudeness. Nicolas ignored them, but he had to admit the bank robbers had vanished.

"Where did they go?" Hands propped on his hips, he took a deep breath, still hoping he'd spot the suspect in the crowd, but after a minute realized he'd been outwitted by three clever robbers. He ran a hand over his hair and jogged back to his partner.

Police officers fanned out, searching the station and its vicinity. Nicolas' description of the three robbers was passed to the staff attached to the case, and two officers were assigned to check the video surveillance of the time frame. Additional forces were ordered to search the vicinity of the bank building for evidence.

Nicolas heard the siren of the ambulance until it stopped outside the station. Jason was still sitting on the steps leading to the platforms, sweating. He pressed his lips tight but couldn't seem to suppress a groan.

"Sorry, pal, that was a stupid accident," Jason mumbled, trying to smile but failing.

"I should've been faster." Nicolas wiped his brow. Despite the November cold, his shirt was clammy and clung to his back. The thick woolen jacket he wore was too small and constricting. "I don't know how I could've missed him."

"Police got the video surveillance. We'll find him. Them. They can't have vanished so easily." Jason touched his arm to get his attention. "Keep going. Look at me. I'll be some freaking three-legged creature for a week."

Two medics arrived, and Nicolas made way for them as they asked Jason questions about the accident and his condition. Nicolas only half listened to Jason's clipped replies, his mind still on the quick disappearance of the three men. He had heard of a rapid change of clothes, even hairdos, but had thought the gangsters would have needed more time to change so completely.

"Maybe they had help," Jason said when the medics helped him stand on one foot to carry him upstairs. "Check the videos. I bet you'll find them."

Nicolas nodded without agreeing and followed toward the sidewalk. "Going to the George Washington University Hospital?"

"Yes, sir." The medic was a good-natured Afro-American with a round face and short graying hair. "You following?"

Nicolas smiled wryly. "I'll help make sure you don't drop wisenheimer on the way."

Jacklyn raised her brows at the unexpected visitor in front of her apartment door. "Harry Fuller. What brings you here on this rainy afternoon?"

"May I come in?"

Jacklyn stepped back, and Harry walked past her, his smile quickly dying and his chin dropping to his chest. His eyes were deeply shadowed, like he hadn't slept for days. He appeared older than his forty-five years as he shuffled through the room. She remembered him smelling of expensive cologne instead of sweat, but she was far from feeling commiserative. "You'd better have a good reason to drop by on my day off instead of calling me. I do have a phone, you know." She closed the door and followed him as he took off his thick winter coat. "Don't get too comfortable. Spill the beans."

Harry put the coat across the couch and turned back to her with an all-encompassing gesture. "Nice home. Very cozy. And still with a man's touch to it. I imagined you'd have more knickknacks."

"Wrong answer." Jacklyn buttoned her blouse and wished she hadn't dressed casually, but she didn't intend on inviting Harry to stay and chat about old times. "What do you want?"

Though impeccably dressed, Harry was in a state of disarray. He needed a shave, and his hair was long and shaggy. "Don't you understand that I need some . . . comfort after what happened?" He released a shuddering breath and slumped on the couch. His smile indicated he was close to crying. "My only son's been imprisoned."

"For committing serious crimes." She brought a pitcher of juice and two glasses from the kitchen. She sat down on the couch, keeping plenty of space between them. "Don't even ask for wine or anything else. It's way too early for booze."

"I'm not complaining." Harry took the glass she offered. Once more, his lips twitched, as if he'd forgotten how to smile. The wrinkles on his face seemed deeper than before. "Thanks. You know, so far, the public prosecutor has built his case against Kevin attempting to kill Greg Woolsey on circumstantial evidence." He sipped some juice and held the glass in his trembling hands. "A psychiatrist was called to assist in the interrogation, and I bet now that he knows him, he'll try some dirty tricks to lure Kevin to confess."

"You still think Kevin isn't the serial killer?" Jacklyn had goosebumps all over her body. The memory of the murders and her boyfriend's involvement in catching the killer was still vivid.

It was true, though, that the evidence collected didn't suffice to bring Kevin down and sentence him if he didn't confess. Harry looked at her, and she understood that—as a father—he would believe in his son's innocence to the last moment.

"The murders stopped after his arrest, and his friend confessed he helped him prepare at least one crime site." Jacklyn kept her voice flat. "Don't think Kevin will be treated unfairly.

The trial will be held soon, then we'll see how much can be proven."

Harry shook his head and went on after a pause. "So much violence. So much bad influence on the business. It's terrible . . . and not over yet."

"Have you come to complain about your company taking the blame for your son's actions? Get real!" Jacklyn frowned.

"No. Of course not."

She didn't believe his contrite look.

"But . . . still . . . the last four months haven't been easy. Police questioned my employees and me several times. We've been under scrutiny as if we had something to do with the case! Can you imagine? And I have to appear in court to explain for the umpteenth time that I didn't know of my son's . . . activities. If there were any." He hung his head. "I employed him like many other young men and women. And while I'm feeling bad enough for whatever happened, my business goes down the drain because people don't want to be associated with the club and me." He looked up with pain-filled eyes. "Don't you understand? I'll need a year to get back on track. And the club's my baby. I don't want to close it, but at the moment, it's not making any profits."

Jacklyn was touched by his despair. "You probably need a marketing change. Maybe change the program, too, to appeal to a different audience and make them forget about the . . .connection."

Harry's face lit up. He took a deep breath, and this time, his smile was honest. "Wow, that's . . . really a great idea! Hey, it's perfect. Thank you."

"As if you haven't tried—"

"No. So far, I've been occupied with writing statements, contacting my lawyer about everything and nothing, and trying to run the rest of my business smoothly and not lose money." He reached out, but Jacklyn's warning gaze made him drop his hand. "Okay, so I'll just say a heartfelt *thank you*. I knew it'd be a good idea to come to you." He put down the glass on the table. His voice was light. "You know, Richard understands, but he's a guy . . . well, most of the day, I'd say. You, on the other hand, have the female touch I needed right now."

Jacklyn emptied her glass and got up to put more distance between them. "I still think it wasn't one of your best ideas to come to the home of the FBI agent who arrested your son. So, before Nick walks through that door and sees you, I'm asking you to leave."

"It's your home, Jacky. He's just a fucking roommate." He leaned back into the cushions, portraying the sincere businessman. "I could change that."

Jacklyn counted to ten before she answered. "If you're about to offer me another apartment in DC, I say no. Not in this lifetime. Please, leave."

"First, you'll listen to my offer."

Nicolas spent part of the afternoon at the hospital to learn that Jason had suffered a grade-two sprain of the medial ligament of his left knee and would stay for a day or two to make sure there wasn't more damage. Jason had endured the examinations stoically, pressing his lips tight. His relief at seeing the new love in his life, Elaine, walk through the door of the hospital room was obvious. Nicolas understood the message and left.

Back at the office, reports about the robbers' vehicle were in his email. The city had been lucky the van hadn't blown up as the criminals had planned. There had been an incendiary device behind the front seats, but for some reason, it hadn't ignited. An explosion at the Federal Triangle resulting in numerous people wounded or dead would have been a disaster.

The van had been taken to the CSU department for further inspection.

Police forces had searched the vicinity of the bank for evidence of their preparations. So far, no traces had been found.

Police officers had secured video surveillance of the metro station for Nicolas to check, and he spent two hours looking at various camera angles. Watching the three robbers blend in with such elegance, he was—in a wicked way—astonished at their professionalism. While hurrying through the station, they had quickly taken off their backpacks, reversed their jackets, and put on wigs and false beards they had under their clothes. None of them had dumped suspicious material or lost parts of the disguise during the hectic chase. They had also escaped direct face recognition by pulling up hoods or putting on baseball caps, which they had carried in the inner pockets of their jackets.

Their escape appeared planned, rehearsed, and practiced, which led Nicolas to search data banks for more information concerning bank robberies in the vicinity using the same modus operandi. To increase the number of hits, he expanded his query to include up to four robbers, which according to the reports on his desk was how the robbery had been pulled off.

While waiting for the results, Nicholas continued his review of the reports. The robbers had worn gloves and face masks inside the bank. They had shot a guard behind the entrance, and he was in critical condition. The police officers outside the bank had gotten away unharmed, but their service car was totaled. The robbers' *93Rs* had been found in the van and were currently being checked for hints concerning their origin.

The query results showed two similar robberies. The first one had taken place in Germantown in a small and minimally secured bank. A guard had been clubbed unconscious with the butt of a hand gun, and the employees had handed out the money quickly without further resistance. Three days later, the second robbery had occurred in Tysons Corner. The robbers had looted ten thousand dollars within three minutes after injuring a guard with a bullet in the shoulder. A cashier had told the police he'd thought the robbers would shoot all the people present, so he and two colleagues had placed the money on the counters for the thugs to grab.

In both cases, the men's disguises had been similar but with different wigs and bulky biker jackets. The report stated one man had worn a green hoodie with—supposedly—the logo of the *New York Jets*.

The FBI had gotten notice of the robberies but hadn't mandated an extensive investigation. After the third robbery and the increased violence, the call was out now for a thorough operation.

Senior Agent Sullivan officially dropped the case on Nicolas' desk, stating that his experience at the Federal Triangle made him the expert for solving this crime. With his usual grumpy order to *get the job done yesterday,* Sullivan went into his office, ignoring Nicolas' rebuke that solving bank robberies wasn't one of his tasks. Sullivan hissed that they were short on active agents and slammed his door.

Nicolas reclined, reviewed the reports, and added them to the profile he'd laid out on the whiteboard. He missed Jason's input as much as his jokes to lighten the mood—even more so when he overheard their boss browbeating a colleague over a minor mistake in an investigation.

Nicolas finished the first report for his superior and quickly headed out of the office.

The hand across his mouth was calloused and so strong Matthew feared his teeth would break. He tasted blood in his mouth. The man's thumb at his nose cut off his breath and left him suffocating and in such pain that his eyes watered. In a panic, he grabbed for the strong upper arms but couldn't break his opponent's grip.

White dots danced in front of his eyes, and he was about to lose consciousness. Fear gave him strength for another attempt, so he rammed his elbow into the man's belly, but to no avail. The attacker pressed harder and punched Matthew's liver with his other hand. Pain shot through his body, breaking his resistance, and his knees buckled.

"Listen carefully, Montagna, we don't suffer scum like you here!"

He knew the dark voice hissing in his ear. He knew the portly man who had wrestled him to the floor, and the distinct smell of his cranberry-flavored breath mints.

"Leave for good, or take your last breath on the street! There're ways to get rid of you, asshole!"

The pressure was suddenly gone, and Matthew lay on the floor of his house, coughing and panting for air. The heavy door banged shut, and steps faded across the porch. The last thing he heard was a heavy Italian curse.

Matthew Montagna woke, soaked with sweat, his hands clenching the pillow. A guttural sound escaped him as his body shook uncontrollably. He squinted into the darkness, illuminated by the faint streetlight shining through the curtains. His heart was beating fast, and for a minute, he listened to his strained breathing and the low sounds of traffic before he was able to sit on the side of the bed. He ran both hands through his hair and across his bearded face. Shivering, he discarded the clammy t-shirt and groped for a fresh one in the drawer beside his bed.

Unable to go back to sleep, he shuffled into the kitchen to get a drink of water and looked around the half-decorated rooms. He had moved from Chicago two weeks earlier. Most of his stuff was still packed. Friends had stated he was just changing one big city for another, but Matthew had lived in the concrete jungle of Illinois for too long to go anywhere else and feel at home. For now, DC was just a place he had to live.

He touched the coffee maker he'd bought three years ago. Nerina had commented it was way too expensive and useless, and that she'd be glad to get rid of it. Matthew sighed. He had left behind so much more than his house in the suburbs of Chicago.

He put the empty glass in the dishwasher that still smelled new. FBI headquarters had generously paid for his move, and the other employees provided assistance of different kinds, including generous proposals to show him around so he could get acquainted with his new workplace. He had accepted the offers for tours through downtown to learn street names and places. He had carefully listened to tidbits about the DC agents and their work attitude.

The apartment the real estate agent had found for him was spacious, freshly renovated, and would serve until he could find a house in the suburbs—more like his old place. He wouldn't call the apartment a *home*, even if he stacked the bookshelves with his books and filled the cupboards and walk-in closets with his wardrobe and other items he had brought. Most of the boxes were still unopened, and he had no intention of opening them soon. Too many memories were connected to photographs, medals, and knickknacks collected over the years. A neighbor had regretfully claimed he packed his life in boxes, and Matthew had agreed heavyheartedly.

So far, he'd only unpacked his business suits and dress shirts, the two pairs of shoes he needed, and accessories for the kitchen and bathroom.

He leaned against the counter and grabbed the telephone to call his best friend, Bert, in Chicago, but put it back after glancing at the wall clock. It was way too early for a chat. Bert would call him the *nasty Italian*, drawl his nickname—*Monty*—as if he was drunk, and sink back into his bed after a gush of swear words.

The image of his feisty friend and his abnormal desire for sleep, triggered a quick smile. Matthew checked the alarm clock and returned to bed.

Jacklyn could tell by the way Nicolas put down his backpack and took off his coat and shoes he'd had a stressful day. She cocked her head as she approached him, smiling tentatively. In the year they had been together, she'd learned to read the signs—how he walked in, how he doffed his clothes, how he looked at her. Right then, his eyes were bloodshot, his movements slow and weary. She worried he'd drop what he was holding, so she stood behind him and helped him peel off his suit jacket.

"Too much hard work, hmm?"

"You can't imagine." Nicolas pulled her in his arms and whispered in her hair. "But I'm glad I'm home."

Jacklyn had goosebumps on her arms and a bad feeling in her stomach. "Did anything terrible happen?" They parted, and she put the jacket on a hanger.

"That depends." He walked to the bathroom and left her no choice but to follow. He took off his dress shirt and pants and swayed on one foot to get rid of the socks. "I botched up catching three bank robbers, and Jason fell down the stairs at the metro and is in the hospital with an injured knee." He glanced at her. "So, judge for yourself if it was terrible."

She rubbed his shoulder gently. His muscles were tense, and he reeked of sweat. "I know you work hard and try your best, but . . . in my eyes, you are perfect. I'm glad Jason wasn't hurt severely, and I'm convinced you'll catch the bad guys. You're good at your job, no matter what happened today." She kissed him chastely, enjoying the stubble tickling her skin. "Take a shower, and I . . . or do you want me to stay?" She frowned at his begging gaze. "Just say it."

"Stay."

Jacklyn bit her lower lip, trying and failing to suppress a smile. "As you wish."

She took off her clothes and joined him in the shower. Standing behind him, she reached for the shower gel as he leaned against her, moaning quietly. He rolled his shoulders in the warm spray and grabbed her hips. Giggling because she had trouble reaching around him to pour gel in her hand, she kissed him between the shoulder blades, content with his reaction. He pressed his hands against the tiles and hung his head in the rain of water while she took pleasure in washing his body.

Never in her life, had she had a lover with such a trained physique—a man used to sports and martial arts, a man who kept himself lean and healthy without a woman urging him. Nicolas Hayes was six foot two, a gentleman, and a very talented special agent with the FBI, a fact she had learned to respect. In consequence, Jacklyn accepted his odd working hours, tiredness, and—occasionally—his bad moods. However, after she had won him over, she hadn't regretted a single day.

"If I scrub you any longer, your skin will peel off."

He turned and wiped the water off his face. "We could change places."

She burst out laughing. "Naw, it wasn't me stinking like a bear after hibernation!"

"Oh, that's how you see me? A bear? Thanks a lot!"

"Minus the fur, but—"

Nicolas pulled her close and kissed her. When they parted, he smiled and appeared much more at ease.

Jacklyn sighed. "I so love the way you make up for your grumpiness."

He put his hands on her butt. "Do you want me to help you make dinner?"

She frowned and pointedly looked down along their touching bodies. "What kind of dinner are you talking about?"

He turned off the water. "The one with you being my dessert, which I—since it's my choice—will devour before the main course."

Jacklyn lifted her chin and raised her brows. "You're talking about devouring me? What about me and my hunger? I've been deprived of your presence the whole day." She fetched another kiss. "How hungry are you?"

His next kiss was the answer and then some, and Jacklyn melted in his arms.

Katherine smashed her bag on the table, took off her coat, and glared at the joyous group of four men handing out beer bottles and chips and giving high-fives to each other as if celebrating the super bowl win. She counted to five before she opened her mouth.

"Tell me, all of you, are you out of your fucking minds?" The men fell silent. "Is that what you call *professional*? You busted this! You almost got caught!" She looked at Herman—*Manny* to his friends—her eldest brother, who was the only one able to stand her glare. "Tell me, Manny, how's it possible that officer was so close on your heels you could smell his cologne?"

Herman, tall and broadly built, flashed a cocky smile and opened his arms wide. He could've embraced his younger brothers and his sister in one swoop. "He wore aftershave? Man, I didn't notice that!" The other men laughed. Herman quickly lifted a hand to stop Kate's reply. "Hey, calm down, okay? We got away. Plans B and C worked smoothly. No one got hurt—"

"None of us," Benjamin cut in, lifting a bottle of beer and

receiving nods and cheers from his brothers.

"Okay, none of us." Herman exchanged a high-five with Benjamin. "We saved most of the money and escaped smooth as a baby's butt. That's all that counts."

"Don't say . . ." Katherine looked from Herman to Benjamin and his twin, Theodor, then to their friend, Tom, who had driven the van. Their expressions were of mild amusement and—to her chagrin—contentment. "That's how you see it? It's enough for you that you had such a narrow escape?"

She took the small glass Benjamin handed her and looked around. The scent of malt whiskey reminded her of the evening before when they had sat together to review the plan one last time. She had anticipated the robbery would run as smoothly as the previous ones. Katherine had thought they all knew their places and actions by heart.

She took a deep breath before she continued. "And that the van didn't burn? That's just bad karma, or what? Come on, don't gimme that shit!" She gulped down the whiskey and slammed the glass on the table, then pointed at Herman. "You screwed up! What about the cameras at the metro station? Are you sure you didn't get caught? Seen? You know nothing."

"Fuck, Kate, stop bickering! I just can't take it anymore." Theodor poured himself a drink while he shook his head. "You're right. The van didn't blow up, and one of us might or might not be on tape. So what?" He shrugged. "We've changed disguises every time. Who'll know it's us?"

Katherine loved her brothers dearly, but at that moment, she wanted to knock their heads on the table. She only restrained herself because they were stronger, and she'd have embarrassed herself trying to wrestle one of them. Instead, she turned her glare on Theodor. "*Who'll know?* The fucking FBI will know. The two who chased you through the station were with the FBI, not metro police. That means they have stacked up personnel and will be much more alert to every unusual move around the banks in DC. We've got to leave this turf, or we'll get caught."

"Well, *we'll* get caught. That's right. Not you." Herman's deep voice carried, though he spoke quietly. "You'll sit somewhere safe in a car and judge our work."

Before Katherine replied, Herman lifted his hand to stop her.

"Right, you do the planning. We got that. And you worry. Fine. But, hey, did you notice that our asses are at stake every time we go out there?" He looked around for the other men's approval. "So, stop throwing shade at us, will ya? Give us some credit. We do what we can. And we *did* get away, okay? Acknowledge that at least." Smiling like a winner, he toasted her with a bottle of beer.

"I've planned these robberies meticulously."

She watched Tom take off his overcoat to reveal muscled arms. If you didn't look closely, you could mistake him for the fourth brother of the group—the introverted thinker in contrast to the boasting others. Looking at him, mellowed her anger. He met her gaze, and his apparent desire sped up her heartbeat. She wanted to embrace him and call it a day.

She collected her thoughts and continued in the same stern voice. "I work hard to make sure you all get out. Don't gimme that blah-blah about *credit* because it's your ass that'd be taken to jail. If you had followed my plan every step, no one would've been in danger." Katherine accepted a second glass of whiskey and knocked it back quickly.

"Who could've known the FBI would show up?" Herman put down the already empty bottle with a frown and stretched for another one. "We thought the police were occupied with guarding the demonstrations. You can't put the blame on us. We made the best of it."

Katherine fumbled for a hair tie to bind back her curly hair. "Why didn't the van blow up? Was something wrong with the fuse? Ben, didn't you check it?"

"Why not watch the news?" Benjamin hit the button of the remote. "I bet it's the top story of the night."

Katherine felt the alcohol kick in and dissolve the tension she'd endured since the FBI car had sped up behind the van. For fifteen painful minutes, she'd been afraid that her brothers and Tom would get caught. Though she'd been relieved seeing them unharmed, their sloppiness bothered her.

She shrugged, discarded her cardigan, and slumped on the couch. Theodor glanced at her with his dark blue eyes. Like his twin, Benjamin, he had an angelic face, a fair complexion, and blond hair. Without effort, he could charm the ladies and get any woman he wanted, no matter what the time or place. He smiled at her, then turned toward the kitchen to take care of dinner. She heard him open the fridge as her stomach grumbled.

Herman pulled up a chair and sat with his bulky forearms propped on the backrest. It galled her to find him at ease, even smiling, but that was his way of dealing with stress. He joked and moved on as if danger didn't mean anything to him. Katherine was torn between scolding and applauding his attitude. She'd always envied his easy-going manner.

The anchorman of the local news station had a serious expression. "According to police sources, the bank robbery was executed with brutal force. The wounded guard is still in critical condition. The bank's tellers and customers are being treated for shock and minor injuries. The robbers looted about fifteen thousand dollars—"

"Yeah, and we almost got it all!" Theodor clapped his hands.

"—and got away by dumping their van at the Federal Triangle to slip through police forces securing the station. One officer was injured during the chase, and the police assume the three robbers escaped on one of the trains during the turmoil. So far, the perpetrators haven't been identified. The FBI has taken over the investigation and is examining video surveillance footage. If you have any information about the robbers, contact your local police department or the FBI. There is a reward for clues leading to their arrest."

Benjamin turned to Katherine. "See? They don't know shit."

Katherine lowered her chin and snorted. "Since when do the police give all their information to the media? The FBI will strip down the van and the weapons for evidence. Is there anything you haven't told me so far?" Once more, she glared at the men. "Like leaving chewing gum for their DNA experts? Or someone working without gloves? No? Okay, so you may have survived this one." She got up again to pace back and forth through the room, gesturing with both hands. "Still, I don't understand why the van didn't blow up. What the fuck happened?" She stopped and turned her attention back to her brothers. "Ben? What happened?"

"I don't know." Ben dropped his gaze and then—as if gathering strength—looked back at the TV program. "Must've been something wrong with the fuse," he growled.

Katherine was silent for a moment and pursed her lips. "Fact is, the plan for our next coup is gone, ruined, smashed to smithereens. *Washington Trust and Loan* will live without being looted. I'll need time to come up with another target."

"Fine." Theodor bobbed his head and put down a bowl with fried rice. "As always, we'll stay out of the way, play it cool, and stand at attention whenever you call."

"Very funny." Herman slapped his younger brother's head. "Why not ask what she's got in her mind? Maybe we can help with the preparations." He smiled amiably at her. "What do you want us to do?"

"Stay low-key and don't bully the neighbors."

Herman smirked. "I love you so much, sis."

CHAPTER TWO

"The news about the bank robbery is today's top story." Jacklyn pushed back a strand of her dark brown hair. She turned the paper on the breakfast table for Nicolas to see. "The FBI's holding back information, right? You know more than that or . . . not?"

Nicolas swallowed the last bite of his cereal before he got up. "We know they're hardcore criminals who aren't afraid of killing someone, and that frightens me. I also know they won't stop until they get caught. Imagine two heavily armed men dealing with the bank accountants and another one waiting in the car, ready to break through barriers." He shook his head and emptied the coffee cup. "Not to mention that the van was supposed to blow up. At Federal Triangle! The city's lucky that didn't happen." He put on his jacket and kissed her cheek.

She got a whiff of his aftershave, sending her mind back to the bedroom where their day had started an hour ago. She wanted to pull him close, kiss him, and take him back to bed once more.

"After work, I'll visit Jason for half an hour, okay?"

Jacklyn tried to hide that she was getting grumpier with every delay. "What about your free day tomorrow? Does it still exist?"

"It does. If anything changes, I'll give you a call."

"It better not change. I've got so many plans."

"And I'm looking forward to them." He kissed her again and left.

Jacklyn stood at the window to watch him cross the street and get into his service car. She hadn't had the heart to bring up Harry's proposal and wondered whether Nicolas would approve.

The night before, Nicolas had been tired and taciturn. A satisfying meal, her monologue about funny news she'd heard, and a massage of his back and legs had helped him smile again. They had watched a movie together and gotten to bed early. He had kissed her goodnight and fell asleep immediately with a smile on his lips.

Jacklyn was grateful she was his lover and his support in hard times. Nicolas, six years younger than her, was an independent character. He was born and raised in Lynchburg with his father, a policeman, and his mother, a strong-willed and very strict person who had stayed at home to take care of the kids. He had a down-to-earth attitude and was one of the most hard-working men she knew.

She had the background of four wild and naughty years in Philadelphia and New York, was proud of her wide-ranging experience, and wouldn't give up her lifestyle under any circumstances. Some of her friends called her monogamous life boring these days. Some were happy she'd settled with the right man and called her blessed.

Jacklyn turned away from the window to get dressed.

During the first month of sharing her home, she'd agonized over whether their attitudes and ways of life matched. She had wanted to give her heart and herself to someone deserving her love, but without altering her expectations of a fulfilling relationship. She wasn't a woman to adopt a subordinate role and feel great. Her independence meant the world to her, and if any man tried to take it, she would revolt and leave. However, Nicolas hadn't challenged her. He wanted a coequal partner who spoke her mind, and he'd gotten much more.

Jacklyn sniggered when she left the kitchen to drive to her physiotherapist office. On Nicolas' next day off, he would find out—and not to his chagrin—how dominant she could be.

Matthew lifted his gaze off the memo he was reading when Senior Agent Sullivan called out to a new arrival striding into the large office. The agent wore the standard dark gray suit, was taller than six feet, blond with a crew cut, clean-shaven, and carried his broad shoulders well without straining for an upright bearing. His blue eyes made quick contact but focused on Mr. *No-nonsense* Sullivan a moment later. According to FBI regulations, the guy wore no jewelry, and the suit, tie, and shoes were of good quality but not expensive.

The man's shoulders dropped as he listened to Sullivan's words. Once more, his gaze met with Matthew's. In an instant, his look darkened, and Matthew got damp palms. He swallowed and looked at the page in front of him without reading.

Sullivan's smile looked as false as the *Breitling* watch he was wearing when both men approached Matt, who got up from his chair, trying for a friendly smile. The blond man seemed to resent him silently, his stoical expression meant to be blank.

"This is Agent Nicholas Hayes. You'll work with him," Sullivan grumbled. "Agent Matthew Montagna, from the field office in Chicago."

Agent Hayes shook Matthew's hand for the briefest time, then let go with an equally stoic nod of approval. Matthew rubbed his chin, telling himself he wouldn't act differently if the roles were reversed. Matthew dropped his sweaty hands to his sides and accidentally knocked on the table.

"Agent Beckham will be on sick leave for six weeks,"

Sullivan explained. He looked from Matthew to Agent Hayes, making it clear they were to behave professionally.

Matthew had already learned the senior agent accepted no irony, sarcasm, or humor of any flavor.

"Agent Montagna will support your investigation. He's dealt with bank robberies before." After a brief pause, he scowled at Matthew. "By the way, take an hour to get rid of that . . . scrubby beard. It might fit the Windy City, but it's certainly out of place here."

Matthew frowned, but held his tongue and broke eye contact.

Sullivan nodded to both of them curtly, and after briefly glancing at his watch, returned to his office.

Matt turned to his new partner. "I was already informed about the *Sun Savings Bank* robbery yesterday." He cleared his throat. "What have you got so far?"

Agent Hayes waited until Sullivan closed the door to his office. "My stomach's grumbling. I'll show you the cafeteria and brief you over a second breakfast."

Matthew smiled, relieved. "Sounds like a great idea."

"Let's see how many great ideas you've got after the biggest sandwich in DC."

Matthew didn't know whether this would turn into a competition, but he was game.

Katherine sat straight on her yoga mat, eyes wide open, focusing on her breathing as she put her palms together in front of her heart and dropped her shoulder blades. The turmoil in her mind was settled by practicing yoga whenever she found the time. She had started the art of yoga six years ago. Troubled in a way she couldn't comprehend, she'd turned to an old lady in the neighborhood who had performed her daily exercises on the porch. Her instructions had changed

Katherine's mood within two days. She had thanked the old lady profusely for guiding her to a new way of living. In the following years, she had learned about the secrets of yoga and the power it unleashed. The shelf behind her was stacked with yoga DVDs, and she knew most of the exercises by heart.

Done with her lesson, Katherine sat cross-legged and watched Herman bench-press two hundred pounds. His biceps and chest muscles bulged as he repeated the drill five times before he put down the barbell. Tom stood behind the bench, quietly waiting to see if his help was needed. He made eye contact with Katherine and broke it three seconds later when Herman sat up, running a hand through his short, sweaty hair.

"Did you make up your mind, sis?" Herman asked.

She studied Tom's face but was unable to decipher his mood. Even though he'd been on the team for a year, he hadn't told her much about his life in spite of their temporary closeness. When Herman followed Katherine's gaze, Tom broke eye contact once more. She couldn't tell if he wanted to be secretive or if he was ashamed.

"I'm still shocked about what happened yesterday."

Herman grinned. In the sunlight, his blond stubble looked like little spikes protruding from his angular chin. "You're too damn tough to be shocked or frightened." He got up, grabbed a towel, and wiped his face and upper body.

Tom's glance told Katherine he shared Herman's assumption. Their trust in her abilities made her heart beat fast and her stomach churn.

"So, what's next? A bank out of town?" her brother queried.

"We've got to change the approach completely." Katherine got up and rolled the mat to put it against the wall. She kept her voice flat. "No bank. The FBI will put up a profile. They might know about the other two banks and put them on the list with the others back in Illinois and Minnesota." She turned to grab her water bottle. "We might get caught if we try the same kind of assault another time."

"We'll be famous." Herman exchanged glances with Theodor who was rope-skipping on the other side of their private gym. "What's on your mind? I guess coffee shops like in the past won't do."

Katherine's glare triggered laughter. "Money transport," she said with conviction and walked through the room to open the patio door for a breath of fresh air. Looking into the garden always soothed her. She had planted rose bushes in three different colors around the well-trimmed lawn. Some of them still carried blossoms in spite of the chilly weather. Tom had stated the garden had a female touch. His words had been a warm rain of affection, and she remembered his hands on her shoulders and his breath against her neck. "And we won't do it in DC."

"Great," Herman said, and Tom nodded. "And when?"

"I haven't started planning yet! Three weeks, maybe four. I don't know. Herman, take some time and shave, please. You look like a scoundrel."

"Four weeks?" Theodor stopped skipping. His eyes were wide. "But . . . the money we got won't last that long!"

"You'll have to tighten your belt. If you try rushing me, then do your stuff alone, okay? And, no, Theo, that angry look won't change my mind. Take one whore less in town, and maybe . . . maybe party only on weekends."

"You don't—"

"Cut it out!" Herman lifted his hand to stop Katherine's anger, but his look was directed at his brother. "You heard her. Get a grip. Maybe start putting some money aside for another day." He turned to Katherine, grinning. "You don't like scoundrels? Since when?"

Theodor dropped the skipping rope and approached his

elder brother. "Oh, now you want to tell me how I've got to live my life?" He was almost as tall as Herman, yet narrow in the shoulders. He lifted his chin as he tried and failed to sound older than twenty-five. "I can do what I want with my money, okay? I can spend it on booze, games, women . . . don't you ever dare to put your nose in my stuff! I'm not asking what you do with your share of the loot, okay?"

"Yeah, bang another slut in town." Herman snorted and stood straight. "If that's all you want, go ahead. But don't come up to me again to ask for money." He slapped Theodor's shoulder and turned away. "Tom? It's okay. I'm done for now."

"It was my bro, bro!" Theodor shouted.

"No, it wasn't! Try to fool the rest of the world, but not your family, damn it!"

Katherine looked at Theodor. "He's right. You're a damn fool when it comes to money."

Theodor picked up the skipping rope and cocked his head. "Really? So what? Do you want to lecture me, too?"

She shook her head. "Don't go there. Spending all the money might seem fine right now, but one day I won't be there anymore and—"

"Why should you leave us?" Theo turned the rope in his hands. "We're a great team!"

Tom wiped the barbell with a towel and left the gym, taking his water bottle with him. The look he gave Katherine made her heart ache even more. He appeared so shy when others were around, and more than anything she wanted to spend time with him alone. With an effort, she turned to watch Theo rope-skipping again.

"Do you really think I'll do this for the rest of my life? Get real. I'll turn thirty this month, and though you might thrive on the thrill, I don't. I was shocked yesterday. That's no lie." She put down the bottle to retrieve her towel from the rowing machine. "While Benny got away from the roof undetected, the three of you almost got caught. I'm worried every time you walk into a bank and don't come out for five minutes. Don't you see that I want this family safe?"

"Well, winning a lottery could help with that. But so far . . ." Theodor flipped the rope twice as fast, speeding it up to a blur before he slowed down again. "And, yes, I know you'll say I wouldn't last a week with a fortune." He shrugged without missing a jump. "Yeah, you might be right. Hell, I like what we do. It's fun."

"Only until you get caught." Katherine shook her head when Theo laughed the danger away. She left the gym to take a shower and have a private word with Tom. After that, she'd start searching for a manageable goal.

Nicolas took his sandwich with ham and cheese, chose a coke and followed Agent Montagna, who ordered a salad with grilled chicken and a bottle of water. Montagna was of average height and weight, and the tailored suit indicated he did work out on a regular basis without stressing for a muscled appearance. The classic wardrobe was freshly pressed, the shoes polished. He had the quick walk of a man having served in the army.

"Did your wife put you on a diet?" Nicolas asked with a smile as he sat down on the other side of the table.

Matthew glanced at him. "I'm divorced."

"Oh. Sorry to hear that."

"No sorry. It's better this way. I mean, I'm glad it's over. It was . . ." Matthew's lips twitched, and his left thumb played with the empty spot at the ring finger. "Let's say, it was a hard time." He took a deep breath. "Hell, I'm starving."

They ate in silence. Matthew Montagna appeared to be ten years older than him, if he read the wrinkles on his face right.

Some gray mixed in the dark brown hair as well as in his beard. His moves were controlled, yet with an undercurrent of restlessness. Nicolas assumed he was a trained agent with a recent history of either private or official violence. His knuckles bore healing scratches, and the backs of his hands were chafed, as were his wrists. The face of his watch was shattered on one side, leaving it hardly readable. Upon a closer look, Nicolas detected a dark bruise beside his Adam's apple, partly covered by the dress shirt's lapels.

"Stop staring at me, Agent Hayes," Matthew said looking at his plate. "I'm not a suspect."

"Sorry. And it's Nicolas. Or Nick."

"Matt." The briefest of smiles followed.

Nicolas frowned. "Thought you'd have a more unique nickname . . . something made of your surname. Doesn't it mean *mountain*?"

"Yes." Matthew evaded Nicolas' gaze. He put the fork in the empty bowl and pushed it to the center of the table. "What have you got on the bank robbery that I couldn't read in the short time?"

Nicolas sipped coke and wiped his lips with the napkin. "First of all, two other bank robberies with different disguises but the same MO. Three men, local banks, two inside the bank, one waiting in the car. They were quick, they acted with brutal determination, and scared the tellers and the customers to the point that they didn't remember much of what happened. All of them agreed they were afraid the men would shoot to kill. Additionally, the disguises prevented them from being identified by cameras or people."

"They've got a MO that works. Fine. They'll try again."

"Yes, that's also my impression. Twice, their transport was blown up and burnt down. This time, the fuse didn't ignite. Not even the tip was burnt. CSU is to find the reason and hopefully some evidence."

Matthew wiped his chin. "Did one of them shy away from causing an explosion at the Federal Triangle? Where did the other two blow up?"

Nicolas leaned back and looked at Matt for a moment. "Lonely alleys." He nodded. "Good point. However . . . they were determined to shoot."

"They haven't killed anyone."

"So far. One man's in critical condition."

"What about the other two robberies? Anything special that went with them? Anything . . . recognizable? Do they repeat parts of their outfits? Like clothes, hair, hats?"

"I've pinned the evidence on the whiteboard. What jumped my mind was the false roadblock to fake street repairs. The preparation was done way ahead. I called the service, and they said there wasn't any repair planned. The robbers drove through the barriers, and their escape route was planned to the last detail. Without our coincidental appearance, they'd have cleared away. There were two demonstrations going on, police forces were thin, and reaction time was delayed. They didn't expect a harsh pursuit, that's for sure."

"Again . . . what about the other two? Good road access to highways or freeways?"

"Yes. In both cases, CSU assumes the vans were stolen. The plates were also false. We can't tell about the weapons' origins because they, too, got burned inside the vans."

"Interesting. They plan way ahead with the transports, so at least one of them will be an expert in car theft. They've got new weapons for every robbery, which means they've got a fresh supply whenever they need them."

"Or they bought a lot of weaponry once."

"Nah, that would've been too obvious. I bet they know some arms dealers who sell to them without asking questions." Matthew played with the napkin. "Three men. They could take turns buying weapons so the dealers wouldn't know."

"Yes."

"What about the men? Any distinctive clues that might lead to their identification?"

"We might get DNA from the van and weapons this time." Nicolas emptied the can and rolled it between his fingers before he crushed it. "The three men are tall, broad-shouldered, which might or might not be part of the disguise, and they're agile, fast, and skillful. By the way they move . . . not older than twenty-five and used to running. They're clever and escaped face recognition at the station."

"This means they checked the escape route in all details. Three men, agile, young, brutal, and very clever." Matthew shook his head. "Call me old-fashioned, but this sounds like an older man in the background directing their moves."

"A mastermind?" Nicolas dropped the crushed can on the table and pushed it toward Matthew's bowl. "A man staying in the background all the time?"

"Maybe he planned the robberies and watched their performance. If they're connected via radio, he could give them directions. Afterward, they share the loot. Just an idea."

"Let's go upstairs and check this idea against the facts we have so far. CSU report should come in today." Nicolas got up. "Welcome to the team."

Matthew pointed at Nicolas' fact sheet. "The three bank robberies indicate they weren't out for the most money. In comparison, the loot at the end of the month would've been much bigger."

"Yes, but security would've expected a robbery. They would've been much more watchful." Nicolas crossed his arms and leaned against the desk behind him. "They took what they could get—"

"But without high risk. They used the surprise to their advantage. Their plan had been to get the money facing two guards instead of, say, five at the end of the month."

"Which means their planning includes an evaluation of the possible loot, and they only take what's at the teller windows. They aren't out to empty the safes. It would take too much time. Still, they must watch the banks way ahead to count the customers and find out when firms bring in cash."

Matthew nodded. "Exactly. They do their homework. But that leads to another facet. The first two robberies took place within a week, one on Monday, the other on Thursday. The third one—yesterday—was four weeks *after* the second one. Which leads to two possible consequences. Either the first two were so easy they decided to cash all in and be sure to get away, or they had men watching a bank each to pile information and pull the robberies through in a short time. Thus, they avoided police forces digging deep into the investigation. In addition, the banks were quite far apart from each other, and none of them a major target."

Nicolas clicked his tongue. "We have to check surveillance videos of three to four weeks prior to the robbery to find out whether the robbers visited the banks frequently or had a car parked outside to count the customers."

"Given their clever disguises, they might not show up like normal customers, but maybe dressed as businessmen or old men with beards." Matthew smiled and stopped seeing Agent Hayes didn't join. "I wouldn't put it beyond them to have fun evaluating their targets."

"The profiler is with you on this one. The three men appear to enjoy what they're doing. He compared them to the gang in *Point Break*. If there was only one thing in common or . . . a part of disguise they use repeatedly, it'd be much easier." He got off the table. "I'll call the local police to ask them and check the videos of the weeks prior to the crimes."

"Was the money marked in any way?"

"No. The money at the tellers isn't marked. That's why the robberies were less risky than others."

"Again, clever." Matthew stepped back from the board and wiped his chin. The excitement of the chase got to him. He hadn't worked in the field for a year. "They minimize the risk of getting caught by choosing a day when there's less protection—"

"And they choose banks which are easy targets and less protected anyway."

"And they're brutal enough to shoot and risk killing." He turned to Nicolas, frowning. "Still, they didn't blow up the van at the metro station. I'm at odds with this incident. Did they truly make a mistake?"

Nicolas checked his emails. "The preliminary CSU report doesn't point to already known criminals. Ballistics identifies the weapons as those used in the robbery. The bullet matches the one extracted from the wounded guard. Serial numbers were professionally erased, so they can't be retraced. They're now comparing the bullets to find out if the weapons were used in other crimes. The fuse didn't fire, and the explosive charge remained intact. The examination of the components hasn't come in yet." He looked up. "They haven't found positive ID of any of the men yet, but also haven't examined everything they found in the van."

"That would be too easy," Mathew replied with a wry smile. He looked at his watch, then took a step back to look at the large clock on the opposite wall. "Do you want to go on for another hour? Then I really need a cig now."

"You smoke? I hadn't thought—"

"I compensate, okay?"

Nicolas looked at him until Matthew huffed.

"I quit, but started over about a year ago. It's hard to—" Matthew finished the sentence with a gesture. "It's already late. I'd like to visit the crime scenes of all three robberies tomorrow."

"Tomorrow's my day off." Nicolas printed the report for Matthew to read.

"But the ongoing investigation . . ."

"I said I have a day off." Nicolas handed him the pages.

"Thanks. Would your girlfriend be angry if you worked?"

Nicolas frowned. "Yeah, she'd be angry. And believe me, we'll spend many hours on this case during the next few weeks, so I don't see a reason to forego my long-planned free day, okay?"

"I get it." He lifted the papers in his hand. "Hope you don't mind that I'll drive around tomorrow."

"Just go ahead." Nicolas curled his lips to a short-lived smile. "I won't be thinking about you."

"That I get, too."

Chapter Three

Nicolas unlocked the door, and the whiff of a heavy perfume crinkled his nose. He was about to ask whether Jacklyn had changed labels when she approached him, smiling conspicuously.

He frowned, taking off his jacket. "What happened?"

"Don't be grumpy. We've got a visitor." She stepped aside to put the jacket on a hanger. Her smile brightened. "My aunt Georgette—who is my mother's sister—is here for a day, and she wants to get to know you."

Nicolas dropped his backpack into a corner and crouched to take off his shoes. "Anything wrong with calling ahead?"

"She's my aunt! She's family. Why should she call? She doesn't mind you looking kinda crinkled."

He looked up and tried to cover his irritation. "I had a long day, Jacky, and—"

"Don't worry. Say hello, take a shower, and then we'll have dinner together, okay? Nothing else. No obligations. And I bet she won't stay long."

"I can't even think straight, so how can I lead a conversation?"

"Leave this to me and to her, of course. She's an entertainer." She knelt beside him and placed a light kiss on his stubbly cheek. "Hey, just be friendly. She's great, and she won't judge every word you say. And . . ." She cocked her head. "There's the night ahead. And tomorrow we'll have . . . some special fun, hmm, Caspar? That'll be great."

Nicolas exhaled loudly. "You're manipulating me again.

Now I can't think about talking to your aunt without hoping you'll reward me for my—"

"Ah, no." She put a finger across his lips. "No rewarding. I'll take you to heaven as I always do." She kissed his lips and took his hand when they got up. "You don't have to impress her."

"Where is she?"

"In the kitchen, cooking. She's a French woman with . . . *the taste*. Unlike me, she represents French cuisine like only a lady with experience can do."

Nicolas exhaled as they entered the kitchen. Georgette put a casserole into the oven, closed the door with her knee, and set the timer. She turned around, straightened, and gently put back a strand of her wavy brown hair. Nicolas was speechless over the family resemblance. He supposed she was about sixty years old, but she could've passed for younger. There was joy in her dark brown eyes, and her welcome smile genuine.

"Ah, you grace me with your presence, as I hoped." They shook hands. "So nice to finally meet you!" She looked at Jacklyn. "You prefer blonds now, hmm? And a young dude this time? I'm impressed . . . and surprised in a good way."

Jacklyn ran a hand through the hair on Nicolas' back of the head from neck to top. "Is it that obvious?"

"It's very nice to meet you," Nicolas said, trying to cloak the thrill Jacklyn's hand caused. "And I'm sorry, Misses . . . I'm sorry, Jacky didn't mention your last name."

She made a dismissive gesture. "Georgette will do. Other than my wonderful diplomatic sister, I'm not into formalities."

"Georgette, then. I'm sorry, I must look like I've come out of a coal mine to you."

"Please, don't apologize that you work and smell like a man. It's appreciated and much better than those lazy bones who rely on their women to bring home the money." She looked at her niece pointedly.

"That was an option?"

She laughed and playfully slapped his shoulder with the back of her hand. "Oh, you rascal! Off you go! Shower! In the meantime, I'll work my magic with the meager provisions Jacklyn's got in her fridge."

"I'm sure it'll be delicious."

"Come on, sweet Nick, not even you can sugarcoat that this young lady doesn't know how to run a kitchen."

Nicolas laughed and kissed Jacklyn's cheek. "I think she does great."

"And I bet you compliment her way too much!"

Nicolas left for the bathroom.

"Does he always behave like a gentleman?" Georgette asked.

"He does, even in bed, if that was your next question."

Nicolas blushed and hurriedly closed the bathroom door.

Matthew worked through the file and all the attached information until he knew the details by heart. He memorized the street maps and followed the criminals' escape routes of the first two robberies. He bet the head of the group had done the same—selecting a target, observing it, planning the streets and turns to take and where to ditch the escape van. He imagined the mastermind brooding over maps and photographs to choose the perfect time for the assault. Matthew called the local heads of police to ask for surveillance tapes of the weeks prior to the crimes and was rewarded with a reluctant agreement for help.

On the way home, he stopped at a liquor store and bought a bottle of expensive whiskey, which he put on the silver tray with glasses in the living room.

After a shower, he opened the top box in the bedroom to unpack piles of t-shirts, pullovers, pants, and sports shorts. He had a lump in his throat as he filled the shelves of the walk-in closet. Nerina's voice was in his ear, mocking him for his soldier-like attitude when it came to order in the closets and cupboards. He sorted shirts and pullovers by color and also by use—official and private. He had extra piles for business shirts and separated a suit, dress shirt, underwear, socks, and shoes for easy access in case of emergency. Nerina had laughed about his tendency to be prepared for any eventuality regarding his job. Not a day had passed without her whispering in his ear how much she loved her *G-man*. They had talked about starting a family, and she'd playfully slapped his chest and told him he had to make more than an effort to make her pregnant. He'd laughed and argued he couldn't do more in the short time they shared, but they hadn't been rewarded with a child.

Matthew turned around and knocked over a small box with personal correspondence. The letter from the judge confirming the divorce lay on top. He stuffed the papers back and put the lid back on. With more force than necessary, he folded three empty moving boxes and put them beside the apartment door, then headed for the bottle of whiskey. He poured a finger's breadth and hesitated. He hadn't eaten much throughout the day. Sighing, he put down the glass to prepare a sandwich. Once he shut the fridge door, he expected Bouncer, their German shepherd, to sit close to his feet waiting for some morsels, his tail wagging on the tiles. The lump was back in his throat thinking of the dog being with friends in his old neighborhood in Chicago, lost and confused. He hadn't expected parting with a dog would be as hard as selling his house to strangers.

Matthew swallowed, took a can of beer, and sat in front of the TV to have dinner.

Nicolas wanted to skip good manners and grab the casserole from the oven. He was hungry enough for two, and the aroma in the kitchen was overwhelming. Jacklyn and her aunt spoke with each other in rapid French. Judging by the tone, they were exchanging bedroom stories.

"There you are!" Georgette smiled as she turned around. "I thought I heard your stomach grumble all the way through the bathroom door. Am I right?"

Nicolas nodded and opened his palms.

"Ah! Well, sit down. We'll be there in a minute." Her smile brightened. "I like men who come from work and are still hungry."

Nicolas looked questioningly at Jacklyn, but she was hiding behind a meaningless smile.

Georgette gazed from her niece to Nicolas and made a dismissive gesture. "Oh, come on, don't take everything I'm saying as sexual. I do like insinuations but don't over-interpret." She put the casserole on a trivet, pressed a large spoon into it, and invited Nicolas to help himself. "Yes, I know, good manners. My sweetie here told me all about you."

"In five minutes?" Nicolas took the spoon. "I thought you'd need more time for a summary."

"I talk fast." Jacklyn sat down with a sweet smile and held her plate for Nicolas to fill. "How's Jason?"

"Grumpy." Nicolas chortled. "He asked me if I got a *handsome* partner to replace him."

"And? Is your new partner handsome?"

Nicolas read amusement as well as curiosity in her eyes. "Nope. He's about forty, the grumpy type, and only *handsome* in a rugged way. Wears a terrible beard that doesn't suit him and that looks patchy at best. But he dresses to the nines, and I bet the shoes he wears were quite expensive. Was transferred from Chicago for unknown reasons, but I'll find out. He appears to know his job, so"—he shrugged—"we either get along with each other or . . . well, we'll work together for six weeks, that's all. Then Jason will be back on deck."

"What happened, anyway?"

Nicolas' grin widened as he lifted a hand off the table. "Get this, he stumbled over the leash of a dog and now—and you can bet they're innovative—all of our colleagues showed up with some dog stuff." He shook his head when Georgette and Jacklyn laughed. "No, he didn't think it was funny. He got stuffed toys, dog toys, books about dog education, and leashes in different colors. Not to mention some dog treats packed like chocolates."

Jacklyn flinched. "Oh, did he get mad?"

"He did. Until the moment Elaine entered his room and was all for it. She even asked him whether he wanted to buy a dog and just hadn't told her." Nicolas paused to dig his fork into the meal. "For a moment, I thought he'd go for it and promise to buy a dog in a week, but reason prevailed." He took a bite and sighed. "Mmm, that's good. Thank you, Georgette, for this great meal."

"Oh, dear. If you take that many words to thank me so effusively, the situation in this kitchen is worse than I thought."

Nicolas stopped laughing and choked.

Georgette looked at him pointedly, like an old and experienced teacher without leniency.

"See? That's what I mean. You better eat, shut your hatch, and let the women take over." Then she turned to Jacklyn and continued their conversation in rapid French.

Nicolas relished the casserole made of potatoes, bacon, and cheese with tasty spices he couldn't name. He helped himself to a second serving and emptied the plate listening to the background of the women's chatter. When Georgette asked him about the meal, Nicolas lifted his head, waking from a trance.

"Great. Honestly, I'm stuffed now."

"Good." She stood and came back with a decanter of red wine and three glasses. "Now, let's see. Some important questions are still on my mind. What have you two lovebirds planned? I mean, you've been together for a year now, if I'm correct. Is this the status quo? Will you move on from here?" She poured wine and handed Jacklyn and Nicolas their glasses. "Don't look at me as if I'd asked the most stupid question ever. My sister's getting on my nerves, so I don't have a choice but to ask."

Jacklyn let the wine turn in the glass. "My parents want a bunch of grandchildren to add to the family tree."

Georgette snorted but didn't appear to disagree. "Your mom wants to know whether you finally found a man for life—after a long list of scalawags, if you don't mind my saying—and what she's got to expect." She toasted and drank. "And if anything needs planning, you know your parents need to know in advance. Long months ahead, no kidding. Their schedule is worse than mine."

Jacklyn turned to Nicolas and lowered her voice. "My father will probably squeeze our wedding in between meetings with ambassadors and senate members."

"Don't be mean." Georgette put down her glass. Her look spoke of love. "My sister always tells me he's constantly trying to establish decent communication between many formally hostile dignitaries, and sometimes it feels like swimming against a heavy current. She didn't name the dignitaries—as you can easily imagine—but your dad's a valuable member of the diplomatic corps, and his credits include recent negotiations between the US and some Arabic countries." She laughed. "End of quote!"

"This means they've got more travel miles than they'll be able to spend in their lifetime." Jacklyn flinched.

"But that doesn't answer my question. Or to be precise, it doesn't stop your parents' worries." She rolled her eyes and raised her brows, looking from Jacklyn to Nicolas. "Hey, I'm not one to pry into your privacy, but—what shall I tell my sister? Come on, don't make it too hard. How do you get along with each other? As I see it, you must be tough in your job, and I know that my sweet Jaqueline can be very dominant."

Nicolas' eyes widened, and he exchanged glances with Jacklyn, who pretended to disappear behind her wine glass.

Georgette sighed exasperatedly. "Both of you . . . did I say something wrong? Hit a soft spot?"

Jacklyn burst out laughing. "Soft spot! Ha!"

"We do get along well with each other," Nicolas hastened to say. "But we haven't thought about . . . changing anything yet. And you're right . . . my job's very demanding. I don't spend much time at home, which . . ."

Jacklyn laughed so hard she had tears in her eyes.

Georgette lifted a hand. "Oh, sweetie, stop that! You're behaving *non compos mentis,* as your mom would say."

"Just say *nutty as a fruitcake,* and everyone gets it." Jacklyn wiped her eyes, still chortling. "Ah, auntie, that was priceless."

"I know I am like that, even though I don't really understand what's so hilarious."

Jacklyn made a face qualifying her as a fruitcake.

Georgette turned her attention to Nicolas. "Before the interruption, you were trying to tell me about the status quo."

"We're happy together, but we both think it's way too early to think about getting married or having children."

"Now that's an answer I can live with." She looked around the room. "You could start by moving into a decent home." She pointed at Jacklyn. "If you ever want something truly outstanding, you should move to Florida. Much more sunshine, and the houses are truly affordable. This place here's kinda shabby and too small."

"Auntie, we haven't decided about moving, either." Jacklyn shook her head and poured more wine. "Let's think about that later, too."

Georgette made a face. "However, you need a more decent place to stay. DC has changed for the worse since I lived here. The suburbs are more or less okay, and if you want me to, I can look around. You know I've got a good view from above." She wiggled her brows, and when Nicolas looked confused, said, "I was an army pilot a long time ago. I changed to private flights."

Jacklyn made a face. "She owns a flight service in Florida with ten planes and two helicopters."

Georgette shrugged. "It's a small company. I like flying, that's all. But let's get back to your housing problem. I could—"

"When we think about steps two and three, we'll make a decision. Promise." Jacklyn toasted her with the glass. "Now, to you. What's going on in your not-so-quiet life?"

Katherine dropped the binoculars in her lap and wiped her burning eyes. Sighing, she reached for a water bottle, drank, and while she screwed the cap, she sank deeper in her seat behind the wheel. The large black armored car stopped in front of the *Federal Bank of Baltimore,* and two men in the uniforms of the security company got out. She checked her watch and nodded. The men—one heavy and puffing, the other one in better shape—went into the building and came back six minutes later laden with two thick black sacks each. The sacks had to be heavy, because both men made a wide swing to put them inside the armored car. An armed guard from the bank stood at the entrance like a sentinel until the driver and his companion got back inside the large van and drove off.

Satisfied with her observations, she took down notes and, considering her empty stomach, decided to head back to her motel and grab a bite on the way.

Matthew switched channels and saw Cary Grant's growing amusement as his film partner Irene Dunne made herself look ridiculous on the dancefloor, being turned around helplessly by an Oklahoma rancher. Cary Grant smiled and suppressed his outburst of hilarity in his unique way. Matthew heard Nerina's laughter in his ears. She loved Cary Grant, Rock Hudson, James Stewart, and many other actors from the thirties and forties. Screwball comedies were her favorite waste of time, and while watching the scene evolve, Matthew was unable to drag his thoughts away from his ex-wife. She knew many of the dialogues from her favorite movies by heart, and while cooking or showering, she sang songs from the musicals. Once, she'd performed *Singin' in the Rain* on their way home, hopping through puddles included. She was a decent singer, even though her father called her a *bathroom soprano.*

Matthew switched channels again, hoping the lump in his throat would go away while he watched Jim Carrey's eyes pop out gaping at Cameron Diaz' night club performance, but even she looked like Nerina, though she was a brunette with a smaller bosom and hips. He reached for the third can from the six-pack, opened it, and once he had drunk, lit another cigarette. A sore throat would be inevitable. The bottle of whiskey beside the TV set waved at him, and he had no choice but to wave back.

Nerina was on his mind, day in and day out, constantly nagging at his heart. Once more, he tried to list the reasons which had led to their divorce, but reason didn't work at this hour. The whiskey helped mute the pain of loss and loneliness. He reached for the phone, and Bert, who lived close to Chicago, took the call, wide awake at this odd hour.

Chapter Four

"Hey, there, Monty, what's up in the wilderness of DC?"

Matthew wiped his beard and ran a hand through his hair. "Don't know. Can't think straight."

"You sound rat-assed to me, my friend. That bad?"

"Don't mention it." He muted the TV and leaned back into the cushions of his old couch. "I tried to unpack my stuff but got stuck in the middle. Guess I can't believe I'll be here for . . . what? Eternity? What about you?"

"You know me, the broker. I took my share of today's fat chances and made decent money selling Optronic shares. It's been said the company's selling some non-profit sections, and I bet the numbers will go down next week."

"I'd better not ask how much decent money you made."

"Let's say you'd weep." Bert roared a deep belly laugh in Matthew's ear. "But okay, that's not the point. What can I do to make you feel better?"

"Beam me back? No, forget that. It's a moot point."

"Did you meet your new colleagues? How are they?"

"The senior agent's a desk-politician with quite an ego and no sense of humor whatsoever. He appears to like no one, including himself. I bet he'd prefer being someplace else. On a scale he's even lower than Fredericks, you know, my old boss. And my new partner . . ." Matthew wiped his eyes. "Could be an okay guy. I'm not sure. He appears to know his moves, though I bet he's not even thirty. I wonder how many years of service he has under his belt. He acts like he knows it all. Maybe he just wants to hold his ground. He's watching me like a suspect. And I bet he'll hurry and get rid of me as soon as his sick partner returns."

"Not that surprising, though."

"Maybe not, but it doesn't feel like a welcome, you know?" He looked at the bottle on the table and sighed.

"I guess that's only getting to you because—"

"Don't say I miss my old colleagues. That's BS! They gave me a farewell gift I won't forget for another week."

"I remember. Does it still hurt?"

Matthew touched the spot at his neck that was still sensitive. "Would that satisfy your sadistic ego?"

"Don't attack me, pal."

"Guess why they left out my face while the rest of my body looks like I barely survived playing football without protection."

Bert sighed loudly. "I knew they were bastards, but that mean . . . naw, I hadn't thought it'd come to that."

"Me neither." Matt wiped his brow and closing his eyes, he felt like being choked. He looked around gasping for air. "I'm so sick of it all, Bert. I want to forget, wipe out the memories, the entire last year, if ever possible. I want to leave it all behind and yet . . . how long will it take?"

"A lot of booze included? Hey, come on. You sound like a wounded dog missing the hand that slapped him. Don't get me wrong," Bert went on before Matt could contradict. "You dealt your cards professionally, but it was clear as mud from the beginning that you wouldn't get out without bruises. Okay, bad pun. But you understand what I mean?"

"It's not a logical point or argument, buddy. I know what happened and that my friends . . . *ex*-friends are pissed with me. That didn't give them the right to rough me up the day before I left for good."

"Surely not. But the brawl's but one part of your misery, right? Nerina's betrayal will weigh you down for months.

You can't change that, Monty, you can't wash away your feelings with a shower or with bottles of whiskey. It was the right decision to ask for the transfer—"

"Hell! As if I had much of a choice."

"And now you'll find your place among the bunch of agents in DC. Look at it in a positive way. Show them you're a good agent. You've been on this job for fifteen years! You're a professional." He sighed. "As for your feelings—give yourself time."

"I still want to see her," Matt whispered. "I miss her so much. Her laughter. Her kisses. Every touch. Oh, I'm so fucked-up." For the umpteenth time, he saw Nerina's pretty face with the little dimples in his mind's eye. She had such an attractive face and friendly manners. She was easy to love, and everyone did. "I know it's silly, and yet I can't help thinking of how she moved, how she sang, and how happy she was when we moved into the new house. She had so much fun furnishing it. We had a good life. Together. And we talked about—" He choked on his words.

"Love, Monty, isn't rational. I wish I could tell you differently, but I went through the same ordeal and spent a lot of money on psychiatrists. Nothing helped."

Matt pulled himself together to snort. "Your ex-wife walked away with a millionaire from Hawaii. Excuse me, but that story's quite different from mine."

"But she told me she didn't leave me for the money—I've got plenty of that, too—but for the *thrill* of him being a climber, a sportsman, a sailor, and some freaking skydiver—all in one person! It was a hard punch in the guts at that time."

"You're overweight, Bert, don't sugarcoat that. You'll never be a true sportsman, and from what I know you don't want to be."

"Thanks for stating the obvious. In retrospect, she wasn't good for me in any way. She spent my money, had attitudes, and always wanted to go out partying. She wasn't truly giving. I'm looking for a more homely woman now."

"Don't lie when you put up a picture on the dating sites. It'll backfire."

Bert was quiet for a moment. "It could help, so they won't be scared in the first place. I'm a charming entertainer. I'm intelligent. I've got inner values, many of them don't show at first glance."

Matthew laughed. "You're lying on a website. Bert, how many dates will you get if you start them with a lie? They'll meet you once and turn away. Women don't like being cheated." Another pause followed. Matthew reached for the glass and bottle to pour a drink. "Come on, be yourself."

Bert sighed again. "I'm trying. I don't want to be alone, and I don't want to lure them with money, you know? I don't mention my penthouse or the cars. They should be attracted by me, not by my bank account."

"I'm convinced you'll find the right lady. Just don't pretend to be someone else. I had such a specimen at my house, and I didn't like it a bit."

"Did you eat today? Something healthy?"

"I had a salad for second breakfast. Why're you asking?"

"I hear you're still on your liquid dinner. That, my friend, won't help you either."

"As if I didn't know."

"My aunt's gone, so—" Jacklyn closed the door and turned around. "Is there anything else on your mind you need to do right now?"

"Getting sober?"

She caressed his chest with both hands. "Funny." They made eye contact. "I could, of course, slap your naked body with a wet towel which would—"

"Hurt my sorry body."

"Maybe." She cocked her head and directed him to the bedroom. "I could also rub your back with ice cubes until you squirm."

He took her by the shoulders and kissed her lips. "What about dropping our clothes and hopping into this wonderful bed together? If you don't look at the loops and the built-in pillory, it's a cozy place."

"You mean—"

"Exactly what I say." He kissed her with feeling and pulled her blouse out of the skirt. "You feel great, by the way. Soft and warm. And you smell great. I missed you the whole day." He caressed her belly and slipped his hands behind her back to unclasp her bra while she unfastened his pants. "Your aunt knew exactly what we'd be doing later," he whispered in her ear.

"Not that much." Jacklyn pushed down his pants and underwear.

Nicolas gasped in pretended shock. "You aren't playing this by the book."

"Never do." She took off her skirt and blouse and slipped out of the bra. Once he caressed her breasts, her nipples got hard and her breathing accelerated. "You got the wrong woman for that." Amid kissing, they landed on the bed. "Get ready to do me, Caspar, drunk or not."

He kissed her breasts and belly. "Couldn't get so drunk I wouldn't be able to lay you."

"Prove it."

A short, stocky man with a graying mustache approached Matthew's desk, frowning while he greeted him. "I hoped I'd find the agents Hayes or Beckham here." Matthew looked up. The arrival cocked his head, and one strand of his too-long hair fell over his forehead. He wore a lab coat with an assembly of unidentifiable spots, and the buttons were mismatched with the buttonholes. "I'm Dr. Dave Miller from CSU. I've got something they might be interested in."

"I'm Agent Matthew Montagna. I'm new on the team and work with Hayes. You can hand me the report."

"Oh." Miller corrected his glasses that didn't need correction. "You know, that van . . . was really interesting. You know the case of the robberies, yes?"

Matthew nodded.

"Fine." Miller pushed away the strand of hair, which fell back immediately. "The two other vans exploded and in consequence burned down completely, so no DNA, no fingerprints, nothing. Zip useful information if you put a lot of metal shards etcetera aside." He made a dramatic pause and smiled. "Here, there are five different kinds of hair in the van, one belonging to a dog. I guess we can rule him out as a suspect."

"Four people in the van? One more than we assumed was hiding in there. But—" He paused, and Miller maintained a broad smile, which made Matthew wonder what the guy had smoked during the last hour. "There were only three thugs running toward the station. Did you find . . ."

"No, we didn't find a body hidden under the seats." Miller snorted.

Matthew understood it was his way of laughter.

Miller went on quickly. "That would indeed have been an interesting finding! But, hey, I shouldn't complain! We've got four people's DNA and that of an Australian shepherd. Though the van's VIN was erased, just like on the weapons, I cross-checked the list of stolen vans in the vicinity of Maryland with owners who also have a dog." He was about to hand Matthew the report but kept it at the last moment. "The van was stolen from Mr. and Mrs. Calhoun, who—not surprisingly—own an Australian shepherd. Nice, yes?"

"Nice. Yes." Matthew held back laughter. "And what did the Calhouns say about their stolen van?"

"It was taken from the parking lot at a small grocery store eight weeks ago. No, no video surveillance. Nothing. I tried to trace it on the streets, but . . . well, not every area is completely covered, and the older recordings get deleted. You got that?" He opened his eyes wide and went on when Matthew nodded. "It means the robbers made a grave mistake, and we can trace their way, maybe even back to where they started. In the other two cases Agent Hayes listed, the vans couldn't be identified and traced back to their owners. You'd be surprised how many vans are on the streets and how many are reported stolen in a month." He cleared his throat. "Anyway, we've got the van's ID, so to speak, and . . . yes?"

"Does the DNA of two samples belong to the Calhouns?"

"We haven't had time to test that, but we are on it." Miller bobbed his head. "I wanted to deliver the news right to you . . . well, to Agent Hayes, to be precise." His eyes shone with eagerness.

"I understand. And the other DNA? Do you have any hits with robbers or others?"

"No." Miller's voice dropped, and he turned out his free hand. "You've got an interesting voice, not as deep as I'd have supposed by a man of your inches."

Matthew raised his brows. "You're saying?"

"I'm addicted to audio books, okay? They keep me focused when examining stuff. That's why I hear a lot of different voices and yours—"

"Did you identify the suspects?"

"No hits so far. If one of them was ever involved in a crime, there was no DNA sample taken and saved for further comparison." He handed Matthew the crumpled pages. "I'll send it via email to Agent Hayes and Beckham."

"Yes, do that. Thank you."

"You're welcome." Miller frowned. "You aren't from around here, are you?"

"I'm from Chicago."

"Ah! I've been there once. You get a terrific view of Lake Michigan. I couldn't get enough." He shrugged. "But it was just a vacation. I suppose it's great living there."

"Yes."

"Homesick?"

"A bit. I'll get over it," he said quickly when Miller's gaze turned sympathetic. "It's a . . . privilege to serve in DC."

"If you see it like that—" Miller's lips curled into a wry, mocking smile. One more time, he glanced at the empty desk before he turned and headed back.

Matthew whistled through his teeth, wondering how many strange enthusiasts he'd meet on his way.

Nicolas stopped on the way out of the bathroom, eyes wide, and exhaled in surprise. Jacklyn was waiting for him dressed in some patches of black leather that barely covered intimate areas. She stood with her legs apart, which was impressive because of the sharp looking high heels that dug into the carpet. Her legs appeared a foot longer than usual, and he wanted nothing more than to sink on his knees and caress her perfect beauty.

He raised his brows. "You want to start this before I've had breakfast?"

"I want to do this instead of breakfast." Jacklyn's sweet smile was a contradiction to the black leather mittens with silver rings dangling on her fingers. The crop at her belt was an indicator of whatever she had in mind. "You'd better get down on your knees, Caspar, and be obedient, or this will be a very long morning without a bite." She rolled her eyes. "Pun intended."

"But I really like breakfast." He knelt, cloaking a smile. "It's the most important meal of the day."

She bent and kissed his forehead. "And it'll be a long day. Promise."

He made a move to crawl toward the kitchen, and she stepped in his way.

Nicolas kissed her knees. "Please, let me have breakfast. I'm starving!"

She fastened the mittens around his hands. "No dice."

Nicolas flinched at her resolute tone and nuzzled her belly. "Please." When she looked at him impatiently, he couldn't help but smile. "I could do this all day."

"Back to the bedroom."

"You could feed me."

"Bedroom."

"Discussion?"

"No."

"Struggle?"

"Don't you dare!" She pointed toward the bedroom. "Kneel on the bed, and don't make a fuss."

"Because you're gonna make a fuss?"

She slapped the back of his head. "You're having too much fun, Caspar."

"Aww . . ." He climbed the bed and knelt between the posts. "You look very eager."

She bound his hands to the sides, then put an arm around his throat to hiss in his ear. "And if you don't shut your trap, I'll gag and blindfold you and make you wish you'd been a gentleman." Jacklyn bit his earlobe before she pulled down his boxer shorts. "Shut up," she warned.

Nicolas lowered his chin and closed his eyes when Jacklyn slapped his butt. His mouth was dry, and he stopped thinking about breakfast.

On his way to the first crime scene, Matthew stayed in one lane on the highway and strictly kept to the speed limit, listening to his favorite *REM* album. *Losing my Religion* filled the car, and Matthew gently tapped the rhythm on the wheel. His eyesight was dimmed by the headache that had been steadily building behind his brow and was clawing through his eyeballs. He rubbed his temples, to no avail. A truck honked behind him, waking him from his daydream. His speed had dropped to thirty-five miles per hour, and a column of cars was driving by, dispersing sleet. The truck overtook him with roaring engines, and the headache accepted the invitation and grew in intensity. Probably the truck driver had to keep an appointment and was angry about the lazy fellow in the middle lane.

Once more, Matthew wiped his eyes and almost missed the exit. In his haste, he cut off two cars as he sped for the right lane. Honking followed him when he slowed down to make a right turn at the traffic light. He stopped at the next burger point for some strong coffee. His stomach was still turning over, and the black coffee didn't improve his condition. He drank it anyway, smoked a cigarette outside the small diner, and walked back to his service car.

He parked close to the bank and took a stroll around the block to get acquainted with the surroundings before he talked to the police sergeant in charge of the investigation. He got the surveillance tapes on a USB stick with the information that in spite of a careful check, nothing suspicious had been found. Matthew thanked the young man, walked through the bank, and after a break in the sun, entered the building on the other side of the street. He knocked on doors and asked for information concerning the day of the assault. Some residents were helpful, some grunted that they hadn't seen anything.

An old woman in a dark blue bathrobe hanging loosely around her slim body squinted at him, then shook her head.

"You know, officer, those questions have been asked, more than once, I'd say, and nothing was found. I didn't look out of the window that day. I was knitting, and after the commotion, I went out."

"Did you see someone on the staircase? Going up or down? Someone you didn't know?" The smallest of dogs appeared from right behind the woman's thin legs. Matt went down on one knee and reached out, smiling.

The old woman raised her graying brows as high as they would get. "Are you one of those dudes who want to look a lady under the skirt?"

On the other side of the landing, the door opened to reveal a six-foot-four giant with shoulders as wide as the frame. His voice was deep, his rolling accent difficult to understand. "Is he bothering you, momma?"

"No, no, Jimmy, not bothering. Not right now." She looked down to where Matt was coaxing the dog. "And you aren't up to, hmm?"

"A Chihuahua, right?"

"Right." The old woman cocked her head. "Beware, he's not friendly to strangers."

"He could still try to bother you." The young man's voice slurred. He shifted from one foot to the other. "That man, I mean."

The small dog sniffed Matt's hand, and after a moment's hesitation got closer to have his head and ears tickled. Matt looked up when the woman made a sound of surprise.

"Usually, he bites." She huffed quietly. "Now, you're a dog person, right? He knows that. I'm sure he knows that. But I bet you haven't come for a chat with Mr. Cincinnati."

"What d'ya want?" the man on the other side asked.

Matt turned his head. "I want to solve a crime. The bank

robbery that took place here four weeks ago. Can you tell me something about it?"

"Wasn't home that day." Jimmy scratched his tousled hair, sniffled, and set his gaze on *momma* again. "Do you need anything? Gonna go grocery shopping later."

"Thank you, Jimmy, I'm fine." She took a deep breath and faced Matthew again, putting a finger on her lips. "Thinking of it . . . sometimes there's a dipshit on the roof, sleeping there. Ah, don't look at me like that, Mr. Police. They're good for nothing. Hanging around, just wasting time. Though . . ." She pondered, and a smile broke through once Mr. Cincinnati jumped on Matthew's knee to get closer to both hands petting him. "The man I saw, he carried a bag. Not just some old backpack-thingy or a rolled mat, but a sports bag. Dark blue."

"How big?"

She cocked her head and squinted. "Big enough for clothes, shoes, and such. Or for a rifle."

"I understand."

"Yes, you do."

"Do you have a description for me?"

"Of the rifle?" She made a sly face.

Matthew laughed out loud and quickly kept the dog from falling off his knee. His hands and wrists were wet where the dog had licked him. Just then it tried to reach for Matthew's beard. "Yeah, if you can do that."

"Naw, can't. But the man was tall and broad but not like Jimmy and also not as tall." She looked at her neighbor who stood more erect and held his chin high. "I saw him coming down. He was quick on his feet. Took two steps at a time. And he carried a bag on his shoulder."

"Young?"

She nodded, frowning. "Early twenties, maybe. Didn't make eye contact and rushed down without a word."

"And he came down from the roof?"

"I think so. It's just another level up."

"And this was after the bank robbery?" The dog barked in a high voice. Matthew kept him from going for his face and almost sat on his butt. He balanced himself and became aware of the old woman's smile.

"Yes. I heard the shots, but didn't go looking, of course. Instead, I took my purse and was on my way out to the other side of the building."

"To the back yard?"

"So to speak. And he ran past me." She pointed at the floor. "Right here where you spoil my dog. He's supposed to protect me." They laughed before she turned serious again. "Blue bag and . . . sports shoes. Black. Or dark blue."

Matthew frowned. He put down the dog to take notes and added the name of the lady. Carefully, aware of his headache, he straightened. Mr. Cincinnati yelped and jumped at his leg. "Excuse me, but why didn't you tell that to the police?"

"Nobody asked." She shrugged and pulled down the corners of her mouth. "I didn't think of him, either. Like I said . . . the scum comes and goes."

"Any facial description?"

"Dark brown hair, hanging in his face. He wore a hoodie. He was a white man, for sure, but—" She shrugged again. "No, I can't think of anything else that'd help you find him."

"Thank you, ma'am."

She laughed and gently touched his lower arm. "Call me *momma*. Everybody does."

Jacklyn had wound a thin rope around Nicolas' balls and tied a knot at the canopy. The rope passed between his butt cheeks, which were reddened by her spanking. He had to remain upright, or he'd tighten the rope so much he couldn't stand. Nicolas' thighs trembled. The stench of his sweat was in the air, mingling with her perfume as she knelt in front of him, displaying her female assets in their entire splendor.

She stroked his hard cock lovingly, yet no more than teasingly. It was enough to spur his arousal to a new high. He moved forward to her hand and—with a wicked smile—she took her hand away.

He craved for contact, for fulfillment and was about to tell her when she whispered, "Lick me, Caspar, and make me come like you never did before."

She held tight to slings bound at the canopy, and he understood her flawless morning plan as she drew closer for him to kiss her vulva and lick in between. His arousal grew with every intimate contact and her loud breathing. She closed her eyes and lowered her head.

"Gimme more, my little Caspar, you can do better than that."

"Fuck you, Wendy, it's your fault that I can hardly move."

Jacklyn giggled. "I only turned your fantasy to reality. You're hard as a rock, and now you . . . uh, that's good."

He strained to please her even if it meant enduring the hard pull on his balls and the resulting pain. He felt her trembling and heard her whispered wishes as she drew closer to the climax. He evaded her sudden shudder by accident as she stood on wobbly legs, riding the pleasure he caused. When she slumped on the mattress, her gaze was hazy.

She kissed his sweaty chest while her hands caressed his lower belly. "Do you want more?"

"Damn you, yes!" He tore at the ropes holding him. "Cut me loose, and I'll show you what I fucking want!"

"That's so not gonna happen." Jacklyn bit his nipples and pulled his aching cock to increase pressure on his testicles. Once he gritted his teeth, she pulled the fraction of an inch that forced a small cry. "You'll make up for your saucy words."

"Not when you ruin me."

Jacklyn caressed his member and gently blew on it. "Better?" She opened the knot around his balls. "I think I know the best way to punish you."

He had an idea, seeing her mischievous smile.

Matthew went up to the roof. The wind picked up the moment he opened the door, and he squinted against the gusts blowing dust and dirt as he focused on the wall to the street side, looking for clues. There was a narrow brick ledge, about two feet high, partly crumbling. Some of the debris was crushed to dust. Matthew walked closer and knelt on the concrete to look across. The bank entrance was in clear sight. At the time of the robbery, the sun had been in the man's back.

"Nice position for a shooter." Matthew looked left and right along the ledge, but he couldn't determine whether the fourth man—if the old woman was right about her observation—had been here to survey the assault. There was no evidence that a rifle had been put up, and after four weeks, there were no signs in the dust anymore.

Frustrated, Matthew left the building to head for the second crime scene at Tysons Corner.

After a conversation with the bank manager, who appeared surprised seeing yet another FBI agent on duty, he had a friendly chat with the local police chief. The surveillance videos of the three weeks prior to the assault displayed a lot of people, but Matthew couldn't pin down a face that showed up more often than others. The tapes were sent to the FBI headquarters for closer analysis but without hope for different results.

After a cup of coffee at the nearest diner, Matthew made the same approach to the residents of the houses on the opposite side. On the stairway, he swayed and held tight to the handrail, catching his breath. He wanted to crawl into his bed and not run around at a four-week-old crime scene. It didn't make sense. Cursing under his breath, he knocked on yet another door. A teenager in a washed-out shirt, jeans, and with a baseball cap worn back to front opened the door. He was chewing gum and pretended to be annoyed and bored when Matthew showed his ID.

The questioning strained Matthew's nerves. His instincts told him the young man knew something but was unwilling to explain it to a stranger, no matter his credential.

"Maybe you don't know, but the gang committed two other crimes, and if we don't catch them fast, they'll commit another one." Matthew cocked his head. "Just imagine—you could be the one who nails them before they can do that."

The young man leaned against the door and put his long-fingered hands into his pants pockets. "Risking my bro's freedom?"

Matthew looked into dark brown eyes full of mischief. "You know, if you consider him your *bro*, I consider you his accomplice. Would a visit to the DC headquarters of the FBI mean anything to you or your family? I mean I can certainly come up with a scenario based on your statement that you had something in common with those *bros*."

"Dude, hey, no!" The teenager lifted his hands in defense. He huffed. "Okay, I saw one man coming down, okay? He ran into me, knocked me two steps down, and hurried out." He shook his head, breaking eye contact. Matthew was under the impression the young man was ashamed he'd been pushed easily. "Didn't see anything of his face, hair, or anything else." He shrugged. "Hey, I know from TV what you need to identify him, but—"

"How tall was he?"

"Tall and broad." The teenager seemed sullen. "He was quick, so—" He shrugged. "Young, I'd say."

"Did he say a word? An apology maybe?"

"Yeah, he said *sorry* and was out faster than my fat brother when someone announces there's cake."

"Was he white or black? From around here? Any dialect you recognized?"

"By one word? Get real." He chewed more intensely and pulled up his nose. "He said it and was gone."

"Did you see a car waiting for him outside or did he walk along the street?"

"No fucking idea."

Matthew frowned. "Did he carry a bag?"

"Yeah, some expensive sports bag." He pointed at Matt and nodded rapidly. "*Nike*. Dark blue with the swish. Looked kinda dusty."

"Very used?"

"No, more like he put it down in the dust somewhere."

"On the rooftop, maybe? Is it accessible?"

The teenager grinned and cocked his head. "Yeah, sure. It's got a small door, nothing special. It's not even locked. I'll show you."

"Do you have a name?"

"Robert. Rob." He sniffled and didn't meet Matthew's gaze.

He ran upstairs, and Matthew followed more slowly, fighting another assault of a headache. On the roof, he caught his breath and held tight to the frame.

"You'd better quit smoking," Robert said, grinning broadly. "My dad always says that . . . before he lights another one."

"I know that feeling." Matthew assessed the area and had a look across the ledge toward the bank's main entrance. When he found cigarette stubs on the dusty concrete, he turned to the young man. "Do you or your friends come up here often?"

Robert's hands were back in his pockets, and he lifted his shoulders, grimacing as if Matt had accused him of having sex in public. "It's forbidden . . . so, well, yes . . . we do come up here, but only when our folks aren't watching."

"Do your friends smoke?"

"We're careful not to leave anything, if you mean that. Won't want anyone to know and—" He nodded with his chin toward the wall. "You found something?"

Matthew had already pulled out a small plastic bag to collect the stubs. "If these weren't left by your friends, maybe the young man you saw smoked while watching."

"Wow!" Robert's eyes widened. "You think he was up here to . . . what? Watch and—" He stopped and cocked his head. "You think he's a sharpshooter, some Special Forces type like Gibbs from *NCIS*?"

"A sharpshooter?" Matthew stowed the bag. "Well, why not?" He examined the area more closely, checked the ledge, and walked around the roof without detecting further clues. He had played with the idea of a sniper backing the robbers and was eager to check the idea against the facts of the last crime site.

Robert shuffled behind him, and they left the roof together. "Can you catch him just with these . . . stubs?"

"Maybe not, but we can determine whether the same man was present at other crime scenes."

Robert whistled through his teeth. "So, it's real, and you've got an Abby Schuto in your team, huh?" When Matthew raised his brows, Robert said, "You know, the TV series. She's a cool expert. A scientist. You got one like her? And is she doing great things?"

"Maybe not a hot scientist, but crime scene investigation is real, and we've got experts, too. Some criminals get caught because they were sloppy or didn't know they left behind valuable evidence." He looked into the young man's face.

"Thank you for your help."

"Sure." Robert grinned and quickly quashed it.

Smiling while thinking of Miller being everything but *hot,* Matthew walked back to his car.

Chapter Five

Jacklyn knew Nicolas didn't approve of a blindfold and gag, so his compliance after a brief struggle was more than she'd hoped for. Still tied to the bedposts, Nicolas was panting with anticipation. She stood behind him to knead his reddened butt cheeks and extended her caressing to his cock and balls. He spread his trembling legs wide to give her access, but she moved to his front once he got closer to the climax. He let out a frustrated sigh that turned to hissing when she closed her lips around his rod. He strained in the shackles, and all she wanted to do was touch his bulging biceps and enjoy his struggle. She curbed her desire to lick and suck his member. Nicolas put his head back, urging her wordlessly to push him over the top.

She couldn't help but change her mind. In haste, she undid the buckles of the mittens. "Don't you dare take off the rest," she hissed while he lowered his arms. "I want to see you like this when you do me."

Nicolas made a sound she interpreted as unwilling but complying. Horny in a way that felt unreal, Jacklyn reclined and pulled her lover with her. She couldn't wait to feel him inside her, feel him push relentlessly and urgently. She wound her legs around his waist as he slid inside.

"Harder!"

Nicolas moved forward, pressing his cock as deep as her body allowed. Jacklyn gasped into the orgasm that seemed to fill her entire body. Nicolas groaned with the same desire and let loose that moment. She dug her nails into his shoulder muscles and—biting her lips—rode out the welcome pain he caused, her gaze fixed on his face. She wanted to memorize the minute of their greatest intimacy. She couldn't have been more content.

Nicolas collapsed beside her, shivering in the aftermath.

"I think I gotta change your name," she said and laughed while she undid the blindfold and gag. She cherished his squinting and heavy breathing. "You're much more than a ghost." Jacklyn caressed his sweaty hair while kissing and straddling him. "More like . . . *the Beast*."

Nicolas moved his jaw left and right and flinched. The corners of his mouth were reddened. "That'd make you *Belle*, hmm?"

She crinkled her nose. "But as I said over and over while watching the movie, I want the Beast. So don't change." She kissed him sensuously. "Please, stay the way you are."

"Exhausted and sweaty?"

Jacklyn burst out laughing. "Oh, you're ruining the moment!" Playfully, she boxed his arm, and he pretended to be hurt. "Come on, I don't think I could do you any harm."

"My butt's telling a different story. And let me remind you—I'm still hungry." He gently nipped her chin. "Ravenously hungry by now."

"I feel your rumbling stomach." She slipped off him to stand beside the bed. "May I invite the beast in you to shower with me and have a feast in the kitchen afterward?"

"If it involves food, I'm in."

Matthew bought coffee and a sandwich at a shop close to the bank in DC. Munching and shivering in the wind-driven sleet, he watched the entrance of the bank, the surrounding street, and its characteristics. He was convinced the gang had used the four weeks between the crimes to check out bank routines and customer behavior. He bet they had appeared inside the bank several times to get familiar with the cashiers, the director, and the security guards. Maybe they had even chatted with one of them. The profiler had compared the men to the gang from *Point Break*. They were young and reckless and used violence to scare the victims. In the end, he remembered, they got caught. But that was a movie, and Matthew knew from experience, there wasn't a *happily ever after* scenario for everyone in real life.

He finished eating and crossed the street to access the roof of the opposite building after questioning the tenants. He had no luck. It was an office building, and the employees shrugged and told him they had minded their own business. If there had been someone up on the roof or coming down from there, they wouldn't have noticed, since there were many strangers entering and leaving throughout the day. Any messenger boy could enter the building without being watched, and video surveillance was only stored for one day.

The roof's door lock had been picked. Matthew saw the fine lines in the metal and wondered why his DC colleagues hadn't mentioned it. On the roof at the wall facing the street, the dust and dirt were disturbed. He took pictures with his cell phone before he went closer. The ledge was new, the concrete hardly a month old. He didn't find scratches or any other sign of an intruder who had waited. There were no cigarette stubs, either.

After taking notes of the evidence, Matthew walked downstairs like a sailor with a bad hangover. A wave of nausea made him grab the rail. He stopped and took deep breaths until he felt better, happy that no one saw him shuffle toward the first floor. Back in his car, Matthew decided to stop at his apartment for a nap before going back to the office.

Katherine heard the quarrel when she left the car in front of the house. She took a look around to see whether neighbors were gawking, but it was early afternoon, and nobody was mowing the lawn or washing their cars in the front yard. Frowning, she stepped into the hallway. Tom appeared and took the two bags of groceries but quickly evaded her inquisitive stare. He pressed his lips too tight to make his whispered words understandable, then vanished into the kitchen like a robot going about its work.

"I didn't knock over your bike, you stupid moron!" Theo was shouting in the living room.

Benjamin threw his empty coke can at his brother, yelling even louder. "Yes, you did! You pay for the repairs!"

"You didn't pull out the side stand correctly! Your fucking fault!" Theo was searching for something to throw when Katherine stepped in between.

"Are you nuts? Totally out of your mind?" She dropped her handbag on the table loud enough to get the men's attention. "The neighbors can hear your fight! They're already gathering on their patios for a front row seat. Tom just went out to hand them snacks and beer." She propped her hands on her hips. "You're both morons, stupid like shit!" She looked at the twins. They pouted and shuffled on the wooden floor, evading her glare. "I told you I don't want to move again. I told you to rein in your temper, even if it means bullying each other in private behind closed doors, okay? I told you to stay low-key. What's so fucking hard about that?"

"He ruined my bike," Benjamin said sullenly, still glaring at his brother. "He drove into it. On purpose!"

"I didn't even get close to it. Okay? You don't have a fucking clue about driving, and you don't know fuck how to handle a bike!" Theo thrust his arms in the air. "It's not my fault you parked it on a slope."

"You're jealous I bought the bike, and you can't afford one.

Maybe you'd better save money next time and do something useful with it."

Theo gaped at his twin. "For fuck's sake, don't tell her what she wants to hear, damn you! You're spending your money just as quickly, and I know you're already broke. Again."

"I've had enough." Katherine took a deep breath. She wondered what had gone wrong that the twins fought so much more than other siblings. "You might be twenty-five on paper, but you act like toddlers. Figure out how the bike can be fixed without getting into a fistfight. Then prepare dinner. I'm starving. I'm taking a long shower now, and when I get back, you'd better be ready."

"Or?" Theo raised his brows and pouted.

From the corner of her eye, she saw Benjamin twitch his brows and knew he was on his brother's train of thought. "Or I'll have both of you spanked. Naked. With a crop. Across your asses." She grabbed her handbag and walked off, ignoring laughter and wolf whistles behind her.

"When did you start to figure out what turns you on?"

Taking a break in the living room, Jacklyn adjusted her butt on his thighs, putting her hands on his naked shoulders. She cocked her head and bit her lower lip, knowing he loved the pose.

"A part of me always wanted it that way, but you know, girls like me are educated to become conservative, well-behaved, sophisticated young women who might or might not work, depending on the husband they have to marry and raise a bunch of children." She kissed Nicolas' tip of his nose, then leaned back, frowning. "You really mean that. You really wanna know."

"Absolutely. I wanna know why I put my ass out for you to spank."

"And enjoy it."

He nodded. "And enjoy it. Tell me."

Jacklyn caressed his cheeks, exhaling blissfully. "You're a remarkable man. Usually, the men I met already had the urge to become subs."

"The *scalawags*, as your aunt called them?"

They both chuckled. "Yeah, it was something in their genes or in their expectation of fulfillment. You're different."

Nicolas looked down along his bare body. "Not that much."

"Aside from your extraordinary equipment, you've played the sex game . . ." She sighed.

"Conservatively?"

"Yeah, pretty much by the book. But I love that you didn't push me away when I came along and wanted something different." She met his gaze and finger-combed his hair. "I love the play of muscles, the way you behave when bound. I love your moaning and how you silently beg for more. I love the control you give me and how you play along, even if I make your head spin on some occasions."

Nicolas made a face. "I hit the brakes here and there."

Her sensuous kiss led to more intimate kisses, as if he'd fall apart if she didn't keep him connected to her lips. She ran her hands along his upper arms and shoulders and again through his hair. "You've never scolded me for trying something new. You didn't stop me when I started shaving you." She leaned back to look in his eyes. "And you haven't protested when I did it again."

He flashed a smile. "How could I resist you?"

"Aww, getting mushy on me?"

Once more, Nicolas looked at his assets. "Nope. Definitely not."

Jacklyn played her hands along his ribcage, then attacked his nipples. "I know what I want to—"

He held her wrists, laughing uncontrollably. "Stop that! You're tickling me!"

"Am I?" She escaped his grip to tickle his sides and armpits. He squirmed, and when she didn't stop, he grabbed her upper arms to thrust her to the side on the couch. "Now we'll see—"

Jacklyn brought up her knee against his belly for leverage and pushed him back. She laughed when his eyes went wide, and when he attacked her again with monster howls, she dodged his hands to run for the bedroom. Squealing, she jumped on the bed and swiveled around to face him. He followed her, imitating the Beast marvelously, wild eyes and outstretched hands included. Jacklyn scrutinized her opponent, biting her lips not to laugh. Nicolas charged her and realized too late she'd anticipated his move to trap his right wrist in a shackle tied to a belt around the mattress. He made a sound of disappointment when she locked his second wrist, restricting his movement even further.

"You got me. Again." Nicolas lifted his shackled hands. "I bet with that look on your face you're up to nothing good."

She could tell by his chuckle he made a vain effort to remain serious. "You're so mistaken." Jacklyn panted and pushed back a strand of her hair. "I'm making all this effort to help you get satisfied."

"Aww . . ." He lowered his chin. "I'm so not buying this crap. I'd have loved to cuddle with you, talk silly nonsense, and maybe even love you a little." He looked up again, smiling impishly. "And you're out to ruin my careful planning."

"I made the plans for this day." Jacklyn slipped between his tied-up hands. "You've got no say in this." She bit his nipples and only stopped once he hissed through his teeth. "I could put a collar—"

"No."

Jacklyn traced his neck and shoulder line and moved up

once more to look in his eyes. "It's been a year ago and you could—"

"No."

She frowned with sympathy. "Okay. I was just . . . forget it." She kissed his lips, trying to make up for her move. "I love you so much, my great, wonderful Beast."

He roared and pretended to bite her nose. She could see in his eyes, though, that his mind juggled with her doomed intention.

Matthew arrived at his interim desk just as Sullivan was browbeating a gray-haired agent over a report. Before Matt had a chance to switch on his computer, Sullivan had already chased away the sweating and angry colleague. He came over, ignoring a question his secretary asked about the meeting with someone called *Prescott.* He made a dismissive gesture and kept his gaze set on Matthew.

"Why didn't you answer your phone?" His eyes were slits and his mouth drawn to a thin line. Though he wore cologne, Matthew smelled sweat beneath. "Why didn't you react to any message? Is there a reason you were absent throughout the day without reporting in?"

Matthew swallowed the question of whether he'd been demoted to high school and had to show up at the principal's office. Sullivan breathed down his neck, and his hands were tight fists.

Matthew kept his voice low and calm. "I investigated the crime scenes and found—"

"There were *two more* bank robberies, and your colleagues already got there to investigate. Only you—praised by your former superior for being so experienced—were missing. I was close to sending agents after your GPS signal. Where the hell have you been?"

"The gang consists of one more member, a young man who observes the entrances of the banks and waits—probably with a gun—whether his assistance is needed. If not, he disappears."

Sullivan wiped away the statement with a flip of his hand. "There were no such indications for another bank robber. And I still demand to know where you've been all day."

"I drove to Germantown, Tyson's Corner, and revisited the bank in DC. If you want a full report right now, just say it. Otherwise, I'll give you a complete version in an hour."

Sullivan narrowed his eyes. "Are you getting fresh with me? Is that it? Are you trying to establish a good standing here by insulting me? You'd better not go that way." He tapped the desk. "Without my permission, no one goes out to investigate, especially not at crime sites already thoroughly checked by my agents."

Matthew cleared his throat. "Sorry, sir, but I didn't know that. Additionally, if the other agents had thoroughly interviewed the residents, they'd have found out about the young man with the blue sports bag in which he—most probably—carried a gun." He shrugged intentionally. "I assume it was a sharpshooter gun, folded."

"Where's the evidence?"

"Eyewitnesses at both buildings stated they saw a young man run down from the roof with a bag across his shoulder."

"Oh, and now you assume he carried a gun?" Sullivan's eyebrows shot up. "You're quick to jump to conclusions, huh?"

"I found cigarette stubs at one site. They're with Miller from CSU right now."

Sullivan shook his head. "Don't play that lone cowboy game, Montagna. We're a team here." Upon turning, he said, "You could've asked Hayes to accompany you. And I want that report in thirty minutes. Get acquainted with the reports

Addleton and Spring brought in and look for matches."

"Yes, of course, as you wish. I'll stop breathing until I'll have that one finished." Matthew stopped mumbling as he browsed the rudimentary reports on two bank robberies in the DC vicinity, but he knew instantly they had nothing in common with the gang of four.

"You're shaking your head," a man in a dark gray suit said standing beside the desk.

Matthew looked up, startled. "Yeah, it's loose, and I can't stop. Addleton, or Spring?"

"Spring." He had a firm handshake, suiting his square built. "Addleton is the classy guy with that slicked-back black hair. You find him constantly fighting off women the moment he leaves the safety of this office."

Matthew's grin widened as he followed Spring's pointing finger. Addleton had the physique and the looks of Christiano Ronaldo, and his moves showed restrained strength and restlessness. He fidgeted with the knot of his tie as he scanned the room.

"You're his . . ."

"Bodyguard." Agent Spring nodded gravely. The overhead light shone on his bald, dark brown head. "Besides chasing bank robbers, my prime task is to keep women away from him in order to save his outfits. He had bad weeks when none of his suits survived."

"I see." Matthew curbed his laughter to a chuckle. "Difficult tasks."

"Especially to get him back to the office in his underwear. He's a bit fickle when it comes to that. And now back to those two robberies." Spring put his fleshy hands on the table. "I'm with you that the MO doesn't fit the other three crimes the gang committed. You've got new insight?" He moved his head left and right and pointed across his shoulder. "Couldn't help but hear a part of the conversation, if you wanna call it a conversation at all. You think there was another man involved?"

"Yes. I hope the stubs belong to that man, and that we'll know more tomorrow." He pointed at his monitor. "I'm gonna write this down for Sullivan and send you copies."

"Thanks. By the way, welcome to DC. What made you come here? It's not the *Ritz Carlton* of all FBI field offices."

"Fate." Matthew mimicked Spring's grave nod. "Simple fate to lift the team spirit. Maybe in a decade or sometime later, I'll win."

Jacklyn accompanied Nicolas on a run through the Meridian Hill Park. He was taciturn and hid it by increasing his speed to stay ahead of her. The last quarter mile he left her behind, running upstairs as if competing for the Olympics. She didn't try to catch up, hoping he'd run off steam and get home in a better mood. She couldn't stop thinking that her proposal had so profoundly ruined his willingness. Though she'd have loved to see him with one of the studded collars she kept in her drawers, she had so far accepted his refusal, based on his terrible experience a year ago while he'd been at the mercy of a serial killer.

The bastard had tortured him with a shock collar to force him into obedience. After that ordeal, Nicolas had refused to fasten the top button of his dress shirt or wear a tie for more than two months. An FBI psychiatrist had helped him deal with the consequences of his imprisonment, and as long as there was no pressure of any kind on his Adam's apple, Nicolas could shake off his anxiety.

She cursed her misbehavior for the tenth time on the four-mile run and was close to tears when Nicolas sped on the level path toward the parking lot. Her sides were in flames, and she slowed to a walk as she pressed her hands on her hips. She couldn't remember having run so fast in her lifetime. The cold air stung her lungs.

"Breathe evenly," Nicolas said, handing her a water bottle from the trunk. "Drink and do some stretching." He frowned. "Usually, you have better control of your breathing. We didn't run any further than usual."

He opened the second bottle while Jacklyn tried to come out of her self-pity. She was also jealous he didn't seem out of breath. She bet he could've run the distance in half the time or overtaken her while she was on the first lap.

"I . . . I owe you an apology and don't know what to say. I pondered the whole time, but—" She finished with a gesture of loss.

Nicolas lowered the bottle to look at her with wide open eyes. "An apology? For what?"

Jacklyn straightened and touched her neck. "I was about to force you into something you still don't wanna do. Obviously, I ignored the signs."

"You stopped." His smile was accompanied by a nonchalant shrug. "After all, I'm grateful you backed down." His frown deepened. "That's why you look so miserable?"

Jacklyn nodded, swallowing the lump in her throat. Nicolas put the bottle back in the trunk to embrace her.

"Jacky, honestly, I'd already forgotten about that." He kissed her forehead. "Please, don't think you did something wrong."

"But it was wrong. I know I shouldn't have said a word about collars. I know you don't want them. But I—"

"Ssh. It's all right." He bent to kiss her lips and looked her in the eyes. "There's nothing to forgive, and you don't have to apologize. I'm a big boy. No, don't cry. Please." He caressed her cheeks and kissed her again. "I love you, Jacky. Nothing you do can change that."

"But . . . this game . . . *our* game . . . it's still set by my rules.

And I try to be patient, to not push you too far. I don't want you to lose trust in me. It's all about trust." She embraced Nicolas and pressed her cheek against his chest. "I want to play with you. It's such a thrill ride every time, and I can't imagine a better partner."

He kissed her hair. "I love what you do. How you do it. I want you to feel free to try new things." He moved backward to make eye contact. "I haven't had such fulfillment in my sex life before. I've always been the one trying to be careful, to not harm my lover."

"Yes, you're well endowed."

"Yes, I am." He smiled lopsidedly and pushed a strand of hair from her temple. "You allow me to rage and romp and don't dread me."

"Well, there's no need to . . . with enough chains around your wrists and ankles."

"Exactly." Nicolas pulled her close again. "Sounds like a plan to me for the evening."

Chapter Six

For two weeks, Katherine and Herman took terms observing the bank entrance and the guards of the security company who came to fetch the money. The routines varied but had a pattern, and the three teams remained the same. Katherine created detailed files on every man, his family ties, abilities, and habits. She made Herman write down every single move the bank guard and the men of the security service company made on their daily encounter. Katherine and Herman used different disguises and visited the bank in the early evening to find out what happened inside while the tellers brought out the cash sacks on a trolley.

She didn't trust Theo or Ben with the task of exploring the interior. They had proved in the past they were like pranksters in a toy shop, ready to try out everything and end up being charged by the owner. Herman was more considerate and followed her orders by the book, so she set him on certain tasks.

He observed the employees and customers. He learned about frequent visitors to the director and was talented in counting the cash delivered at the tellers' desks. While Katherine walked in and out to check for cameras and other surveillance, Herman challenged the guards and tested their attention, shuffling into the room dressed in rags and pestering customers. The guards didn't hesitate to politely but firmly walk him out. They made sure he stayed on the sidewalk, and they threatened to call the police if he didn't leave. Herman had told her that he judged they were decisive but weak when it came to violence. They weren't trained to defend the bank with weapons, and Katherine agreed with him that once a shot was fired, they'd back down and hope someone called the Baltimore Police.

"I guess we're ready to strike?" Herman leaned back in the passenger seat to open a soda can.

"Fasten your seatbelt, please."

He did, smiling impishly.

Katherine considered him a satisfied lion stretching his paws in the sunshine. She felt anxiety deep down, no matter how many facets of the crime she had evaluated. There was always a chance she'd overseen something essential, something that would lead to the arrest or injury of her brothers. She demanded that if the routine didn't work, the brothers must abort the plan and run. She wasn't sure they'd follow the rule.

"I'll go over the plan tomorrow. Did Ben steal the van?"

"Yep." Herman drank and lowered the can to his lap to get rid of the false beard while Katherine steered her Lincoln through traffic. "It's another *Toyota,* and they've already exchanged the windshield with bullet-proof glass."

"How did he get that?"

"Don't ask." Herman shook his head. "Really. You don't wanna know, and he won't tell you."

"But I—"

"He knows a woman who knows a man who knows another man ready to do everything as long as the money's okay." He raised his brows. "He's a charmer. The vendor doesn't know Ben, so our anonymity is still guaranteed. Any further questions?"

"Are they behaving?"

"I guess Tom's giving them a hard time." He laughed. "That sounds like he's a kindergarten teacher."

"Ben and Theo are worse than toddlers sometimes. They

don't even know about appropriate behavior, and I feel guilty that Tom's expected to keep them in check. That's not right."

Herman hummed. "He does it for you, and you know it. Is he a good lover?"

She ignored the remark. "I don't know what I did wrong. I tried everything to keep them out of trouble, but they don't see the dangers. Or don't want to." She shook her head when Herman laughed even louder. "How dare you laugh at me? I was the one who brought you up after Mom ran away."

"Hey, hey, sis, it's okay!" He touched her arm, still chuckling. "No one doubts you tried your best. They're reckless sometimes, yes, but they also cherish what you did for them. For all of us." His look was sincere. "We'd all be dead or in prison without you. Don't you ever think we're ungrateful." For a fleeting moment, pain showed in his eyes. "We all carry enough scars from our father to never forget you saved our lives when we were little."

"You were never little," Katherine replied, trying to smile. "You were like a ram at the age of four."

Herman traced her upper ear with his fingers. "You're only two years older. How can you remember me being four?"

She pushed his hand away but still smiled. The memory of their childhood was as painful as any playwright could imagine. "You pushed me over the edge of the couch, and I hit my head so hard I saw double."

"I still regret that, but—in my defense—I was on the run."

"From the neighbor's dog!" Katherine giggled. "He wasn't out to bite you. He just wanted to cuddle."

"He was a damn mastiff!"

"Then you were about the same weight class at that time."

"Thank you so much. If you weren't driving, I'd chase and tickle you until you squirm."

"Hey, that'd be fun." Katherine laughed, seeing his amusement. "Except that you wouldn't catch me, and I'd be the one tickling you until midnight."

Herman clicked his tongue, pouting, and imitating the voice of a toddler "You're so mean."

A red traffic light saved her. She hit the brakes, and when the car stopped, burst into laughter that had her eyes watering. "Now . . . who's the kid here?"

Matthew rifled through the evidence once again without hope of detecting anything new. The whiteboard with photographs of the video surveillance hadn't been updated in the last two weeks. The weapons had no records and appeared unused, maybe stolen from a truck. The stubs Miller had examined belonged to a man with similar DNA to one of the men who had been in the DC van. *Similar,* Matthew knew, meant he was a close relative, most probably a twin brother. The fact confirmed his assumption that the fourth man being on the lookout for the other three.

The hairs detected in the van belonged to the Calhouns and two members of the gang. They were in their twenties, male, white, and without any significant gene defects or illnesses that would allow further investigation. The findings didn't help, since no member of the group had a criminal record. Matthew couldn't explain the fact of how a trained group of men acting like professionals could have gone unnoticed by police authorities over a longer period. Even though they were robbing banks now, he assumed they had looted small shops before. No one starts out big.

Nicolas hadn't discarded his theory of a mastermind in the background, but they hadn't found proof. The gang of four hadn't committed another crime yet, and Nicolas was getting restless, acidly stating that the FBI stood a better chance catching them if they attacked another bank. Sullivan increased the pressure every day that they didn't present a suspect. His annoying insistence depressed Nicolas' mood even further, if that was humanly possible.

While at work, Matthew hardly spoke a word with him, expecting a harsh rebuke if he tried. So far, they had filled their workdays with interrogating a large number of local thieves, paying unfriendly visits to known arms' dealers, and bothering car dealers known to do crooked deals. Upon Matt's suggestion, they'd checked bars, betting offices, and drug dealers in the area to look for young men with unusual sums of cash in their pockets. But even that extended search didn't obtain any results. The news that the wounded guard had died from infection didn't help, either.

The gang remained in an unknown hideout.

Matthew glanced at Sullivan's office, hoping against hope his superior would refrain from asking the same stupid question. Nicolas hurried through the office, gesturing for Matthew to get up and grab his gear.

"There's a robbery at the Union Trade Bank," he explained on their way to the garage. "Police were alarmed immediately and are holding the fort."

"So the gangsters didn't get out?"

"Not yet." Nicolas got behind the wheel and switched on lights and siren as they left for the street. The car jumped across the speed bump, and Matthew's stomach flipped.

"Where're we going?"

"Arlington."

"That's around the corner."

"You wanna jog?"

"No! I like driving with a madman."

"Consider this my civil way. I can do—" Nicolas swerved around a truck swinging into the right lane. The driver obviously hadn't seen the *Oldsmobile* behind him. "Worse."

"Don't doubt that." Matthew held tight to the door handle and pursed his lips. Though he didn't mind car racing, it was different with unsuspecting participants. Nicolas managed to pass the truck without accident. Other drivers were already pulling over to clear the middle lane. Nicolas hit the gas pedal, and the *Oldsmobile* jumped toward the next intersection.

"What do we know so far?"

Nicolas kept his focus fixed on the road and, to Matt's relief, both hands on the wheel. "Policemen reported at least three robbers. Two inside, the third one outside, but escaping in the van when police arrived. He's on the run. The other two—if there're only two—are trapped inside."

"Hostages?"

"Estimated five plus the tellers. It's not a busy hour."

Matthew frowned. "Reaction time of the police is way faster than normal."

"Yes, one of the clerks hit the red button the moment the men walked in. Can't tell what made them suspicious. Maybe the guns at level."

Matthew's reply stuck in his throat when the car rushed the corner with squealing tires. No matter his sturdy stomach, he was feeling sick.

"Hostage Rescue Team was also alerted," Nicolas said evenly. "But maybe the situation can be solved quickly."

Matthew swallowed. He knew the local Hostage Rescue Team, or HRT, were good at their jobs. "What's on the other side of the street?"

"We're there. See for yourself." Nicolas parked at the curb.

Police cars had lined up, blocking the road on both sides, and traffic officers redirected the cars at the next corner. The front of the bank consisted of huge glass windows with advertisements. Behind the posters, the vertical blinds had been pulled shut, with only small slits left. Two of the blinds hung haphazardly by their threads. Because of sunlight and the darker interior, they couldn't see movement inside the bank.

The wide space opposite the bank building was empty, a

gaping hole of soil and stones. Excavators and tower cranes were parked at the sides. A big sign at the fence announced a new shopping center in the making, but no workers were present. Passersby were stopped by policemen and scurried back toward the intersection. Matthew got out of the car, slammed the door shut, and turned toward Nicolas, but his partner was hurrying across the street, his badge held high to signal for the captain of the task force.

Matthew sighed and jogged after him. "Nick! Hey, wait!" He touched Nicolas' upper arm. "This doesn't look like the same gang. It's just not right."

"Because?"

"There's no possible lookout for the fourth man."

Nicolas frowned and pointed toward the intersection. "The other details fit. Easy bank access, no major bank, not the last day of the month, an easy escape route."

"Yet no support if anything went awry. Like it did."

Nicolas nodded without granting assent, then turned to listen to the police captain.

"At least two robbers inside. They threatened to kill all hostages if we don't pull back."

"You got them on the phone?"

"No. One of them shouted through the front door with a young woman held in front of him so we couldn't shoot." The captain wiped his gray mustache and adjusted the fit of his hat. "I'm glad to see you here. What's the plan? Shall my men retreat?"

"We aren't HRT, just the special agents attached to the series of bank robberies."

"Oh." The captain's face fell. "I thought we could get this solved quickly." He took a deep breath as he looked over his shoulder. His haggard shoulders dropped. "So, we gonna wait?"

"We have to. What can you tell us about the bank robbers?"

The captain was interrupted by shots fired inside the bank. One of the large windows cracked when two bullets struck. Instantly, the police officers ducked behind their cars. The captain shouted to hold fire. The bullet-proof glass showed a web of destruction. Matthew worried about the people inside.

More shots resounded.

Nicolas turned on his heels, ran for the car, and came back with two bullet-proof vests and two automatic rifles.

"No time to wait for HRT," he said, gearing up. "They're about to lose it. Are you with me getting inside?"

"Sure." Matthew felt the surge of excitement and fear churning his stomach and vibrating his nerves as he fastened the vest and checked the rifle magazine. He'd been assigned to a desk job for a year, and though he'd continued training, he'd been disconnected from active duty. His heart raced so badly he fought nausea and hoped his partner wouldn't notice.

"You okay?" Nicolas asked. "Can I count on you?"

"Yes." More words were strangled in his throat, and Matthew nodded he'd follow Nicolas' lead as he wiped his sweaty hands on his pants.

"There's a back entrance."

They took the captain and four police officers with shotguns to the rear side of the building, moving swiftly through a narrow service alley. As ordered, the policemen waiting in front of the bank called to the robbers via megaphone to give up and leave the building with their hands up. Nicolas pulled out a small black device, clipped it to the lock and had it detonated ten seconds later. The sound was drowned by yet another shot and a shrill cry inside the bank. Nicolas and Matthew rushed through the entrance quick enough to evade to the left and to the right when shots were fired in their direction.

Matthew dodged at the corner of a corridor leading toward

the counter area.

"Stand back, or we kill the fucking people!" a man shouted. His voice was ear-piercing, on the verge of panic, and made Matthew's hair stand on end. "Back off, you assholes! I'll kill you all!"

Matthew let out his breath and leveled the gun to turn the corner quickly. "FBI! Put down your weapon and raise your hands above your head!" He made another step, blood pulsing in his ears. He heard someone talking behind him, but couldn't make out any words. Another step brought him closer to the shadow of a man. A woman wept loudly, another one shrieked, and Matthew had the urge to rush the counter area and kill the bastards.

Nicolas appeared beside him on the other side of the corridor. He crouched low, gun leveled, and moved forward with slow, measured steps.

A tall, lanky man stepped into the corridor. His left arm was pressed around the throat of a woman in a dark red two-piece outfit. A large brooch shaped like an owl glittered with every heave of her bosom. She fought to breathe, and small cries escaped her lips. The bank robber pressed the muzzle of a *Browning* handgun against her temple. His finger moved at the trigger, ready to pull through. The man's face was covered by a white mask, and his arm pressed harder when the woman grabbed helplessly to pull him off. Her round face was reddened and her eyes full of terror. Tears had smeared her careful eye make-up.

"Drop your weapons!" the thug screamed. "Drop them, or I'll kill her!"

The woman opened her mouth for another, now suppressed cry, and her eyes turned inward as her knees buckled. She became dead weight and slipped down despite the gangster's attempt to hold her. He turned the muzzle toward the policemen.

Nicolas shot the moment the woman's head was below the man's shoulder and hit his throat. The impact thrust him backward to the floor where his head bounced once. The gun slithered to the wall as he reached for the wound with both hands. His breath was but a gargle with blood pulsing out of the hole. The hostage slipped to the floor and lay on her belly, motionless. Nicolas gave up his stance and knelt at her side to check her pulse.

A woman in jeans and leather jacket appeared in the corridor, taking Matthew by surprise.

"You miserable bastards!"

Her brunette hair and tanned complexion as well as her female physique caught his attention and pushed him back memory lane so vehemently, he whispered Nerina's name.

"Fuck you all!" She pulled up the pistol with both hands and aimed at Nicolas' head.

Matthew inhaled, shocked, frozen in his crouch. He raised the shotgun when on his left, two police officers fired simultaneously, rocking the woman with a volley so viciously she was pushed back three steps and collapsed on the floor. Matthew stared at the body, feeling a fist tightening around his ribcage. He couldn't breathe. His thoughts were reduced to imagining Nerina might have ended the same way—bleeding to death in a hail of bullets.

"She should've surrendered," he whispered, hardly hearing his words through the ringing in his ears.

"The lady's fine," Nicolas said in a clear, commanding tone to the officers closing in. "Just unconscious. Get an ambulance!" He got up from the spot beside the teller. "Hey, Matt, you coming?"

Matthew was already moving forward to kick the weapon away from the dead bank robber. The woman's upper body had been pierced by four bullets. Her lifeless eyes seemed to accuse him, and Matthew hurried on, weapon at the ready to face the next target. He hoped there'd be another robber, someone who deserved punishment for the pain he had caused.

Nicolas was moving at his left side, the role model of an FBI agent with outstanding field training. The smell of gun powder and sweat was in the air, and the noise after the sudden screams was muffled. They checked the large area thoroughly but didn't see another man or woman with a gun. There were only bank employees and customers prone on the floor, shaken and terrified. Some lifted their heads tentatively, while two women next to the counters remained in their position, whimpering.

"Are you all right? Anyone hurt?" Nicolas shouted. "Is there another one around?"

"No," a young man with a ponytail answered. His eyes were wide and full of fright. "There were only two."

Upon a nodded agreement, Matthew gave up his stance and turned to an elderly man who sat slumped against a desk. He was barely conscious and bleeding from a shoulder wound close to his neck. Matthew stowed his weapon to deliver first aid, listening to the employee's mumbling. At second glance, he realized the man was wearing a uniform and had probably tried to protect the customers. Behind Matthew, more policemen poured in to assist employees and customers who were able to walk out of the bank. On the street, sirens announced the incoming ambulances.

Matthew looked into Nicolas' stern face. His eyes were still wide, his face sweaty, but his breathing appeared under control. After the briefest moment of eye contact, Nicolas directed the officers with clear orders, let in the medics, and shooed an eager young sergeant away from the female body. Without the vest and the shotgun, Agent Hayes might've been a bank teller, but with more self-confidence than the others.

Katherine could tell from Benjamin's furtive glance something was wrong. He avoided her approach and left the room quickly. Heart beating in her throat, she hurried through the living room onto the porch. The stench of smoke filled the area, and she squinted, quickening her steps.

Tom was fighting flames among the rose bushes with a fire extinguisher, leaving the branches with white, blossom-like decoration. He inhaled sharply when she stopped beside him.

"I'm sorry, I tried to save . . ." He shook his head and put down the extinguisher. "It was too late."

"Tom? Tom, are you all right?" She reached out for him, but he sidestepped, shaking his head once more.

"I'm really sorry. I wasn't fast enough."

"My rose bushes . . ." Katherine exhaled, gaze fixed on the pitiable remnants dripping with foam.

Two feet away, the barbecue coals were still smoking, and some pieces lay scattered on the blackened grass. The slices of raw meat waited on a small table. The rising rage in her head needed a vent.

She stepped back, facing the gray sky, and praying for composure. "Theo or Ben?"

Tom secured the extinguisher's latch and was about to pass her by.

"Theo or Ben?" she repeated.

"I don't know." Tom kept his chin low, still not meeting her gaze. "And I won't tell."

"Don't fucking try to protect them!"

"I'm not." He evaded her hand once more and left.

Katherine turned around, feeling suffocated. Fear was gaining a hold on her. She thought of Ben and Theo and a burning shed in Joliet. Sitting in the grass and watching the fire, they had smiled as if granted their greatest wish and were surprised when Katherine yelled at them. Their father had quickly grabbed and lambasted them until they screamed while Katherine and Herman had run to fight the fire with water buckets. Their efforts had been in vain. Within minutes, the shed and everything in it had burned to ashes. They had been lucky the shed hadn't held any diesel canisters.

The twins, at nine years old, had cried for hours, partly because of pain and partly because their wonderful party idea had turned into a disaster.

She turned to head to the training room, but Herman blocked her way. He lifted his hands and mimicked her move when she sidestepped. "Hey, wait, I just heard. Don't . . . don't go there. Please, I know they misbehaved. Let me deal with them."

"You?" Katherine pushed his chest. "You'll give them a high-five and laugh with them." She pushed again, harder. And when it felt good, she put more weight into it. "They could've burned down the house. The entire fucking house! With you and me inside."

"I won't laugh with them. Believe me, I know they've overstepped a line. I'm not stupid."

"Yes, you are!" She drummed her fists on his chest. "You and Ben and Theo. You're a fucking bunch of retarded twits, good-for-nothing idiots who are only happy destroying everything beautiful in this world." Tears trickled down her cheeks. "No matter what I try to build up, you rip it down with your asses and laugh." Her voice rose. "I can't take no more! No more!" She broke free from Herman to stumble a few steps. "I'll leave you." She lifted her hands. "I need to leave you."

"I know. I understand." He followed her. "But we'd be lost without you. Probably dead."

"Yes, you would be. So what?" She sobbed and wiped her eyes. "I shouldn't mess about with you. You only cause trouble."

Herman embraced her and didn't let go when she fought his grip. He kissed her hair. "I'll buy you new bushes and make the twins plant them. You can stand behind them and whip them while they kneel in the soil. Okay? Will that do?"

Katherine wept, and while he still held her fast, she nodded with her forehead pressed against his chest.

"Their naked asses, if you want to," Herman said, chuckling.

"With a cat-o-nine-tails."

Herman's chuckle rose in volume. "I'll buy that, too."

The investigation of the crime scene, including interrogating the customers and employees, took three hours. CSU secured evidence, and the coroner showed up to transport the dead robbers and a victim who had been killed in the first eruption of violence. The tellers described under tears what had happened, and Matthew and Nicolas did their best to lead them through the protocol before they allowed them to leave.

Matthew was bathed in sweat, had a headache, and was hungry and thirsty. He hadn't had breakfast prior to the operation, and while police and CSU wrapped up, he waited impatiently for Nicolas to show up at the car. He made a mental note to stock the car with food and drink. The wind was picking up, and he longed to get inside.

Nicolas arrived, carrying his vest and shotgun one-handed while he opened the trunk with the other. "The captain will hand over his report later today. Coroner and CSU are briefed to deliver their results ASAP." They dropped the gear in the trunk and got in the car. "Sullivan won't be satisfied we just solved a crime."

"But didn't catch the serial robbers." Matthew shook his head. "No brownie points from his side."

Nicolas grunted something unintelligible, put the car in

gear, and drove past the police barrier. He sped down the avenue, out of Arlington, and left downtown behind to exit the highway at the parking lot of a small diner. It was empty but for two cars, and Nicolas parked at the end of the row close to a painted wall that hid the garbage cans. Matthew opened his mouth to thank Nicolas for the smartest idea he'd had so far but caught his partner's glare. The words stuck in his throat.

"Get out!" Nicolas ordered, opened the seat belt, and was out first.

Matthew followed. As he closed the door, Nicolas was already around the hood, grabbed his lapels, and pressed his back against the metal. Matt felt a sharp pain at his spine.

"Are you out of your fucking mind?" Nicolas shook him hard. His eyes were wide. "Did you wanna kill me? Let me die on the first job we've got together?"

"I didn't—"

"She was pointing at me, you bastard! I looked into the muzzle!"

Matthew brought up his arms to break his partner's fierce grip and get his back away from the car. "Stop that, damn it! I would've shot!"

"Right after she'd have pulled the trigger!" Nicolas grabbed his shoulders again hard enough to hurt him. "You would've been too fucking late! She would've shot me in the face!"

"No!" Matthew fought his way out, and they wrestled until Matthew had Nicolas in a chokehold. His voice was strained. "Get a grip, damn it! I didn't want to get you killed. Okay? I was shocked for a moment seeing a woman, but that's all. Man, stop fighting!"

Nicolas grunted, fought, and stopped when he didn't break free. They stood, breathing laboriously like two deer struggling with their antlers.

"Can I let go without risking you going for my face?"

Matthew asked, cautiously easing his grip.

Nicolas nodded, and once Matthew loosened his hold stepped back at the hood to straighten his shirt and jacket. His face had an unhealthy red hue, and despite his wordless promise, Matthew didn't trust the truce. Given the fury he was in, Matthew didn't put it beyond his partner to assault him again.

Nicolas ran a hand through his hair as he caught his breath. "You let me down in there. And I wanna know why. Don't gimme that shit that you've never seen a female gangster."

"No." Matthew felt a weight pulling him down. He steadied himself at the door frame. "No, that's not it. I . . . I thought . . . she looked like . . ." He closed his eyes, but the parking lot turned around him, and he swayed. "She looked like my wife. Ex-wife." He blinked and waited for Nicolas' outburst of anger, knowing he wouldn't withstand another round. "It was just a split-second. Her picture . . . I'm a good shot, Nick. I won't let you down."

Nicolas pursed his lips and propped his hands on his hips. "Don't put my life at risk, okay? Get your ex off your mind or get another partner. I don't wanna live through that again."

"Okay." Matthew frowned. "You gonna report me for my mistake?"

"Wouldn't have wrestled you here if I was going to vilify you." Nicolas locked the car. "You pay for breakfast."

Matthew nodded compliantly while he checked his tie and lapels in the side window. "I pay for breakfast."

"This month."

"Hell, may I remind you? You just lost—"

"You pay for breakfast."

Chapter Seven

They ordered breakfast and coffee. To the waitress' astonishment, Matthew asked for a large glass of water along with his coffee. Nicolas granted him time to drink and studied the small crowd sitting on the other side at the window. Six men in work clothes were debating the current football season results, louder with each argument. One of them slapped the table, and the waitress asked them politely to tone down their conversation. He was about to talk back when his gaze fell on Nicolas, who casually pulled back the lower part of his jacket. His badge shone for a second, and the guest nodded toward the waitress, grunting an excuse. Twitching his brows, Nicolas let the jacket fall in place again.

When the waitress looked in his direction quizzically, he smiled and toasted her with his cup of coffee.

"I wouldn't mind some hands-on argument," Matthew said quietly. He put both hands around his mug, staring at the steaming coffee. "I'm glad the bank robbers are dead. Wouldn't want them to have a long trial and . . ." He sighed and took a sip.

"Tell me about your ex-wife, and you'd better not put me off with nonsense about your tragic relationship."

"And if it was just that?" Matthew set down the mug with more care than necessary.

Nicolas wished he hadn't made the remark. Matthew sounded deeply wounded.

"You put the officers and me in danger today."

"Yes, this one's on me. When it comes to my relationship—

that's something totally different." He took another sip. "Women let you run over razor-sharp blades and laugh at you while you're bleeding." He paused. "What I lived through . . . there's nothing I can sum up in a few words."

Their breakfast orders were served, and they ate in silence. A family with three children took another booth at the window. The parents tried to calm the kids down, yet they were climbing the seats and slipping down again, only to continue playing under the table. The eldest was about ten years old, the younger ones about seven and five. They were excited about eating in a diner. The waitress was all smiles and helpfulness to take their orders, even showed them they could combine kids' menus. She accepted all kinds of side orders and had a joke for the youngest that the cook would make him dinosaur pancakes if he wished.

Nicolas watched Matthew's demeanor change from grumpy and sad to mildly amused. The parents thanked the waitress for having brought their orders quickly, and the kids settled to eat in surprising peacefulness.

Matthew pushed the empty plate to the edge of the table and put his hands around the mug again. "My wife cheated on me. Badly. More than once. She betrayed me with a smile and made me believe I was the love of her life. She misused my trust, and finally, after almost three years, I was the last one to find out about her true character." He lifted and dropped his left hand on the table, and his thumb played with the empty spot at his ring finger. "You aren't married, huh?" he asked, looking up.

"No."

"But in a relationship?"

"Yes."

"A rough one, as it appears to me."

Nicolas frowned. "No, not at all."

Matthew shook his head and wiped his chin. "Not my

business, but you don't chafe your wrists with a hard sponge. Those abrasions come from cuffs."

"I don't–" He pulled down the shirt sleeves. "This really isn't the subject here, Matt, so don't try to digress."

Matthew huffed. "I get it." He took a deep breath. "My wife betrayed me in the worst way possible, and I filed for divorce. Papers from the judge came four weeks ago and confirmed I'm free and single again."

"I've been working with a partner who's been through a divorce for more than four years by now. He's never hesitated because he saw the face of his former wife on a job."

"We're all different."

"You were shocked."

"I was shocked because I feared that one day, Nerina might become the target of a sniper because of my job. It's not unheard of that the wives of agents get into some criminals' focus."

Nicolas raised his brows. "The moment a thug's got a weapon she's a threat, okay? You'd better not think–"

"It's not going to happen again."

"No? Because from now on you'll be sober in the morning?"

Matthew sat up straight. "What's this about?"

Nicolas wanted to shake Matthew for his pretended innocence. "You dare ask? I haven't said a word because I know it's hard to start over in a new city with new people around you. Okay. But I expected this to last for a few days, not two weeks."

"I don't–"

"Yes, you do! Even now you look like–"

"Shit. I know." He made a face. "My partner wrestled me in the parking lot."

"You look like you're having a very bad hangover. Again."

"That's not true. Come on–"

"You thought if you don't talk I wouldn't notice? But I did. I don't know how bad your divorce was, and to be honest, I don't care. But I need a partner who focuses on the job and helps me solve crimes. I don't care how you spend your evenings and nights, but from the moment you arrive at the office, you must be awake and fully alert. This isn't an office job. My life depends on you and your reaction."

"Are you done?"

"I've spared this lecture for today. Why did you ask for a transfer? Or didn't you?"

Again, Matthew seemed taken aback by the question. "I asked for it. I needed distance after my divorce."

"That bad?"

"That bad." Matthew took a deep breath. His gaze was unsteady. "Can we change the subject? Please? Enough soul stripping for the day." He looked for the waitress to ask her for the check.

"Why DC?"

"It was the first field office with a free spot for another agent." Matthew paid, left a sizeable tip, and stood. "Meeting Senior Agent Sullivan cleared up why that is."

They left for the parking lot. Nicolas put his hands in his pants pockets. "You didn't give preferences? I mean, coming from Chicago, maybe Minneapolis would've been a better choice."

"If I had made a choice." They got into the car, and Nicolas backed up. "But I left it to my superior with the only request to arrange a quick leave. That's what he did."

Nicolas had a list of questions he wanted to be answered, but seeing Matthew's pain, he shut his mouth for the ride.

Nicolas came home thinking about Matthew's confession. Instinct told him there was more behind his colleague's mood swings and hangovers, but at the office, they'd focused on summing up the case with the bank robber couple. The fugitive in the escape car had been stopped by highway police ten miles outside DC and was in custody. Matthew had volunteered to stay late and write the report for Sullivan. In silent understanding, Nicolas had accepted the peace-offering and left.

Jacklyn greeted him wrapped in thick jogging pants and a cardigan. "Heat is off. I already called the service. They'll need four to six hours to repair it." She shivered. "Cuddle?"

Nicolas put down his backpack to embrace her. He felt better instantly. "Sure. Let me freshen up and grab a bite. I'm starving."

"I'll get you something, and we'll eat in bed. It's the only warm place at the moment. Especially with you in it." She slapped his butt and went into the kitchen.

He felt the cold the moment he got out of the shower and quickly dressed to meet Jacklyn in their bed, padded with pillows and warm blankets. Her head stuck out, and her pitiful whimper made him laugh.

"It's never been this cold in DC, ever," she complained as he slipped under the covers.

"Poor little freezing girl." He took her in his arms and kissed her hair. "What'll you do in December? Wear two pairs of pants and a thick winter coat for the Christmas party?"

"There'll be a Christmas party?" she peeped. "And me attending it with you?"

"If you want to. I'd be happy if you accompanied me." He made a face. "I need all the support I can get to stand Sullivan's repeated Christmas speech and how great the FBI is. And not to mention how grateful we should be because we're allowed to work there." He rolled his eyes. "Which means we should bow at his feet because he's our boss."

"What about Jason?"

"You tell me." He made eye contact. "How's his physiotherapy?"

"You didn't tell me he's a sissy. He wants to feel better but avoids pain at all costs. I told him he won't walk the next couple of weeks if he doesn't get over that point."

"You told him he's a sissy? He'll keep a grudge for days."

"I don't care. He must do the exercises. But I guess he enjoys staying at home with Elaine being a mother hen. She's constantly around him. I bet she'd quit working to be there twenty-four-seven if she could afford it. I talked to her, but I don't think she'll push him. Yes, laugh it off! Men are so—"

"Wonderful?" Nicolas kissed the tip of her nose. "Irreplaceable? Lovable?"

Jacklyn put her palms on his cheeks. "I do love you, my Beast. But if you howl and moan about aches, I'll slap you. Promise."

Nicolas burst out laughing and smacked a kiss on her lips. "My little Belle, did you listen to what you just said? You're the one who slaps my sorry butt constantly. And you chain my wrists so tight Matt noticed the abrasions."

"Ouch!" Jacklyn grimaced and checked his arms. "I'd better be careful, hmm? Or your colleagues will come checking on me and claim a case of domestic violence."

"I won't allow that. What we have is between us. I can handle Matt. He's got his own bunch of problems." While he ate, he recapped the events of the day's bank robbery without going into detail. "Let's say we had an argument about his work attitude, and it's settled."

"It doesn't sound like he's easy to work with. Will he watch out for you?"

"He'll have my back if it comes to it." Nicolas kissed her with feeling. "Don't worry. Just put your freezing toes under my legs and cuddle with me."

While *REM* performed *Man on the Moon*, Matthew pondered Nicolas' lecture, disregarding traffic around him until he had a narrow encounter with a large *Lincoln Continental* driven by an old woman who couldn't look across the wheel. He honked, and she steered away, flipping the bird. Matthew gaped at her, distracted once more. More honking from other drivers followed.

Feeling like the survivor of a traffic war, Matthew parked his car and walked home. He got into his apartment, and as he took off his badge and gun, he realized he was out of whiskey. He stood in the hallway for a minute before he cursed, turned, and walked to the liquor store a block down the street. A cold drizzle slapped his face, and he pulled up the lapels of his woolen overcoat. For the umpteenth time, he wished he was back in Chicago. Homesickness washed over him, even colder than the raindrops in his face. Sneezing, he entered the store, bought his favorite whiskey, and headed out again, stowing his wallet. Nicolas' words were in his mind again, and his mood sank. He couldn't remember being so weak-minded and dependent on booze. He had been proud of his strong character, his soldier-like attitude, and his spotless FBI file. If Nicolas reported his failure and hangovers to Sullivan, he'd probably be admonished or—if Sullivan and his peers had a bad day—get the ax.

A sound caught his attention. Matthew stopped at the store corner in time. Holding the bottle in his right hand, he threw the left one up to fend off the blow to his face. He swiveled around, hit the bottle across the black man's head, and when the attacker swayed, he kicked him in the belly. The stranger sat hard on the concrete.

"You damn motherfucker!" Matthew was about to kick the lanky thug again when two more men ran toward him from the dark alley. Matt took a second to break into a run. It was too late.

The guy to his right had a ring in his nose, another one in his brow, and a third one dangled from his left ear. His broad face with the narrow eyes and the flat nose spoke of low intelligence but a lot of fight experience. His fist with brass knuckles shot out for Matthew's face. He missed and hit the bottle instead. Glass broke, and Matthew dropped the paper bag quickly to avoid cutting himself. He reached for his gun, but the holster was empty.

"Fuck!"

The guy to his left, of average built but powerful, boxed Matthew's kidney three times in quick succession. Hurting badly, Matthew stepped back to get both men in view and deflect their attacks. He glanced left and right.

"Stop, you fuckers! I'm a police officer! You don't wanna mess with me!"

"Who do you wanna threaten with that voice? A nun?"

Matthew parried two more blows but was forced against the wall. He dodged the next fist aimed at his face, yet couldn't get out of reach.

"Get his badge and gun! Hurry!" the man with the brass knuckles shouted.

The second thug, a guy in his thirties, hit Matthew's chin with one fist, causing him to see double, while the other one aimed for his chest. Matthew kicked the man's knee, heard him howl and kicked again, harder.

The man went down beside his unconscious companion. "Son of a bitch!"

A blow to his belly cut off Matthew's air, but he freed himself with an uppercut that drove the thug with the rings back. Matthew coughed, and in spite of his fuzzy vision, lashed out against the thug's face again before he kicked his genitals as hard as he could. The man went down, screaming. The other stayed on the ground and held his knee. Matthew kicked his face, and he dropped like a stone, unconscious.

Matthew panted and leaned against the wall, expecting there would be more muggers waiting in line. He wiped his tearing eyes, and when his eyesight cleared, he searched the men's pockets. He found neither wallets nor guns. After dropping their few belongings, he limped out of the shadow behind the liquor store into the streetlights. There were no passersby, and traffic was thin. The store manager was stacking up cigarette packs behind the counter, oblivious to what was happening outside. Matthew's right hand was slick with blood, but it was too dark to see the damage.

Slowly and in pain, Matthew walked back to his apartment.

Jacklyn traced Nicolas' chest with her fingertips. "Don't you think my aunt's right, and we should move into a cozy house in the suburbs?"

"You're joking, right?"

"No, I'm not." She looked up to him and stretched to place kisses on his cheek. "We do have little room here, and you still have stuff in your apartment. It would be wonderful to leave downtown behind. After all, with the money we spend on two apartments, we could easily afford a bigger home in a better district."

Nicolas sat straight in the bed, frowning. "We agreed on staying here because it's the shortest commute to work for both of us. So, how come the change of mind?"

"My parents have a great home on Long Island. It's an old house with a large garden." She released her breath, sighing. She remembered the beautiful garden where she had played as a kid. Back then, she had hoped to earn enough money to call such a mansion her own later in her life. "Old trees, plenty of space. I've always loved being there. It's beautiful."

"Sure, your parents have plenty of money to spend without thinking twice. I'm only a special agent, not an ambassador. Sorry, my little Belle, but I can't afford to buy you a castle in my lifetime."

Jacklyn detected uneasiness and tried to quash it with a smile and a kiss. "Nick, I'm not talking about an old estate with twenty acres of land around, okay? Just a home with three bedrooms, maybe, a small garden, and a porch to sit on at nights."

"You're missing your parents' wealth?"

"Don't say that. I'm not missing anything." She flinched because he had seen through her so easily again. "I shouldn't have mentioned my parents, hmm? Bad me. But think of it—together we can afford a better home, and we should do it now while prices are low."

"I don't care about prices. Aside from my loving this apartment—we don't have the time to go looking for a new place. I don't know when I'd have time to meet with real estate agents and visit open houses." He made a face and sighed, exasperatedly. "Jacky, this is time-consuming, believe me. And as mentioned before, I like it here. With you."

"I know a place where I'd want to live." She bit her lips, watching Nicolas' mood turn from patient to cautious. "You know, I've pondered this idea for some time, and then I spoke to Harry and—"

"*Harry Fuller*?" Nicolas was tense and inched away from her. "You aren't telling me you're thinking about moving into a house Harry offered you to buy, right?"

"I know what you think, but wait and—"

Nicolas' voice sank to a growl. "You and I spent a weekend at his house in the mountains, and he had us *on tape*! Honestly, I don't know whether he erased all the videos as he claimed. I won't set foot in any house he owns. Forget it."

"Nick, please . . ."

Nicolas slipped out of the bed, pointing a finger at her. "You cannot seriously think about dealing with that man. His son's a killer, and he might be involved somehow."

"That hasn't been proven so far, and I doubt it."

"You do? Or is this just you thinking of good ol' times and that you can't imagine any of your friends being a gangster? Get real."

Jacklyn gaped at him. "You're prejudiced. I can't believe it. How could you say that?"

"I've seen enough crooks in my years of service to know. So, if you wanna move . . . okay, but find a different real estate agent. I won't set foot in a house Harry owns. I couldn't sleep there."

"It's really nice," she said meekly.

Nicolas shook his head and left the bedroom.

Matthew looked back at the flight of stairs. There were several drops of blood, dark red against the light brown wooden steps, even more on the doorstep, because he'd searched for the keys. He closed the door behind him and shuffled into the bathroom, keeping his hand pressed against his belly. In the light above the mirror, his face looked ashen, decorated with a purple bruise at his chin. His eyes were dark-rimmed, and now after the tension left him, he was tired, as if he'd run a marathon. He slipped out of his jacket and shirt, both soiled with blood.

Clenching his teeth against the pain, he searched the cabinet for the neatly packed first aid kit. He ripped it open one-handed, using his teeth. The contents spilled across the sink and shelf.

"Fuck! Nerina, I could use a hand here," he mumbled. His right hand was bleeding from a cut close to the wrist, and he moved his fingers carefully. The bleeding had flushed out foreign bodies but didn't stop. He rinsed the wound, decided against driving to a hospital, and used butterfly closures and a tight bandage. Matthew hoped the bleeding would stop sooner than later, but he felt his blood pressure drop while he cleaned up the sink. He had more bruises along his ribcage and sides, one the size of a man's fist. He called himself lucky the brass knuckles hadn't been in play.

He flinched, realizing he was still out of whiskey. Sputtering a row of curses in two languages, he fetched the last six-pack of beer and settled on the couch. He knew Bert's number by heart and when his friend took the call, spilled his day's misery in a clipped version.

"You aren't a happy camper these days, huh?" Bert teased. "I don't like telling you this, but if you don't get a grip, either your partner will throttle you, or you'll kill yourself because of sloppiness. Take your pick."

"That's really helpful." Matthew stood to take a painkiller and washed it down with beer. "How was your day?"

"Well, I didn't try to get shot, I didn't run into thieves. By the way, what were they up to? Money? Your life? If they wanted to kill you—just playing the devil's advocate here, but they could've done that with a bullet."

"Really?" Matt put the cold can against his forehead and closed his eyes. "A knife would've done the job, too, and isn't as loud."

"But you're getting the point here, right? You didn't mention a knife. And you said they were out for your badge and gun? Did they get anything?"

"No. They got nothing." The cold was working against the growing headache. "And I can't think of anything else behind the attack than some muggers out for a quick grab of cash."

"No, no, that doesn't fit. You heard them call for your badge and gun, right?"

Bert's alertness made Matthew grumpy. "I told him I'm a

police officer. I thought it would drive him off. It worked in Chicago. But DC's a different city altogether."

"More brutal muggers? You're kidding me."

"Number one crime city." Matthew drank his beer and put down the can. He couldn't have felt lonelier on a deserted planet.

"But, Monty, I might not be an expert, but they must've expected you to draw your gun, right?"

"They were hard and fast on me and knew what they wanted. When I tried to reach and, yes, realized I didn't have my piece with me, they doubled their efforts to get me down."

"But they weren't out to kill you, right?"

"Nope, obviously not." Matthew closed his eyes. The fight came back in bits and pieces, but he had no energy to follow Bert's analysis further. "How's Bouncer? Did you see him?"

"Hey, if you wanna know about your dog, why don't you call Gladys and Umberto? Do you expect me to check across the street every day?"

Matthew sighed. The pain in his hand was only tolerable if he kept it elevated. He wondered how he was supposed to sleep. "They'd tell me too much. I miss my dog, okay? I don't want stories about the *good life* he's leading now, just if he's okay."

"That's ungrateful, Monty, and you know it."

"Yeah, I know." Matt grunted changing position.

"You sure you don't want to see a doc about your condition? I mean, tough guy and so on, but a brawl's a brawl."

"I'll make it. I don't want to call in sick in the morning. It's just—"

"A no-go? Really? Monty, if you can't walk straight, you're in your partner's way and no help at all. Promise me to think about it in a few hours, okay?"

"You're clucking, Bert. Maybe you shouldn't advertise for a woman for life but for a guy. You've got enough femininity for two."

"Monty!" Bert roared in his ear. "You're a son of a bitch!"

Laughing out loud, Matthew hung up.

Chapter Eight

Katherine drank coffee from a plastic cup and cursed when she spilled drops on the yellow blouse she was wearing under her winter coat. She put the cup away, sighed, and withstood the urge to leave the car and ask for a wet cloth in the next shop. There would be clerks to recognize her later. There would be passersby who could describe her, even though she wore a brown-haired wig, large sunglasses, and clothes she despised as unstylish. The requirement was the same as before—the fewer people who knew about her and her brothers, the fewer people were able to testify.

"Van's coming around the corner," Ben said in her ear. She imagined him on the rooftop, left hand at the barrel, finger of his right hand around the trigger. He would kneel behind the low ledge while spying through the sight. Anytime she watched him shoot, she was amazed at his abilities. "Thirty seconds."

"Roger, buddy," Herman replied in his dark voice full of amusement. "Hope you've got enough bullets. This is going to be a fucking show."

"You're on!"

Katherine bit on her artificial nail when the armored car rounded the corner and stopped at the bank entrance. Two men got out, nodded toward each other, and waited for the guard from the bank to direct them inside. She looked at her watch.

"Five minutes."

"We're there, sweet sis." Herman made a kissing noise, but

Katherine was too tense for a joke.

She repeated the mantra she had invented. Everything would work out. She had the boys prepared to the last detail with escape plans B and C for any eventuality. There was no reason for nervousness.

Her heart beat so fast, she felt a lump in her throat. She glanced at the coffee cup, but though it would look natural for anyone passing by that she was sitting in her car drinking coffee, she didn't pick it up. Her stomach churned. She'd already checked whether the car would jump to action the moment she needed it without running it idle the whole time. This, too, would be suspicious.

After three minutes, the guards appeared, carrying two large sacks each.

"They're early! Go!"

"Roger that." Benjamin sounded eager.

With a popping sound that no pedestrian noticed, two wheels of the armored car lost air, and it listed to the right side. Herman's black van turned the corner and stopped right behind the damaged vehicle. Herman and Theo jumped out on the left side while Tom remained behind the wheel, his mask drawn across his face. Herman leveled the *MP* and shot at the guard close to the entrance. The man broke down on the sidewalk, and Theo ordered the others to drop the sacks. They obeyed immediately and stepped back, hands lifted. As fast as they could, passersby turned and fled in both directions, shrieking in terror. Katherine estimated the police forces would arrive in four minutes if one of the clerks hit the emergency button immediately. The double glass doors of the bank opened, and two guards with their weapons drawn came out. Herman had them in view and shot four bullets to bring them down. They collapsed against the door and didn't get up. The men from the transport service dropped to their knees. Katherine couldn't hear words, but they appeared to beg Herman to spare them.

Theo collected the four sacks, threw them into the van, and was inside first. Katherine heard him grunt with the heavy weight. Herman hurried backward, got in the van and Theo pulled the sliding door. Tom hit the gas, and the van swerved into the street.

Katherine looked at her watch and sighed. The van rushed past her, and she wove into traffic to turn at the next corner. Calming down, she stopped at another parking spot and waited for Benjamin to join her. Her younger brother grinned broadly, but for the life of her, she was still too tense to smile.

Matthew's morning consisted of getting motivated to get out of bed, the ordeal of finally convincing his body to follow his brain's order, and staying on his feet after the two tasks were completed. His upper body was covered with dark purple bruises, and his right hand throbbed painfully with every move. After breakfast, he passed up the first cigarette of the day, took painkillers, and got out of the apartment early.

The morning lit up once he met a Labrador and its owner in the elevator. Without thinking about his aches, he bent to scratch the dog's ears.

"He likes you," the man stated and reached out a manicured and soft hand for a handshake. "I'm Lawrence Binkley. I live in four-o-six."

"Matt Montagna." He continued stroking the dog that couldn't get enough of his hand. "I'm in three-o-six, directly below yours."

"Ah, funny." He pointed at the dog. "He's still young, you know. Do you have a dog? I hardly see him like that." Lawrence laughed. He had a high voice, suiting his average frame with a pouch threatening to blow the buttons of his blue winter coat. "But that's okay. I'd already thought he's kinda weird. Always retreating from people."

"He's a good dog. Looks terrific. In good shape." The elevator stopped on the first floor, and when the doors opened, Matthew made it back to a standing position like an old man with a bad case of arthritis.

"You okay?"

"Will be." Matthew stepped out of the elevator and stopped at the pillar for a moment. "Too much work the last few days."

"Yeah, I know how that feels."

"How do you manage to keep a dog, when you work so much?"

Lawrence beamed at him, and his blue eyes shone with eagerness. "Oh, there's a great daycare lady two blocks south. She takes care of him."

"Professional care?"

"In a way. She knows a lot about dogs, and I think she doesn't have to work, so . . . she plays with him, walks him . . . she's terrific. Do you have a dog, too?"

"I used to. He's with friends of mine."

"Ah, you're new in town, huh? I thought so. Your accent doesn't quite fit DC." He took a calling card out of his wallet. "If you buy a dog, maybe you could give her a call. I bet she wouldn't mind taking care of two."

"Thank you. That's kind."

Lawrence laughed again. He had a clean-shaven, friendly face with a few wrinkles, more from laughing than from grief, it looked like. "And until that happens, just come for a beer and pet Bingo."

"Bingo?"

The dog barked once.

"Yeah," Lawrence confirmed. "It was the only name he reacted to. That's fine with me. He's from a dog shelter, you know. I thought about buying a dog from a breeder, but there're so many puppies in need of a new home." Lawrence sighed. "If possible, I'd have taken two, but circumstances are what they are. Have a pleasant day. We'll see each other, I suppose?"

"Yes, I'll be around."

Matthew slowly walked toward his car, and in spite of his injuries was in a better mood than before.

Their usual happy start to the day had been canceled, and both Jacklyn and Nicolas had left the apartment aloof, with only a chaste kiss at the door. Nicolas had brushed off her attempts to belittle their argument and insisted he wouldn't follow her into a house owned by Harry Fuller under any circumstances. Though he'd seen tears in her eyes, he didn't give in.

He sat at the desk crammed with reports, information sheets, and notes from colleagues about other bank robberies in the area. None of them fit the MO, but Sullivan had made it clear Hayes and Montagna had to collect every bit of information in case a connection showed up. Nicolas couldn't help thinking it was a kind of demotion after the successful hunt for the serial killer six months earlier. Agents Spring and Addleton were ordered to support him if the need occurred. Right now, they were occupied elsewhere. Nicolas wiped his face with both hands, thinking of the morning's development and whether he could've said anything else to make his position clear without breaking Jacklyn's heart. He looked up and refrained from any comment seeing Matthew shuffle toward his side of the desk.

"Anything new?" Matt asked, taking off his coat in slow-motion.

"I should ask you. What happened to you?"

Matthew sat down and turned toward the coffee maker,

sighing. His voice was weak and hoarse. "After our little sparring, I was up to another brawl and, well, you should see the other guys."

"Did you get them?"

"No, this victory came with a price, okay? I didn't wrestle them to unconsciousness." He tried to get up, but Nicolas was faster.

"I'll get you a coffee." Nicolas delivered a cup of fresh-brewed roast.

"Thank you." Matt sipped and let out a breath. His shoulders dropped.

Nicolas smelled soap and cologne on his partner but no booze. In a twisted way, he was relieved. "Did you file charges?"

"Nope. I bashed them, and they ran for their lives." He sipped again. "I'm a tiger."

"You look terrible."

"Up yours."

Nicolas shook his head, passing him by. "You're a good fighter. What were they up to?"

"We didn't chat."

Nicolas made a face. "Come on, maybe I don't know you well, but you've been roughed up badly. Still, you're here and didn't file charges. That's odd."

Matthew's eyes were bloodshot and deeply shadowed. "My work attitude, okay? Not your concern."

"Did a doc have a look at you?"

Matthew exhaled exasperatedly and stared into the coffee cup.

Upon a touch on his shoulder, Matthew looked up.

Nicolas ignored his irritation. "Okay, come with me. We've got a secretary one floor down. She's excellent in first aid and doesn't keep records."

"I'm not—"

"Get up, get moving." Nicolas waited patiently and escorted his partner downstairs. "How good are you with your left?"

"I'm ambidextrous."

"You don't say! That's why you beat me."

The shadow of a smile showed on Matthew's face. "If you say so. I just tried not to get knocked around by a macho man."

Nicolas introduced Matthew to Lily Shepherd, who—as he had expected—went into professional caring mode. He waited with folded arms in the back of her office. She ushered Matthew to sit down, asked questions, and was as polite as possible without a hint of accusation that he ought to have been seen at the ER right after the fight. She exchanged the old bandage with a new one, made sure the bruises weren't severe, and sent him off with a heartwarming smile.

On the way back to their office, Nicolas noticed Matthew's smile as his tension eased, and heard him mumble a quiet *thank you*. The conversation was about to begin when Agent Addleton hurried down the aisle with a sheet of paper in his hand.

"An attack on an armored car in Baltimore! Two gangsters, one driver, and obviously one shooter on the opposite roof! Does that ring a bell?" He put the paper in front of Nicolas, and with a curious glance at Matthew, tapped on it. "Took place about an hour ago. Three guards wounded. One robber shot the guards at the bank without warning, precise and quick. Local police tried to get them but failed. They're searching the vicinity for witnesses and—"

"Will probably find a burnt van." Nicolas put down his coffee mug. The bad feeling was back in his stomach. He had wished for another robbery, but not like this. When the agent turned away, Nicolas lowered his voice. "Shall I take Spring and Addleton with me?"

"No, I'm coming." Matthew's gaze reflected pain. "Don't you dare pamper me. I'll make it."

"Okay." Nicolas put on his coat and kept his opinion to himself.

Herman threw a bunch of paper money like confetti in the air and whooped like his brothers when the bills rained down on them. Even Tom laughed, digging his hands into the large pile they had scattered on the living room floor. Circumspect as he always was, Tom had shut the blinds so that the few neighbors couldn't get a glimpse at the bags and its contents. The smell of smoke was in the air, mixing with beer now as Theo handed cans to each of them, toasting.

"We did it!" Ben clanked his can so hard the liquid spilled and soiled the carpet. He laughed hysterically. "Woohoo! Haven't seen that much cash for ages! Wow! Wow! We're rich! Finally, for fucking's sake! We're rich!"

"Where's Kate, by the way?" Herman asked in a sober moment. He looked around. "She brought you here, didn't she?"

Ben nodded, drinking and spilling more beer. "Yep. Said something about . . . I don't know. Thought she'd wanna be alone. She's queer sometimes." He shrugged. "You know best how she is, right?"

Herman grabbed his shoulder and pressed until his brother squirmed. "You didn't ask? We won the greatest pot of money so far, and you left her alone? Didn't you ask why she wouldn't come home?"

"Hell, bro, lemme go, okay?" Ben wriggled without success. "That hurts!"

"You bet! Answer me!"

"She dropped me on the doorstep and sped off, okay? Didn't look like she was out for explanations. Now take your hands off me!"

Herman turned to call his sister on the cell phone. She didn't answer, and though he told himself she just needed a moment for herself, he couldn't stop worrying. He turned away from the drunken festivity and Theo's bragging about what he'd do with his part of the loot. Though Theo and Ben turned down the possibility of Katherine leaving the brothers alone, Herman doubted her words had been merely meant to shock him. After every coup, she seemed to draw closer to saying goodbye without planning to return.

He tried her cell phone again. Behind him, Ben and Theo started a happy dance to loud techno music that reverberated from the walls. Tom watched with a beer can in his hand and tapped the rhythm. Herman put a finger in his right ear to listen to the phone ringing. His stomach churned. It would be the perfect moment for her to leave town and start all over somewhere else. She was independent, clever, and could make it anywhere in the world. He had seen her new passport a month ago and wondered about her plans.

The twins were dancing, drinking beer, and throwing around money. They would wait a day to start spending the loot on parties and whores. Every time they left the house, Herman hoped they'd be clear-headed enough not to spill information about the robberies. On most occasions, Tom went with them, but he rejected playing nanny all the time.

Lately, Tom had left the group more often than before and had refused to answer questions of his whereabouts. Herman knew how hard it was to watch the twins, and he had often praised Tom's support. He'd often been the voice of reason and kept the twins out of trouble more times than he could count, so Herman would be the last one taking Tom to task about the twins.

After some incidents, Herman wondered if it wasn't better to let them run into trouble and fend for themselves. Much to Tom's and Herman's chagrin, they thought they couldn't be blamed, and the only reason against that option was his anxiety that Kate and he would be under suspicion, too.

Tom made eye contact and raised his brows. Herman shook his head, emptied the can he'd left on the table, and was about to leave the room when Katherine showed up. Her cheeks were flushing red, her hairdo slightly tousled from the wind, and when she took in the scene, Herman was about to offer an explanation and word his worries before he ran for the stereo to turn down the volume.

"Wow!" she shouted across the blaring music and put down two paper bags on the table. "The party's already started without me!"

Theo hugged and kissed her, and Katherine laughed out loud, putting her head back. She took off her shoes and danced and kicked through the bills, whooping like a teenager.

"Hey, don't you think it's time for a dance?" Katherine reached out for Herman's hand. "Come on, don't look like a grumpy old man! We made it! You did it!" She freed herself from Theo to embrace Herman and then Ben and Tom. "You were awesome!"

Herman's mouth was too dry for words. Her exuberance should console him, even convince him she wouldn't leave, but the look in her eyes said something he couldn't decipher, and that muddied his happiness.

"Whatever you want to say, Nick, just say it. You've been biting down so hard the whole time your lips must be bleeding by now."

"It's got nothing to do with our work."

"Yeah, I know that." Matthew changed position on the seat, hissing when the bruises sent waves of pain through his body. "It's about your girlfriend. You had a fight this morning?"

"None of your business."

Matthew cocked his head. "Nope, but I'm working with you and can't stand you ruining your teeth. That grinding is annoying."

Nicolas glanced at him, and a frown came and went.

Matthew fought down the urge to laugh. "I'm not scratching your male ego, Nick, but I was told that—"

"She wants to move, and I don't. End of story." His hands clenched around the wheel.

Matthew nodded toward the windshield. "The woman gets what she wants. You can discuss, delay, resist . . . but in the end—"

"I'm not interested in your opinion, okay? I can handle my relationship. Period." Matthew was about to reply when Nicolas cut him short. "No offense meant, but I won't take advice from a man recently divorced, okay?"

"None taken. But you're in the weaker position, whether you admit it or not. If you want to change her mind, well, you've got to be irresistible."

Nicolas' frown reappeared.

"Yeah, scold me. Say you know better or that you know the woman in your life inside and out. You don't. Women always keep secrets, and unveiling them will feel like hammering mercury. While you think you have a grip on every part of your relationship, you're profoundly mistaken. If you want to get the upper hand, play it gently with her. Make love to her the way she wants it, may it be soft and with lots of cuddling or . . . a tad rougher." He avoided eye contact on purpose when Nicolas looked his way. "Please her, and then, when you think the moment is right, make your move to convince her." He cleared his throat. "Divorced or not, I claim to have more years of experience than you do."

"I don't doubt that."

Matthew took a deep breath before he went on. "I had a loving wife, a great marriage for almost three years. I wasn't prepared for learning about her betrayal. Well, who is? While I gave her my trust and faithfulness, she cheated on me. Apparently, she did that the whole time. So, keep irony to yourself, will you? Take my advice or leave it, but don't kick me in the guts."

"I didn't intend to—"

"I know. I hope for your sake you've got a woman who deserves your love."

Nicolas didn't share his opinion. At last, he stopped clenching his teeth.

The crime scene had been roped off up and down the street. The damaged service van of the security company stood in front of the bank entrance. As Nicolas learned from the captain in charge, three wounded guards had been taken to the hospital. The two guards from the company had been escorted inside, where they waited with the bank tellers and the customers in separate rooms.

"They were incredibly fast," the first guard from the armored car said in a soft and depressed voice. He was of Hispanic origin, about forty years old, and had a crooked nose that looked broken one time too many to be set straight again. He ran a shaky hand through his hair, then used both hands while he spoke. "I mean, we walked out of the bank, and our van suddenly listed to the side, and that other van stopped right behind it. I'd say, simultaneously. Two men got out, with weird pistols in their hands and . . . they shot without warning."

"Both robbers shot?" Matthew asked quietly.

"Yes." The man frowned and faced the floor. "They were so fast and I . . . didn't see that coming. You understand?

There was no way we—"

"Did they shoot at you?"

"No, no. They shot the bank guard who always comes out with us. He's got a gun." He shrugged. "We only have . . . I mean, we have our hands full with the sacks."

"That means their attention was directed at the armed guard."

"Yes. We were ordered to drop the sacks. I . . . I was afraid they'd shoot us all. And they did fire when the other bank guards got out." He shook his head several times. His voice broke. "I thank God I'm still alive." He lowered his head. "Thankful and yet . . ." He looked up again. "Are they . . . I mean, are they alive?"

"Yes. One's in critical condition, but all of them are alive."

"We could all be dead." He shook his head again. "Never thought this job could be this dangerous."

Nicolas considered him naïve but didn't say it out loud. The second man from the armored car told Matthew about the masks and the ordinary clothing, jeans and jackets without logos, nothing that would help with identification. He apologized for his inaccuracy, and Matthew did his best to assure him he'd done what was right. Nicolas was astonished at how empathic his colleague acted in the interrogation.

Once Matthew had those answers, he turned to the bank manager to ask for the surveillance tapes from outside the bank. "There's only one camera?" he asked, frowning.

Nicolas stood to join. "The sidewalk's not monitored?"

The bank manager swallowed and adjusted his glasses before he reached for a cigarette and pointed outside to smoke. They passed through the doors. "It's not my decision," he said with the cigarette between his lips. "The company decides where cameras are placed, and obviously, they didn't think it was necessary to cover every angle of the sidewalk. So, yes, there's surveillance, but not to a full extent." He inhaled deeply and coughed right away. He pointed upward. "See? All you'll have is a part—"

"From the rear angle, which means their backs and not their faces." Matthew huffed. "Well, if it was easy, everyone could do it. I'll go and get the tapes from the technicians."

Nicolas kept a straight face. "Sir, what can you tell me about the assault?"

"I didn't notice anything until the shots were fired." He drew on the cigarette. "See, I trust the guards to take out the money. It's not my duty to escort them. Not my business, okay?"

Nicolas let out his breath and watched Matthew's back as he ushered a sergeant and a technician through the hall. "How much money was stolen?"

"About a hundred thousand dollars. We had a large deposit this morning from a local company. They do this every fourth Friday. Obviously, the robbers knew." He wiped his forehead. "The bank's insured, but I hope . . . well, never mind." His shoulders sagged. "I'll handle the insurance company." He drew one last time and stubbed out the cigarette on the pavement. "It's never happened before. I mean, bank robberies—they happen inside, right?"

"They happen when security's not tight enough." Nicolas looked down the street. "The robbers watched your bank. I suppose they also entered the bank several times. We need every surveillance tape of the last four weeks at least."

Matthew reappeared with a hard drive. "Everything they got, starting with the day after the last robbery." He nodded toward the bank manager. "We also have to look into the files of your tellers and other employees. It's possible the gang had an insider to provide them with the best day for the robbery."

"That's impossible!" The manager reached for another cigarette from his pack and lit it in haste. His hands trembled. "None of my employees would ever . . ." He blew out smoke, shaking his head. "I'll give you what you want, but you'll see there's no evidence whatsoever of my people doing anything illegal."

Nicolas lifted a hand as the rambling went on. "We'll see to that, sir."

"That's going to be a long day," Matthew stated quietly when they left Baltimore with the information stowed for further investigation. The local police had been asked to keep surveillance of the bank employees and inform them if anyone tried to leave the city.

Nicolas smiled lopsidedly. "Let's say I'll stay with you until the evening. And then . . . what about you digging into the surveillance data while I take your advice?"

Matthew lifted his gaze, and after a surprised look broke into laughter. "Yes, you do that!" He shook his head. "Scoundrel."

Chapter Nine

Nicolas stopped after crossing the threshold, gaping. The door locked behind him. His voice was hoarse, and he cleared his throat to no avail.

"Now I know why you asked me to come home *alone*."

Jacklyn had dressed up in a sexy dark blue police uniform that complimented her female waist and well-shaped legs. The hat with the golden badge sat slightly off center on her brown locks. The skirt was so short he knew she wasn't wearing underwear, and the blouse was a wide-open invitation to fall between her breasts. Nicolas' mind was developing sexy images so fast he felt like he was stumbling through a flip-book. She approached him with small steps on black high heels, pointing a crop at him. Her look was as stern as her voice.

"Drop the bag."

He dropped the bag and stood rooted to the floor, heart beating in his throat. He held his tongue, raising his brows. His head spun, and all the sweet memories of their love life flooded his mind. "What does my lady command?"

Jacklyn narrowed her eyes. "You're under arrest for coming home too late, without flowers, but with too many clothes on, and smelling like work." She slapped the crop across his chest. "Drop the clothes! Now!"

Nicolas smiled, uncertain about her intentions. He opened his hands, palms up. "My clothes? Here? Right now? Don't you let me—"

The crop's flat leather tip was at his cheek. Her stare turned fierce. "I order you to take off what you're wearing. No questions. No discussion."

He gasped and lifted his hands. His pants were tight anyway. "Okay." Unhurriedly, watching her flushing red cheeks and seeing the joy in her eyes, he took off coat and jacket and bent to open the shoelaces. "What would you've said if I'd planned to bring company?"

"I'd have told you to tie him up at the next streetlight."

He looked up. "You're mean."

There was no smile on her face. The crop slapped his cheek, but without intention to hurt.

"Ouch."

"Hurry!"

Nicolas took it slow, and the crop slapped his shoulder, not gentle this time, and again when he didn't hurry to take off his pants. Jacklyn had a way of surprising him—it was impossible to predict what she had planned, and he adored her for her ideas. He was aroused by the thought what kind of surprise she had in store for him.

"Okay, you win! I'll hurry." He slipped out of the dress pants and the shirt. As he made a show of lowering his boxer shorts, the crop hit his belly. "You're getting meaner." He added the shorts to the pile.

"Down on all fours, head on the floor! Hands beside your body." She stepped beside his face once he took the position. "And don't you dare look!"

"I would never."

She slapped his bare butt fast and hard. Nicolas moaned in a surge of lust, and even more when she pushed his legs apart to fasten a leather ball divider. He felt a cold metal ring dangling from his scrotum. A part of his mind knew he was being manipulated, but the other parts yelled he'd better shut up and enjoy the ride.

"Wow . . . what're you planning?" he asked, though he

knew he'd follow whatever she had in mind. His memory of the unusual sex games she invented was splendid, and he expected nothing less than an hour of pure excitement.

Jacklyn was already up again to hit him once more. "Shut up! Right hand behind your back!"

Nicolas had once asked her not to use service handcuffs, and though he wouldn't have protested right now, she'd remembered his request. The cuffs were made of thick leather with buckles. "Left hand!"

Nicolas tested the locked cuffs. He liked to confirm that she played for real.

"Up with you!" Jacklyn grabbed his upper arm. "Don't ask what I'm gonna do with you, or I'll gag and blindfold you, and you won't have fun at all!"

To cover the fun he was experiencing, Nicolas averted his face until she ordered him to kneel on the bed. She fit the hook of a thick elastic strap through the ring at his scrotum and tied it to the foot of the bed. It was flexible, but not very. Nicolas realized her intention as she pulled another strap through a ring on the handcuffs and pulled them through a ring at the canopy. He flexed his fists.

Jacklyn appeared in front of him. Her voice still held the edge of severity. "Here. Take this between your teeth. If you drop it, I'll stop."

"No safe word?"

The leather tip of the crop was back at his cheek so fast he jerked. He didn't remember this fierceness from past games.

"This. Now." She pressed the piece of wood between his teeth and turned away. "If you're not a sissy, I might play with you for a while."

Nicolas wanted to say she could start playing right now. He bit the gag when she pulled the strap at his hands, and he bent forward to adjust to the growing strain. The pull was slow, so he had a minute to realize the growing pain in his balls. For a few heartbeats, it was a pleasure, and his arousal grew stronger. Jacklyn knelt in front of him to stroke his hard-on and the passage toward his scrotum. His skin was pulled tight and sensitive to the slightest touch. He breathed loudly.

"Hmm, you're all mine now, my Beast. No escape. Nowhere to go." She stroked him harder. "You'll suffer my punishment for your crimes to its full extent." Jacklyn giggled.

Nicolas loved to see her in such a playful mood and tolerated her kneading and pulling his member painfully. Arousal shot through his body like a drug. Nicolas blew air through his nose and closed his eyes. His body wanted to move upward to ease the pressure on his shoulders and arms, but then the pain in his balls became intolerable. Groaning, he remained still and kept his teeth firmly around the gag, coping with the increasing level of pain. Sweat made him blink, and Jacklyn frowned and knelt in front of him. When he avoided eye contact, she went on all fours to twist and pinch his nipples.

Nicolas couldn't escape her hands—not even wriggle much—and the small, well-measured pain increased his expectation and impatience. He was as hard as he could get, craving her touch, but her fondling was nothing but a slight brush of her fingertips. He became aware that the restriction was too tight when he tried to move into her hand. She ran her fingernails along his length, then let him know with a smile and a wink what she was about to do.

Catlike, she stretched to take his throbbing penis in her mouth to fondle his glans with her tongue. Nicolas hissed around the gag. He was dizzy, and his heart was beating in his ears. He moaned and tried to tell her to bring him over the top. Instead, she moved backward, releasing his pulsing cock to the cool air. He tried to follow and stopped, frustrated. The muscles in his legs and arms quivered like bowstrings drawn too taut. He endured the strain as he flexed his fists. He wanted satisfaction. He wanted her to fulfill his desire, but her look said she wasn't in for granting him release. Painfully immobilized, he lowered his chin, pondering how far he could go.

Her fingernails ran along his sides, found his aching member, and moved to his maltreated balls. Once more, the scale tipped to the pleasure side. He hung his head, grunted behind the gag, and gave in to her hands and lips teasing him, increasing his arousal until he thought he couldn't take any more.

Nicolas made eye contact, and she seemed to understand his plea. Still teasing him, she eased the strain on his scrotum as well as on his arms, so that feeling returned to his limbs. Lovingly, taking her time, she brought him to the verge of orgasm with her lips and hands, let him linger for a heartbeat, then pushed him over the top. He dropped the gag and cried out in pure bliss.

Aside from two telephones ringing and muted conversations, it was quiet in the large FBI office. The night shift had taken over, and the men huddled behind their monitors, hoping no emergency cases fell on their desks. An agent with a deep voice joked about two women checking a flat tire and stating the damage was not so bad since the flat was only on the bottom. The agent's partner choked on laughter, and they exchanged a high-five. Behind him, Matthew heard the low gurgle of a coffee machine while he spread the printed photographs from the surveillance tapes on the table. Their quality was low, but one detail was clear. Matthew used a magnifying glass, and when he was certain of his finding, he sent the video to the lab technician with the urgent request to get a distinct picture of the man's left wrist.

With a coke in his hand, he skimmed through the pictures

and videos of the other bank robberies and smiled once he detected the similarity. He smiled even more brightly when the technician delivered an enhanced version of the last picture.

The night was improving.

Nicolas hung his head, panting. Sweat dropped off his forehead. He made sounds in his throat, and it took him a while to form words.

"This was—"

"One of the best rides you've ever had." Jacklyn tousled his hair as he rested his head on her shoulder. "Wow . . . I'm really jealous."

"Set me free."

"You really want to be freed? That's a first."

"I need my arms at my body, and this is the most stressful position you've put me in so far."

She kissed the curve of his ear and whispered, "I so love you, my Beast." Giggling, she moved around him to undo the bindings and laughed when he collapsed on the mattress with a pitiful groan. "Oh, come on. I know you loved it." She opened the handcuffs.

"Can't tell right now. Ouch! You're ruining me."

She slumped on the mattress beside him, shrugging casually. "I try to give you the best I have.

"Yeah, you do."

Jacklyn loved the minutes after their session—Nicolas' hazy eyes, his smile, and his groaning, a sound he made even if he hadn't been spanked. Still aroused, she caressed his body and felt along the red lines the shackles had caused. She loved to see the adoration in his eyes. He was the lover she had been looking for years. Playfully, she pulled him up from the bed.

"Time for a shower."

Nicolas groaned getting to his feet. "I'd like to stay here and cuddle with you."

"Get up, my Beast."

He followed her to the bathroom where she ran the warm water.

"The last time we cuddled you were asleep after five minutes."

"I'm having long days."

"I know." They stood under the hot shower, and she enjoyed his big hands washing her body, knowing he considered it his reward. She returned the favor, happy that he had played along.

But there was more on her mind. She stepped out of the shower and handed him a towel. "Nick, would you, please, think about moving into a house? Just a small one, where we would be alone and wouldn't need to be quiet while making love. We're running out of space, too." When she noticed his hesitation, she said, "No, don't answer me now. Think about it. Tomorrow. Let me know when you've reached a decision."

Nicolas slipped into shirt and shorts for the night. Judging by his expression, he wouldn't change his mind.

In the dim light of the apartment's corridor and tired from working overtime, Matthew came to a stumbling halt seeing Lawrence approach with Bingo on the leash.

"Ho, my friend! Sleepwalking?"

Matthew caught his breath and bent to stroke the dog behind the ears. "Sorry, pal, I didn't see you. How are you tonight?"

"Awake, so it seems." Lawrence laughed. "And you look like a bad day on two legs."

"Well . . ." Matt pulled the keys out of his pants pocket while the dog sniffed up and down his leg. "Could be worse."

"There's always a worse day, huh? Wanna join me for a drink once I've walked this poor guy?" He moved his head left and right. "Well, if you're too tired, that's okay. I mean, I'll be around—"

"No, a drink seems fine. I'll meet you—" He checked his watch and couldn't read it.

"Holy damn shit, the glass of your watch is shattered!" Lawrence gaped. "How did that happen to such a wonderful piece?"

"You know watches?"

"I do. And I know someone who could repair it."

"That . . . that would be great."

"Well, then—" Lawrence turned to open the door where Bingo waited. "I'll let him run, and we'll meet in an hour, okay?"

"Sure." Matthew shook his head in surprised happiness as he climbed the stairs. He was still smiling as he unlocked the door to his apartment.

"One more, okay? We're doing one more, right? This one was fucking great! And we want one more!" Theo repeated his demand while he brandished his bottle of whiskey. His eyes were wide and feverish. "Bang! Bang! Wow! We did this! Fuck ass shit, we did it!"

"You're drunk as a sailor!" Herman kept his younger brother from spilling liquor all over the carpet. His laughter died. "Hey, hold it for a minute, okay? It's for drinking, not for splashing the floor."

"Who the fuck cares? I'll buy you a new carpet, for fuck's sake!" Theo lost the bottle to Herman in a tug of war. "Fuck you, bro! That's mine, damn it."

"Yeah, and you've had enough." Herman wrestled with him until Theo gave in with a shrug and looked for another bottle. "No! You hit the sack now, got it? No more booze." He put the bottle down and held his brother with his free hand. "It's over, okay? Or do you want me to knock you out?"

"You aren't my *father*!" He spat the last word like a curse. "You've got nothin' to say, got it?" Theo pulled his arm away and swayed as he tried to keep his balance. Herman pushed him, so he sat on the floor. "Man, are you out of your fucking mind?"

"I mean it, Theo, you damn dweeb. You either go and sleep it off, or I'll knock you out and lock you up. Your choice."

Theo made an effort to get on his feet and fell back. Ben laughed out loud.

"Yeah, fuck you, too!" Theo blurted. "Guess I'm gonna sleep right here."

Ben toasted with his beer can. "Yeah, looks like a bed with beer."

"No, you won't." Herman sighed and bent toward his struggling brother. "You're a pain in the ass." He pulled him onto his shoulder and carried him out. Theo laughed hysterically and slapped Herman's back with both hands as if playing percussion.

"Will ya carry me, too?" Ben shouted, equally drunk.

Herman was on the threshold when Katherine rounded the corner. He froze, noticing her disgust. "Hey, I know, they've partied too much. Let me handle this. Tom's cleaning up the floor. Wait!" he yelled when she passed him by. "I said I will—" He sighed and hung his head.

"She's gonna kick your ass for not looking out for us like a nanny." Theo's hilarity stopped when Herman slapped his butt hard enough that it sounded through the corridor.

"Shut your fucking mouth, asshole! It's enough." He slowed Theo's fall onto the bed at the last moment, grunting. "Shut it! I don't wanna hear anything from you at least for ten hours. If you show your face, I'll knock you out. I swear. It won't be pretty." He turned and slammed the door shut.

The noise from the living room was deafening. If the neighbors were home, they'd know about the quarrel. Herman's shoulders sagged. He was tired to the bone.

"Why didn't you wait, sis?" he asked, interrupting the exchange of curses, swearwords, and threats. He couldn't remember a time he'd heard Katherine speak sweetly. He stepped in between, ready to keep Ben from attacking his sister. "Ben's going to bed, and you can have your glass of wine in peace, okay?"

"They're twenty-five, not five!" Katherine huffed and put down the bottle of wine with more force than necessary. "I'm so sick of this! Of all of you!"

By threatening to put him in a cold bathtub, Herman ushered Ben out of the room and collected potato chips back into the bowl.

Tom was on his knees, wiping the carpet. He didn't look up and didn't heed when Kate told him to stop.

Herman made a face. "Listen, Kate, I know how you feel, but—"

"Don't say this ever again, damn it!" Katherine shook her head and switched on the TV. "They're just a day away from spilling the beans and telling everybody in some godforsaken bar what they do for a living. They're rat-assed without a functioning brain." She pointed at Herman. "Don't say anything in their defense, okay? Just don't."

"Okay, I won't." He put the bowl on the table and filled a glass with her favorite wine. "We've been working together for as long as I can remember, and everything went well. That's to your credit, yes, I know." He handed her the glass. "You kept our family together—"

"I wonder if it was worth the effort."

"You don't mean that, sis." He cocked his head. Her gloomy mood gave him the creeps. "Really, you don't mean that."

Katherine sipped wine and pretended to watch the news.

"Just one more, okay? Kate, please, I understand you want away from Theo and Ben, but . . ." He let out a breath and ran a hand through his hair as he searched for words. "Honestly, I'd need another boost of money to leave, too."

"You do?"

He didn't like her incredulous tone but kept a blank face. "I've got something promised, but I need a lot of money for starters."

"You wanna explain that?"

"No, I won't." He glanced at Tom, who picked up the dirty towels and left the living room. "Only this . . . I want to have a real life, just like you do. I want to make something more of it than running from one assault to the next. If I can turn my idea into a venture, I'll earn enough money to make an honest living. Will you help me?"

"I don't buy that crap. This is much too vague." She sipped again. "You do this for the twins, to get them a chance to keep some of the money while they think there'll be a never-ending cash flow. Did you listen to them? They've already planned how to burn it in town." Katherine shook her head and smiled sadly while she caressed his cheek. "You've got a good heart, Manny, and that's why I'll try and find another bank, but let me tell you this . . . it's the end of the line, okay? Do you hear me? No more robberies, nothing. I can't stand the tension anymore, and I won't risk getting caught. Or that *you* will get caught. It would be too much to bear."

Herman took her by the shoulders, and his voice was as gentle as his touch. "You've worried for us for the longest time. It's all right, Kate. One more, and we'll divide the money and—" He kissed her brow and felt drawn to hold her and never let go. He embraced her and held her tight. "We'll go our ways."

Chapter Ten

Lawrence's apartment was prim, like a picture from a style magazine. There was a brown leather couch in the center of the living room, a large TV set built into a shelf that covered most of the wall, and a set of loudspeakers Matthew longed to hear in action. Aside from the faint smell of cleaning agents and leather, Matthew detected fresh paint on the walls, and the absence of pictures of Lawrence, family members or the dog. Knickknacks consisted of dog toys on the carpet, and three glass jars with candy, chocolate, and the largest one with chips, each of them placed on a napkin. Lawrence served the dip in a small glass bowl which he also placed on a napkin. His smile withered when his gaze fell on the carpet at Matt's feet.

"Oh, would you mind taking off your shoes? You know . . . the dirt."

Matthew hurried to oblige and put his shoes on a rack at the front door.

"Thank you." Lawrence's smile was back. "Beer, wine, whiskey? What do you prefer?"

"Whiskey, if you don't mind." The two doors to the adjacent rooms were closed, and his police instinct was hard to control. He wanted to know more about his neighbor but knew it would be rude to ask for a tour through the man's apartment without sufficient reason. "Is it okay if I smoke?"

"At the open window, please. I'm not so fond of—"

Matt held the lighter in his hand and frowned. "I don't have to if it bothers you."

"No, no." Lawrence quickly lifted and dropped his hand, smiling amiably. "I don't mind you smoking, but I don't want the stench of cold smoke in the apartment the whole night."

Matthew opened the brand new and polished window, and after the third attempt, lit a cigarette. The wind was strong enough to turn the light drizzle to an icy shower. As he blew out the rest of the smoke, he stubbed out the cigarette quickly and then closed the window. Lawrence handed him a glass.

"Here you go."

They toasted, and Matt felt better after the first mouthful. "How long have you lived here?"

"Three years, just about." He nodded, looking around the room as if praising himself for his efforts. He pointed with his glass in hand. "I painted the rooms recently. I didn't like the old color. It was too . . . distant, cold." They settled on the couch with Bingo choosing the place between them on the cream-colored carpet that looked and felt new. "What do you do for a living?"

"I'm with the police." Matthew felt uncomfortable, as if mentioning his profession separated him from the rest of the working force. "And you?"

"I'm a manager at a temp agency." Lawrence's laugh seemed forced. "Yeah, I know, I know, it's always said we tend to exploit people, but for some it's better than not working at all, right?"

"I'm not judging."

"Okay, that's a first." Lawrence's head bobbed while he smiled. He emptied his glass in one gulp. "It's nothing I had imagined for life, but, well, some job's gonna pay the rent, don't you agree?" He got up. "You make some decent money?"

"I'm fine. Don't need that much."

"Ah, you got here alone because of . . . parting with a loved one?"

Matthew lowered his glass. He didn't want to talk about Nerina, so he shook his head. "Listen, Lawrence, you're right, I moved here alone, but—"

"My apologies. It's not my business, and I shouldn't have asked." He poured them both another drink, and his look was commiserative. "You look like you need a good drink right now. Go ahead. I've got much more, a cupboard full." He nodded toward the other wall. "We could start a tasting."

Matt stared into the glass, longing to get drunk and forget. "Sorry, but I have to work tomorrow."

"But that's tomorrow, and I bet you're man enough to manage another drink."

Matthew swallowed the whiskey, nodded, and with the alcohol kicking in started talking about everything and nothing. He tried to avoid blurting about Nerina, his wonderful, outstanding woman and ex-wife, and therefore babbled a lot about dogs and living in Chicago. At one point, he was convinced he was boring his neighbor, but Lawrence said *no,* still smiling and bobbing his head.

Matthew plowed on, comfortable that he had found a true listener.

Matthew woke to a screeching headache. His eyes were swollen, his lids heavy, and his muscles protested every move. He remembered drinking and laughing with Lawrence and that he—after stumbling over dog and couch—had made it to the door and down one level to his apartment. He had slept in his clothes and stank of cold smoke as much as of alcohol.

Groaning, he knocked off the alarm clock and sat up, knowing otherwise he'd slip back to sleep instantly. He undressed on the way to the shower, grunted in the cold water, and wasn't awake until after the first cup of coffee. Once more, he skipped the cigarette, felt sick on the way to his car, and wasn't any better upon entering the office. The only advantage was Senior Agent Sullivan's absence from his desk. Matthew switched on the coffee maker and thought about buying breakfast at the cafeteria when Nicolas approached with fast steps.

"You're already here?"

Nicolas put his jacket across the chair and switched on his computer. His hair was wet. "You still look like shit."

"Since when? Six o'clock?" Matthew wiped his eyes, aware that he'd stumble any minute if he didn't hold fast to the edge of the counter. "Man, you've got some serious sleeping problem."

"I was at the gym."

"Did you find a wall for your bare-knuckle fight? For . . . hey, don't grill me that early, but your hands and wrists need first aid. Just giving back the favor." He handed Nicolas a cup of coffee. "How bad was your night?"

"Not as bad as yours, apparently."

Matthew sat down, both hands tight around his cup. "I had a drink with a neighbor."

Nicolas stood beside his desk. "And it got out of hand." He snorted, gazing up from his bloodied hands. "Don't you have any control?"

"What got out of *your* control last night? The severe hand of your girlfriend?"

"Stop right there!"

Matthew lifted a hand and dropped it quickly before his trembling showed. "Don't growl and bite. I'm stopping. Are you ready for some new leads? Do you want to sit down or take them standing?"

"Don't push it, Matt!"

"Sorry, but your flank's wide open—to stick to the metaphor." His smug grin was grudgingly returned. "Now, what

I found out last night . . . before the drinking started . . . is this." He displayed the enlarged photographs on the table.

"A watch?"

"Not any watch, not like some cheap piece you buy at *Target*. This is a *Rolex Cosmograph Daytona*. It's worth more than fifteen thousand dollars."

Nicolas had a good look at the watch and the pictures. "And how does this help?"

"Watches like these aren't sold everywhere."

"Unless it's a fake."

"It's not. Believe me, I know watches. My father was an expert on that subject, and I inherited his knowledge as well as some pieces. This one's genuine, was bought recently, and should be retraceable with some work. And you have to admit—those young robbers wanna show off. I bet he'll show it to the ladies and impress them." Upon Nicolas' nod, he added, "I'll ask the jewelers around the area the robbers are working. This should give us a hint at whom we're dealing with."

"Good work." Nicolas sat down carefully, exhaling with a suppressed whimper. "Don't say a word."

Matt grinned and didn't try to hide it.

"Did you think about my offer, Jacky? I think I gave you plenty of time to discuss it with your boyfriend."

Jacklyn reclined on her office chair and bit her nails. She wanted to curse and blame Harry for his simulated impatience but knew she'd only play into his hands.

"I don't intend to rush you," Harry said nonchalantly, "or not too much anyway, but there are other interested customers, indeed, who want to move out of this dusty city just like you."

In spite of her knowledge about real estate agents and their tricks to lure customers, she felt a twang of anxiety that her chosen object could be sold to a couple just like Nick and her. They would never cherish it so much. Jacklyn recalled the carefully paved driveway, the front porch, the white and blue front. There was a swing in matching colors. She hadn't believed Harry's glossies and had driven to the property after work. In the sunset, she'd been flabbergasted by its beauty. The rooms were suffused with light, the kitchen was modern and close to perfection, and the bathrooms were big enough even for a hunk like her lover. One bathroom featured a round bathtub in which she had imagined them both playing indulgently. The back yard was of average size, not big enough to need a gardener, but large enough for a table and chairs and—if need be—a sandbox and wading pool. The property was well-looked-after, and Harry's chatterbox of an assistant had described the features in more details than she remembered. She'd already imagined Nick and herself playing catch on the lawn around the house.

"My dear former mistress, are you still there? I'd like—"

"Don't push me!" Jacklyn hated her whining undertone. It was unlike her to feel cornered and inferior. "I'm still trying to convince him."

"With a whip or a paddle?"

"Harry!" She sat up, and her anger flared. "Don't you dare talk to me like that. You should be glad and thankful I still talk with you at all. So spare me any of your flippant comments, okay? I said I'll talk to him. That's what I'm going to do."

"Be aware. I won't hold this estate forever." Harry's voice lost its charm. "I offered it to you first because I thought it's what you wanted. I remember your monologues about moving out of town without leaving the town behind. It's up to you, but don't expect me to give away profit just because the two of you can't make up your minds."

Jacklyn looked at her nail. She had scraped off the polish. "Yes, whatever you say. Go ahead, sell it. Maybe it's a couple that'll allow you to film their love life for your entertainment."

"Ah, that's the snag!" He laughed, excessively, and false. "Oh, well, go ahead and scan the rooms, garden, the yard, and even the garage if you want to. You won't find anything. I'm no more interested in—"

"Don't lie! You'd sell your mother . . . if you still had one . . . for a tape of Nick and me."

Harry was quiet, and she heard him breathe.

"I'll talk to Nick. I'll have an answer for you by the end of the week." She hung up and sat on her chair with trembling hands. "What shall I do?"

Matthew looked away from Nicolas' hands. "What about your girlfriend's pressure to change houses?"

"She anticipated my move and made it her own."

Matthew was about to whistle and reply sarcastically but caught the words before they slipped. "And that . . . led to your aching behind?"

Nicolas' smile came and went. His answer was quiet. "Yes."

"This means you're none the wiser. She still wants that new home, and you don't."

"Thanks for stating the obvious."

Matthew had a list of questions that wanted out badly. He remained quiet for half the ride until the words came out unbidden. "I know the most dangerous moment . . . the one triggering resistance . . . is when you put the second handcuff on a suspect. The crook realizes with a start that he's bound, in trouble, caught. It's the moment he'll wriggle and fight. How do you stand that? Giving up your freedom?"

"It's none of your business." Nicolas looked straight through the windshield. "Maybe your old partners in Chicago allowed you to meddle with their affairs, but I won't."

Matthew raised his brows, chewing on that answer like a dog on an old bone. Nerina had once proposed games in the bedroom, role-play, living out some fantasies. Matthew had quietly but decisively resisted. He couldn't imagine being anything but gentle and loving to a woman, and he'd seen too many strange scenes between couples to jump on something new and, as Nerina had called it, *exotic*. In some cases, the excitement had turned to serious harm to one of the partners. He had goosebumps thinking about what she might've done with him bound to a bed. He couldn't shake the image of being molested. It was worse than having a fight in a dark alley.

"Was your father a watchmaker?"

Matthew was glad for the distraction. "It wasn't his main profession, more like a serious hobby. He couldn't stand people throwing away good pieces, and the jewelers robbed the customers blind. He bought the tools and started repairing watches for his friends." He shrugged. "When I was old enough, he taught me some tricks, but I never made it further than changing batteries."

Nicolas huffed. "You could've learned a lot."

"Yes, that might've happened if my father had had more patience with my two left hands. But he was a perfectionist. He didn't understand my teenage troubles, either." He lifted and turned his hands. "I was better at playing basketball, wrestling, swinging a bat sometimes. And protecting my mom when he didn't."

"Sounds like trouble in your childhood."

"Nicely put." Matthew looked out of the window. "I went away from home as soon as my parents could afford to live in a better district."

"So, you started police work early?"

"Yes. You did the same, I suppose?"

"Police in Lynchburg, then Quantico."

Matthew frowned and turned back to his partner. "You're one of those *youngest ever accepted agents*, huh?" He could tell by Nicolas' suppressed growl he was right. "It was meant as praise, not insult."

"Then don't make it sound like one. I've never . . ." He let the sentence trail off with a gesture. "My father supported me. He made me train hard and urged me to apply for a job with the FBI. The rest was up to them."

"The FBI wouldn't take anyone who isn't qualified, so . . . you obviously know your job."

Nicolas' laugh came out like a snort. "That doesn't make it any better, but I get the point." He pulled over and parked at the curb. "Your jeweler. Let's hope he's got some insight for us." Nicolas clambered out of the service car with a suppressed whimper. "Don't say a word. You don't look so good, either."

Matthew was laughing as they walked toward the entrance. "Anyway, I didn't let myself get beat up voluntarily."

The jeweler took his time and a magnifying glass to inspect the pictures Matthew handed him. He mumbled in his gray beard and adjusted his glasses. Finally, after some sighing and moving his head, he pushed the pictures back across the counter.

"Yes, I think it's the one I sold."

"When?" Matthew asked, spirits lifting. "Do you have the copy of the sales slip, Mr. Genaro? Do you know who bought it?"

The jeweler looked at him as if being accused of stealing a nickel. "Agent Montagna, I do keep copies of all my sales throughout the year, and I also save the surveillance tapes. We jewelers have learned on several and always unpleasant encounters with the police that officers are far more willing to believe in fraud than in our stores being robbed by criminals. If we didn't keep records, insurance companies wouldn't pay a dime for our losses. If you would, please, follow me." He ordered an assistant to take over the business at the counter.

In his office, Mr. Genaro opened two files on his computer for them. "These are my sales starting with July this year. As you can see, *Rolex* is a much-wanted brand, and I sold six pieces, but only one *Daytona.* Now that I know the date, I'll show you the footage of the cameras." He mumbled as the program loaded the video.

"We'll need a copy of that tape, sir," Nicolas said. "And of the document. Just the one."

"Sure." Mr. Genaro's eyes narrowed. "Ah, here you see him enter. He's a young man, and I remember I expected at first glance he'd look for a ring or maybe an inexpensive bracelet for his girlfriend. I was astonished that he asked me to show him *Rolex* watches." He glanced at Matthew. "I started with the cheaper ones, as you see, but he was precisely looking for the *Cosmograph Daytona.*"

Matthew watched the video with growing impatience. The face of the customer was hidden by a lot of blond hair hanging into his eyes. A beard covered the lower part, and in addition to a lot of clothes, he wore a scarf around his neck.

"Do you have another tape from another angle?" Matthew asked when the sale was complete and the customer left with the watch in a gift box.

"No, agent, we're obliged to document what goes on in our shops, but this is no movie studio. We don't shoot from different angles or ask for better lighting." Mr. Genaro's look was adamant. "Do you still want a copy?"

"Yes, of course."

"Very well." He saved the copy on the USB stick Nicolas provided.

"Sir, can you describe the customer for us? His eyes, face, language. What about his hands? You have an eye for such details."

Mr. Genaro sat down and reached for a metal pack with cigarillos. He squinted as he fingered for a lighter on his cramped desk, but didn't use it.

"His hands?" The jeweler simpered. "You expect way too much. I can tell you he wasn't a worker with calloused hands, but his hands were big. He was young, the lanky type with a swing in his hips, and he wore cheap jeans and a worn hoodie beneath the jacket."

"A green one? Probably from the *New York Jets*? Was there a logo on the left side?"

"I didn't see it and, yes, the hoodie was dark green. Because of his looks, I thought he was a customer with less money to spend than he did."

"He paid with a credit card?"

"The information is on the sales slip."

Matthew couldn't grasp his luck. "What about his language?"

"Normal. No swearing, no slang, no detectable accent. He tried hard to speak formally with me. His speech was like that of a foreigner pondering the right words." He smiled briefly as he found his lighter. "I gave him plenty of time, of course. After all, he spent a small fortune for a watch that'll last for a lifetime if he takes care of it." He simpered. "Maybe it'll last longer than his girlfriend, if he's got one."

Chapter Eleven

Changing their bed linens, Jacklyn imagined Nicolas lowering his gaze and accepting her demands, no matter how quietly she spoke. Even more, she wanted him to follow her bidding. She wanted his obedience, his longing, his pledge that he couldn't live without her and would accept everything she dished out only to be sure of her love. In her imagination, he fell on his knees and begged her to chastise and tease him all night long.

Jacklyn felt the heat creeping up. Her breathing accelerated, and she paused. Her gaze rested on the pillory at the foot of the bed. She saw Nick standing there, bent over, unable to get away, waiting for her decision and longing to learn of how she would treat him. She would use a flogger on his trained ass to indulge in seeing his flesh redden, call him a misbehaving boy, and strike harder until his legs quivered and he urged her with guttural sounds to stop, knowing she didn't accept begging.

As she closed her eyes, a sigh escaped her lips. Her legs quivered, and her heart raced. The pillow she'd been holding dropped to the bed.

She knew every nuance of his expressions and every sound that showed the level of pain she inflicted. She yearned for Nick as she hadn't yearned for any lover she remembered. She wanted him on his knees—bound, helpless, begging. The more she loved him, the more she longed to control him, not only his body but his mind. She waited for him to confess his desire to become her servant and caress her as if she was a delicate piece of porcelain. Upon an unspoken command, he'd offer his body so she'd tie him up. He wouldn't move a muscle and would be at her whim for the time she set. She would then look him in the eyes and start teasing his beautiful cock and enjoy his growing desire as well as his devotion.

Nicolas was still connected to the love life he'd led earlier. More often than not, he wanted to stay close to her in bed or anywhere in the apartment, preferably with a lot of cuddling, kissing, and whispering lovely nothings in her ear.

Jacklyn opened her eyes with a loud intake of breath. She didn't remember slumping onto the bed, but there she was with her left hand in her panties and her fingertips wet.

"I thought about joining, but . . ." Nicolas grinned like a boy who'd caught his high school crush reading a porn magazine. His brows twitched. "Do you want me to?"

Jacklyn blushed deeply crimson. Nicolas had already taken off his shoes and jacket and stood two feet away, unbuttoning his dress shirt. She swallowed and sat up straight, not knowing where to put her hand.

"I . . . I don't know what . . . I gotta go." She got up and went to the bathroom to wash her hands.

"Hey, it's all right. No need to be embarrassed."

She dried her hands with a towel as she glanced at him, feverishly thinking about what he'd witnessed. He looked so damn handsome and benevolent. "Don't be ridiculous. I was . . . I got distracted by a thought." She pushed him aside to head for the kitchen.

He followed and shook his head, a smile on his juvenile features.

"Gimme some room, damn it!" She shooed him away. "Go, take a shower, change clothes. I'll prepare dinner."

"Don't be mad at me. I don't mind watching you. And you have to admit that, for a woman with your experience, you behave kinda . . . bewildering."

She put a pot on the stove. "Why don't you just leave me alone for a minute?"

Nicolas huffed but left her alone. Jacklyn hung her head, replaying the moment. There was no good reason for her behavior, no valid argument, yet the feeling of being unmasked clung to her mind like thick oil to feathers. She wiped her face with both hands and forced her breathing down. It was a vain effort, for Nick's perfect body appeared before her mental eye again. While the eggs boiled, she cut bread into slices and realized Nicolas was taking a long time in the bathroom. Guilt washed over her, which she considered as stupid as her outburst. At thirty-five, she should be cool, composed, in control of her feelings and actions. She was the dominant part.

"Yeah, so why don't you act like one?" She took the eggs out of the water, set the table with bread and salad, added glasses, and a bottle of juice. Done, she looked around whether there was anything else to do. The image of Nicolas being naked and submissive got stronger.

She wiped her hands on her shirt and entered the bathroom, heart racing. Her voice was breathy. "Stay where you are."

Nicolas stopped as his head popped through the opening of his t-shirt. "Pardon?"

"Out of the clothes." She helped with his boxers, panting so hard she was dizzy. "I just can't stand starting the evening like this."

"No need to shred my underwear." Nicolas laughed, surprised, and judging by his frown, at odds with her behavior.

"I want you," she stated, pretending a one-liner would sufficiently sum up her feelings and explain her behavior. She came up with no more words, as much as she tried. She shook her head.

"That's fine with me." The shirt fell to the tiles beside the tub.

Leniency was in every word, and she loved him even more. He smelled of soap, and beyond that, she relished the scent that was just him. Unaware, she went down on her knees. She kissed his limp penis, licked along the soft skin toward his testicles, and held tight to the back of his legs.

"You can have mood swings any time if this comes out of it."

"Shut up." She made him spread his legs as he stepped back against the sink, then indulged in feeling his skin on her lips and tongue and listening to his heavy breathing. She moved his prick aside to lick and gently suck his balls. Nicolas moaned. She looked up. He leaned his head back and steadied himself with both hands on the rim of the sink. He let out another low moan telling her he'd go the whole nine yards if she let him.

She got out of her clothes one piece at a time to stay close to him and have her hands and lips on his genitals as much as she could. His abs tightened as he moved his loins in her direction. She pulled back his foreskin to lick his glans, and as expected, he jerked with the sudden thrill.

"Jeez, you wanna throw me from a fucking tower?"

The sentence made her grab his balls and pull, not hard enough to cause lasting pain, but noticeably, to tell him his place. Nicolas hissed through his teeth. His legs quivered as he struggled to stay upright.

"You'll act to my bidding."

Nicolas raised his brows as he looked down at her. "Dark voice and dungeon-talk? Are we there yet?"

Jacklyn inched backward, troubled in an unexplainable way. "Stay where you are."

He swallowed and shook his head. "Won't go anywhere."

"On your knees. Put your hands behind your head."

"Shall I cross my ankles, too?"

"Do what I say."

Jacklyn was at the bathroom door. He lowered himself onto the tiles, a small, suppressed smile on his face.

The quiet time at the office was soothing for Matthew's mind, which was running on an all-time high. The Baltimore Police had delivered pictures and a report about the burned-out van the robbers had used. Once more, they had chosen a remote alley to get rid of the compromising vehicle and gotten away without a street camera noticing. CSU was on the case but hadn't delivered any useful information. Matthew didn't expect much of the investigation. Judging by the pictures, the gangsters hadn't made another mistake as they had done at the Federal Triangle.

Instead of brooding over the details of the destroyed van, Matthew watched the video of the young man in the jeweler's store twenty times, hoping he'd find a clue to identifying him. He had correctly assumed the account for the credit card was fake and untraceable. He wondered why the jeweler hadn't complained about losing money, but it was too late for a call to his shop.

Matthew fetched a coke from the vending machine in the hallway and returned to his desk. He didn't want to admit the visit to Mr. Genaro's shop had been a waste of time. He knew the bank robber was out for expensive goods and would buy another valuable piece. The man wanted to spend his money on fancy stuff, probably to impress the ladies. Once more, and with the footage, he asked the agents Spring and Addleton to assist in interrogating nightclub owners, cashiers at horse racing tracks and some illegal betting agencies. He was convinced the young man wouldn't stay away from public places because he expected his masquerade would save him from being identified. The jeweler's observation of his careful way of speaking could be another indicator he acted differently depending on the occasion.

Matthew looked at the large clock and called the jeweler at home. Mr. Genaro was grumpy but awake.

"Why didn't you tell me the credit card didn't work and that you never got your money?" Matthew asked after Genaro was done complaining about *FBI rudeness.*

"Well, I got my money to the last cent."

The sudden hesitation gave Matthew the creeps. "Explain that, sir."

"The next day, after the purchase and my bank's reply that the money couldn't be transferred, there was an envelope in my mailbox with cash and a copy of the sales slip."

"And you didn't think of telling the police?"

"I got my money, okay? No harm was done. Listen, I was robbed two years ago. Twice. Police were everything but helpful, and I'm sick of calling them so that they'd tell me I took money . . . well, I don't know from whom. There was nothing else in that envelope. No note or any clue about the identity of the customer. So, yes, I took the money I wouldn't have gotten any other way! It was my money, for God's sake!"

"Did you think we wouldn't find out?"

"I don't give a damn, Agent Montagna! I run a business, not a convent. Goodnight!"

Matthew sat stunned before he—after gently putting back the receiver—laughed until he had tears in his eyes.

"Who dared to hurt you?" Jacklyn asked when she tied Nicolas spread-eagled on the bed. She pushed away from the superfluous pillows, feeling guilty she hadn't finished her work.

"I did. I was at the gym this morning."

He flexed his fists and avoided her gaze. Jacklyn kissed the tip of his nose, straddled his waist, and caressed his ribcage up and down to get back into the mood. She couldn't tell whether he did it for her, but he tore at the bonds when she gently bit and twisted his nipples. The display of muscles in motion dried her mouth and made her vulva dripping wet. She watched his struggle with the same interest as others watched a pole dancer's intriguing performance.

"Pull harder," she whispered in his ear. "You'll make me come."

Nicolas' eyes narrowed.

Before he could ask a question, she put a finger across his lips. "Do it."

He tested the cuffs and chains and lifted Jacklyn with his hips as if trying to throw her off. He put strength in his moves until he grunted with strain. Jacklyn forced him down again, suppressing a shout of joy. She was the mistress. She commanded him. Seeing his vain struggle was the utmost compliance she had hoped for. She grabbed his cock.

"Lie still now. Enough."

Panting, Nicolas rested his butt on the mattress again, still flexing his muscles. She read puzzlement in his eyes, and yet he refrained from questions. Smiling, Jacklyn teased his cock until he was fully erect, then moved her belly across his length. He pressed against her, striving for more.

"What're you—"

"Ssh." Keeping her hands on the sides of his head, she parted his lips with her tongue, tousled his hair, and pulled him close. She kissed him long and hard until they parted, gasping.

"No flogging."

"I know." She kept his cock between their bodies to feel his heat. She was overwhelmed by her need. Nonchalantly, reining in her desire, she moved between his legs. "But I can still tease you until you cry uncle."

"That's—"

"Ssh." Keeping eye contact, Jacklyn ran her fingernails

along his member and down to his balls, then following his inner thighs and calves. She knew about his confusion that turned to longing as he hoped for fulfillment. She had him under her heel and yet couldn't shake the idea he was still dominating her because of his manliness. "Don't make a sound. Just pretend you're gagged."

Nicolas held his tongue. Once she read in his eyes what he expected, she moved further up until she could sit on his face and yet didn't. Uncertainty of her moves was back in his gaze, and she was content. She lowered her body so he could kiss her vulva, but she didn't stay to be satisfied that way. She put two fingers on his eyes.

"Don't look. Don't speak."

He followed her order. Resting at her favorite position, Jacklyn let him penetrate her. He gasped and shut his mouth quickly to blow air through his nose. Tensing his abs, he lifted his lower body to increase his penetration, and she put her weight against his, attempting to dictate the rhythm. A circumspect and yet ultimately pleasing struggle evolved in which both tried to get the greatest satisfaction. Once Jacklyn had allowed him to use his strength, and now, as they silently but determinedly fought, she enjoyed how he moved his body and was restricted the same moment. She pushed up on her knees and broke contact.

"Fuck!" Nicolas cursed. "Don't do this!"

Gleefully, Jacklyn hovered above his sweating midsection and watched her lover pant. His perfect six-pack glistened with sweat. He lifted his butt off the mattress but couldn't reach her.

"Jacky! Damn it! This is torment!"

"Keep your eyes and mouth closed, or nothing will happen."

"Fuck this!" Nicolas tore at the shackles with all he had, baring his teeth.

Jacklyn gasped. She had a beast in bed and loved watching him. If it hadn't been cruel, she'd have left to fetch a camera and record his fury. Still smiling, she allowed his begging cock back between her legs. Nicolas grunted as if saying it was about time. He thrust up forcefully to the point she thought she couldn't bear it, but then the orgasm hit her amid the pain, and she cried out. Nicolas spilled himself into her, groaning until he was spent, and sank back to the covers.

There was worry in his gaze. "You okay?"

She was lightheaded and breathless as well. "Ask me later." She slumped on his chest, too content for words. Nicolas remained silent, and when she breathed normally again, she kissed his sweaty throat and cheek. "Do I need to tell you how much I love you?"

"Nope. I got the message."

Jacklyn kissed his dry lips. "God, you make it so easy for me."

"You have a way of convincing me that's unrivaled." He looked left and right. "I admit I'd love to hold you in my arms now and then."

Jacklyn caressed his biceps with a dreamy smile. "Oh, you don't know how much your show of force arouses me."

"I'm getting an idea." He shook his head. "Sometimes you're stone crazy, Belle."

"You need a shave," she whispered at his cheek. "A thorough one."

"I need another shower."

"That much water won't do you any good. I promise to keep the important parts clean."

He snorted. "You have to, if you leave me like this."

"Yes, I should untie you." She straddled him to reach for the cuffs. "Though I don't want to. Keeping you like this . . ."

"Jacky . . ."

"I know." She sighed when Nicolas pulled his arms back

and flexed his fists. There were welts around his wrists.

"Guess there's no excuse handy how this could've happened, huh?"

"Don't try to *find* an excuse." She kissed both his wrists and put his hands on her breasts. "We're grown-ups. We can do what we want."

He sat up to hold and kiss her. The emotion in his words made her shiver. "And I love what you do."

Katherine sat up to disentangle the cover and pull it up. She smiled at Tom lying beside her, his hands folded behind his head. She pulled the cover over his naked body and cuddled close for a kiss he didn't return.

"What's wrong, Tommy? What's on your mind?"

He averted his gaze and let out a breath. "Don't think I don't know why you chose me." He flinched when Katherine moved away. "I'm just a rebound guy until you find someone else."

Katherine swallowed. Her heart raced, and she needed a moment to find her voice. "Don't say that, please. First, you're no *rebound guy*. Second, I chose you because I like you."

"You really want to sleep with me? Seriously?"

"I don't own you, Tom. You can do what you want. And if you think—"

Tom smiled, but she could tell he didn't believe her. "You like me though I'm not Mr. Perfect. I guess that's fair enough." He pulled his legs to the side of the bed. "Can't expect more."

Katherine kept him from getting up. "Don't go. Manny and the twins won't come back this soon." Tom leaned against her, and she kissed his bare shoulder. "You don't have to worry."

"Believe me, I'm not worried about the twins." He turned around and pushed a strand of hair off her forehead. He frowned. "You're a wonderful woman, Katherine, so caring and full of love, but will you stay with me? Will you stay with me when we don't rob banks together? When you finally pull the plug and let your brothers go down the drain?"

Katherine looked him in the eyes. After a moment, she pulled him down for a kiss. Tom didn't protest when she put her hand between his legs. She knew he wanted her, no matter her intentions or her plans. He inched closer to her warm hand, as if parting meant to slip into never-ending misery.

She kissed him with fierce love, hoping to convince him he was no part-time lover. However, as he fondled with her and pushed his fingers along her pubic hair, she was glad he didn't say a word. Tom pulled her ankles across his shoulders to change the angle for his shaft as he pushed into her. Katherine relished his vigor and his relentlessness, his strong hands on her breasts, and the kind of rudeness that was part of his character.

Tom pushed on, grunting with strain. Katherine kept her eyes closed and forbade her mind to think further than the length of her lover's rod.

Agent Spring appeared at Matthew's desk with swinging steps and with an overdone gesture, put a sheet of paper in front of him.

Matthew smirked about Spring's exuberant mood. "And a good morning to you, too, Agent Spring. How can I be of service?"

"You're into formalities? Fine. Very good morning to you, Agent Montagna. This is the latest revelation I received from Illinois. If you don't mind putting your sore eyes on the words, you'll find out that our bank robbers might've come a long way to make trouble around our big city."

"More bank robberies?"

"I expanded the radius after the arrest of the couple in Arlington because they had a long list of robberies that took place in Illinois and Wisconsin. And when I talked with a colleague, I thought it would be the right thing to ask for the gang we're searching for, consisting of three or four men. I gave him the details and let him run a query. Even though the robbers we're searching for appear very young, they might've committed other crimes in other cities. I read your assumption about a mastermind behind the group. And I got a clue from the Minneapolis Police HQ. Same MO—a small bank, not much money, no tight security. Three men are held accounted for, but it might have been their first hit. They wore masks and scarfs, and they were very agile and fast. They clubbed the guard with a rifle barrel and escaped. Ten miles away, a burned-out van was found. That's what they did in Germantown, too." He tapped the page. "There's another possible hit that took place close to Chicago. We should have a look at it."

Nicolas took off his winter coat and sat down. "What's up, Agent Spring? Anything new?"

Matthew looked up and quickly averted his gaze again. Nicolas seemed stressed out, and if Matthew wasn't mistaken, the welts around his partner's wrists were fresh and deeper than before.

"I contacted the office in Minneapolis." Spring stood straight like a soldier reporting to his commanding officer. "There was an assault matching the MO of our four men, though only three men were seen. Reports will be here in a few hours. Another clue leads to the Chicago bureau's competence. So—"

"Matt, that's your terrain. Call your colleagues and ask them what they've got. Looks like the robbers tried out their method in major cities and left before the investigation was underway." He sat down and switched on his computer.

"Matt?"

"They won't answer any questions."

"I beg your pardon?"

Matthew clenched his teeth and kept his gaze on the sheet of paper. "I said—"

"I know what you said."

"I'll get in contact with our Minneapolis office for details." Agent Spring turned on his heels. His shoes made a squishy noise on the floor as he moved to his desk.

Matthew took a deep breath and finally looked up into Nicolas' clean-shaven face. "We didn't part as friends, okay?"

"This is a professional—"

"Stop that!" Matthew hit the desk with his flat hand. "Don't lecture me, okay? My old colleagues hate me for reasons I don't want to explain. Call them, get your answers. Task me with something else or leave me alone, but I won't give those—" He caught himself. "I'm not going to call the Chicago office. If you want all of the juicy information, ask for Agent Whaley. He hates me the most." He pushed the sheet of paper across the desk. "I questioned the jeweler once more. He got the money cash down after the credit card payment failed. Which means, we've got no clue toward the account or the young man who bought the *Daytona*."

"More bad news?" Nicolas reached for the phone.

"You name it." Matthew stood and straightened his shirt cuffs. "I need some air." He grabbed his jacket and left.

Nicolas watched Matthew's hunched back until the door to the hall fell shut. On the phone, he identified himself to the agent in charge in Chicago and explained the situation of the bank robbers and their MO.

An Italian accent tinted the voice of Agent Gandolfo. "Washington, DC, office, huh? Do you know Agent

Montagna?"

"Yes. Sir, would you please answer the question?"

"Sure." Agent Gandolfo cleared his throat. Nicolas heard him type in the background. "I've got two robberies matching your MO. Both took place last September. There's the *Merchants' Bank* in Joliet and the *Clover Bank* in Sycamore. Both banks were robbed within ten days. The robbers took the tellers' money, shot the guards in the shoulders or legs, then emptied a magazine at the ceiling and cleared away with their loot. I can't verify your shooter on the opposite roof, but from the pics I've got here, there are buildings on the other side of the street."

"Can you send me the reports, please?"

"Sure."

"What was done to find them?"

"Local police did the first investigation and came up with nil. When the bank in Sycamore was assaulted shortly after, their chief called us. They expected this to become a series of robberies and didn't want their hands on it."

"Not to mention that robberies with human casualties should be reported to the FBI right away."

Nicolas heard him unwrap something and then Agent Gandolfo's voice sounded as if his mouth was full.

"Just as well. My colleagues did a thorough search and evaluated the evidence, but the robbers disappeared." He smacked his lips. "No repetition of the same MO. Obviously, they feared we'd identify their method."

"Did you find the escape cars?"

"Nope."

Nicolas made a sound of surprise.

"Do you think they parked them at a grocery store, and we didn't look?" Agent Gandolfo asked angrily.

"They might've deep-sixed them. It's just interesting."

"I'll have the reports sent to you today. By the way, if you got the bad luck to work with Montagna, don't turn your back on him."

"I don't understand what you mean." Nicolas looked at the door toward the hall. "You either explain yourself or—"

"Explain? Really? Are you living in some black hole in DC? He sent his wife to spy on his colleagues and then gave the intel to the mafia. What more do you need to know about him? And when she got caught, he claimed he hadn't known what she did! But the mob was way ahead of our raids and always knew where our agents would be. I lost two pals to this fuckwit and his whore."

"I assume he wouldn't be on duty if what you tell me runs true."

Agent Gandolfo's voice grew in volume. "That prick shitted on his pals to save his so-called family from getting caught! He was in league with them the whole time, and just because this can't be proven doesn't mean he's innocent. At least his wife is serving her time. She was sentenced to ten years, and if you ask me—she got a deal."

"If anything else about the robberies turns up, please, call me."

"Will do."

Nicolas put down the receiver. When Agent Spring looked in his direction, he broke eye contact to hide his confusion. He wiped his forehead in order to get rid of the headache that was building as his mind sorted out what he'd heard. Out of the corner of his eye, he saw Senior Agent Sullivan approach. Without losing time, Nicolas was on his feet, took his coat, and walked straight out of the office.

CHAPTER TWELVE

Katherine sat in her limousine and watched the *Federal Trust Bank* entrance in Frederick, Maryland, without seeing who went in or out. Tom's words of the night before troubled her, and while customers walked into the bank, she pondered how she should tell Tom of her plans. The greatest difficulty was she didn't know whether he'd be part of her plans or not. She'd never fought indecision, which added to her trouble.

Herman limped along the sidewalk, grimacing pitifully and mumbling in his thick beard. He leaned on a walking stick and stopped now and then to catch his breath. His coughing was loud enough to cause people to pass him by in a wide arc. An old man asked something, and Herman nodded gravely. He took the banknote and thanked the stranger effusively.

Katherine enjoyed his show until he vanished around the corner. As agreed, he would make appearances in various small banks around town. He didn't know why, and Katherine hadn't explained in detail, for she knew even Manny wasn't the smartest pupil in her bank robbery school.

Two hours later, Herman would reappear in another disguise and pay the *Federal Trust Bank* a second visit to learn about daily routines and cash flow. Kate had already found out the guards were watchful but relaxed. Herman's quick test with a dropped can on the granite floor had revealed that the two men couldn't be provoked easily. They had helped him clean up the mess and laughed at Herman's meager jokes.

She leaned back in her seat, started the car, and drove for half an hour, then returned after shopping for clothes. She parked the car on a parking lot in an alley a block away from the bank. With a woolly hat and a scarf wound tightly around her neck, she strolled toward the bank entrance the moment the armored car arrived. Without haste, Katherine passed by the van, stopped at the curb to tie her shoelaces, and watched the men in uniform do their job. She was fascinated by the similarity of the act. It was like a déjà vu, and she knew it was a piece of cake to figure out how the bank could be looted and how the escape truck would reach safety. She walked on, listing details of her preparation.

Nicolas squinted against the cold wind in the park behind the FBI building. Matthew stood with his collar drawn up in a corner, smoking. He was clearly annoyed, but Nicolas walked on.

"Did Whaley fill you in?"

Nicolas flinched from Matthew's angry but also regretful undertone. He put his hands in his coat pockets. "It was Agent Gandolfo."

"Fatsy Gandolfo, yeah." Matt nodded without looking at Nicolas. He drew on his cigarette. "The righteous one. He told you I'm a son of a bitch, right?"

"Why don't you tell me what happened in Chicago that led to your divorce and your transfer? I'm processing what Agent Gandolfo said to me, but it doesn't make sense."

Matthew dropped the stub and put it out with the tip of his shoe. He fingered for another cigarette. Nicolas patiently waited until Matthew blew out smoke.

"Maybe you know it, or you don't. Chicago's got a great Italian community. That means there're a lot of restaurants, shops, and grocery stores with all the good stuff Italians miss in the US. Italians work in many companies but also for the police and the FBI. They've got a common bond and help each other out. Families have lived in the Chicago area for generations and know each other. Most of them are proud immigrants."

Matthew's hand shook as he lowered the cigarette. "If you're an Italian by heritage, you tend to marry someone from another Italian family. It's certainly not forbidden to marry an American without those roots, but, hey, all of your friends come from one or another Italian family."

He stepped back under a roof, and Nicolas followed, protecting himself from the gusty winds.

"I met Nerina Acardi at an Italian restaurant. She was sweet, kind, and a beauty. I knew her father and some of her brothers who ran similar businesses throughout the city. Nerina and I hit it off quickly, and before I realized it, I was married to her." Matthew smiled sadly. "Nerina was sweet and kind and caring. A typical Italian trait. She asked about my work, and I—the proverbial idiot in love—talked with her about cases, though I knew I shouldn't. She was always interested in my work and wanted to meet with my colleagues, claiming it was her duty to take care of a good relationship with every one of my team. Of course, she cooked like only Italian women can."

Matthew paused and smoked. He kept his focus on the pavement in front of his shoes. "She arranged meetings at our house, and when she considered our home too small, we bought a new one. Her family helped us with money. No, I didn't ask where they got it from. After all, the family was huge, and everyone owned a business. Okay, I didn't ask for references or proof of their revenue. I moved into the new home with my beautiful wife, and because of her exuberance, we also bought a lot of new furniture and even built a small garden house the same summer. A little later, we bought a dog, and I thought we'd hit the jackpot. You know . . . the moment when you think you've got it all, and you only wait for your wife to announce she's pregnant."

Matthew sighed and cleared his throat. "Nerina was a great host, always cheerful. All my colleagues liked her. Oh, yes, they liked her very much." Matthew dropped the second stub to put it out with more force than necessary. "See, I loved Nerina. I accepted her the way she was . . . *is*. I didn't doubt her intentions. I'd never have assumed she lied to me." His voice sank to a painful whisper. "But she did. She framed me big time, and I was the idiot who didn't notice. Maybe I preferred not to notice, but that didn't matter."

"Did she use the FBI internal information for crimes?"

Matthew snorted and glanced at Nicolas. "That's the tame version, Nick. She slept with my colleagues, she handed internal information to her family to help them escape prosecution, and she stole evidence from the vault. Of course, she did this with the help of the officer on duty because she knew him and his . . . well, she had her way with men, and they acted to her bidding and covered it up. I don't know how she did it, but everyone seemed addicted to her, like she was some heavy drug."

Nicolas pondered what to say. Matthew looked like a man thrown into a snake pit he thought he'd survived before. The pain of loss in his eyes was raw.

"How did you find out about her doings?"

"I didn't. I trusted her. I trusted her lies and her confession of love. Whenever I was distrustful, she distracted me. She was a great lover, and she had wound me around her little finger from the beginning. She knew exactly how to get what she wanted. But a new colleague showed up. He'd been sent from Minneapolis to investigate a big fraud in which the Chicago mob was involved, supposedly.

"He caught Nerina and one of my colleagues as they were making out. He reported the incident and . . . that's how I became aware of her doings. He set the ball rolling, and within a week, more details came to light. A team from Minneapolis was sent because suddenly all the Chicago agents were under suspicion." Matthew glanced at Nicolas but looked at his shoes quickly. "I realized she'd used me and all of my colleagues to spy for her family who runs the Chicago area mob. They do this very effectively. They know how to cover their tracks and appear honest. Nerina was sentenced to ten years. Some special agents suffered demotion. Two of our colleagues had been murdered by the mob. That was also uncovered during the six months of investigation." He took a deep breath. "As you can imagine, they blamed me for all occurrences. They insinuated I'd been in league with my wife and supported her doings. After all, the new house was costly, and I couldn't have afforded it with my income."

"Your innocence was proven, I assume?"

Matthew nodded, fingered for a cigarette, but instead of lighting it, played it across his fingers until the wind took it away into a puddle. "On all charges, yes. That didn't keep my colleagues from blaming me. I had to ask for a transfer or—well, I was told insistently that my service in Chicago was no longer wanted."

Nicolas leaned against the cold wall. "I see."

Matthew snorted and looked up. "That's all? No accusation that I should've told you beforehand? Or that you'll ask for another partner right away because you can't trust me? I don't blame you. I was blinded by my wife. Who knows what else will slip my attention?"

"Yes, I would've preferred knowing about the circumstances earlier, but I understand it's not a subject you want to discuss."

Matthew frowned.

Nicolas stood up to his gaze. "I won't ask for another partner, if that's what you're worried about. I want you focused and not half-drunk in the morning. We still have a series of bank robberies to solve, and the men will strike again. Are you with me?"

"Let's see what we've got from Minneapolis and Chicago."

Jacklyn paced the living room, tapping the warm telephone against her chin. She'd known Harry Fuller wouldn't stop pressing her to buy the house, but she hadn't expected him to present her with a couple that was about to sign the contract. His soft words of regret had caused her goosebumps. He had assured her that—so far—the contract wasn't signed, but there was a deadline he was supposed to hold, and she had *one last chance* to change her mind. She dialed Richard's number and blurted out her misery in a summary interrupted by pitiful sighs.

"And then I thought the only person able to help me is you." Jacklyn waited with bated breath and a hammering heart for his answer.

Richard took his time and cleared his throat. She imagined him lifting his hand from the table to use it for his explanation. "Jacklyn, this is no doubt a difficult situation, and you're right it would've been better if you hadn't mentioned Harry's name to Nicolas. But no, I won't pose as the owner of that house, Jacky-darling. Nick's an FBI agent. He'll know, and I'll be in deep shit."

"You're a sissy."

Richard made a sound of anger. "Yes, I'm a sissy when it comes to a hunk with fighting skills and a badge. My poor ass can only take so much."

"He's not violent." She sat down on the edge of the couch and glanced at the clock beside the TV set. Harry expected her to call the next morning.

"He's devoted to you, even obedient when you want him to, but he'd wipe the floor with me if he thinks I'm trying to fool him."

"I need your help, Richard. It's a beautiful house. And it would be perfect for us—in all dimensions. Together, we could afford it, which is the best news."

"I can't pose as the owner, sweetheart. He'd smell a lie."

"You're a lawyer. You're used to lying."

"Maybe, yes. Though I consider that remark very rude, but I can only repeat my words. He's an FBI agent. I won't risk my reputation because of a house you might or might not buy." He paused. "I've got a long list of friends and clients. If you want me to, I could help you find a house."

"Something so gorgeous and so cheap? I doubt it."

"Cheap? Under market value?"

"Well, yes. From what I read, his offer is the best I've seen so far. The house is a gem. Right next to a wide meadow. Wonderful."

His voice indicated a hunter's interest in prey. "Gimme the address. I need to find out something."

Jacklyn stood up, frowning. "Do you think Harry is *lying*?"

Richard hesitated, and his words appeared measured and careful. "I think he wants you to buy it for reasons only he can explain."

"Don't tell me it's a fraud and there's something terrible hidden in the basement. Or that the house was owned by a serial killer."

Richard laughed. In the background, Jacklyn heard a second phone ringing. "You read too many FBI reports. I bet it's nothing that dramatic, but to be honest, Harry's offer intrigues me. I'll call you back."

Jacklyn was about to thank him when the doorbell rang. Before she could say another word, Richard had hung up.

Jacklyn put down the phone, and with her mind on the images of the house she'd visited, walked to the door. She opened her mouth for a grumpy greeting, but when the woman in front of her spread her arms for a hug, Jacklyn squealed with joy.

"Les! You're already in town! Oh, I was so happy when you called! What brings you to DC?"

Lesley laughed and embraced her. She was six inches taller and dressed in black from coat to boots. "Sex—whatever else?"

"Really? Come on in." Jacklyn made way and closed the door. "You come to DC for sex? Are there no men to spank in Philly anymore?"

Lesley's brown eyes widened. "Oh, you didn't know? I bought several sex shops last year and created a new label . . . *Leisurely*. A new shop, certainly with a dungeon, will open in DC shortly, and I have to be there to overlook the preparations."

"You made your hobby your profession. I'm proud of you."

Lesley slipped out of her high-heeled boots and dropped her coat right beside them. "Yep, me, the dungeon queen, and the drags."

With a gesture, Jacklyn invited her to the living room.

Sighing with contentment, Lesley leaned back in the cushions and ran a hand through her black curls, then put both arms on the backrest. "And you still own that—"

"Physiotherapy office. And before you try to talk me out of it . . . I still like it." Jacklyn put a bottle of wine and two glasses on the coffee table. She sat down, still smiling.

Lesley looked the same as two years ago. She was of South African heritage and obviously gifted with spotless skin and a sexy body that she emphasized with tight shirts and tighter pants, both preferably made of leather. No man would take her to be thirty-six, and she would give any man a hard time who dared to estimate her that age.

"You're torturing people your way." She made a gesture with her hand, displaying dark red fingernails. "That's not bad. By the way, the dungeon scene in Amsterdam and Berlin is a blast. I can't tell you how excited I was when I got there the first evening. I felt my eggs pop, believe me."

Jacklyn laughed and spilled wine. "Oops! You do have a way with words, Les!"

"Oh, but not only with words." She toasted and drank. With her lashes lowered seductively, her words appeared an invitation to a bed game. "I learned that my crazy isn't that much different from other people's crazy. That's why my business flourishes. I make a couple of bucks more than I expected." Lesley set down the glass. Her eyes widened. "And you? Are you happy? I mean, kneading people's backs every day isn't boring?"

"No. I like helping people. They're grateful."

Lesley rolled her eyes. When she smiled, little white teeth showed. "Ah, well, as if your clients weren't grateful back then in the dungeons. Come on, Jacky, you can't tell me you live without the thrill of torturing someone. What do you do? Sneak into a club at night, put on a mask, and work as a mistress without anyone recognizing you?" She pointed a finger when Jacklyn lowered her chin. "See? I got ya. I know you need this as much as I do." Lesley emptied the glass and let Jacklyn refill it. "Does the club pay you well? I haven't seen many in DC so far. Is there one you'd recommend?"

"I don't work part-time in a club, Les. Really. I have a boyfriend."

"Fuck me sideways! A real boyfriend? A man you're gonna meet more than once? A man you actually . . . love?" She shook her head when Jacklyn nodded. "Ah, come on, you can't be serious. The times you tried that before you went head over heels and no one was good enough for more than three months."

Jacklyn felt the warmth of love surge through her. "I found someone who likes to play. He lets me play with him. In fact, he wouldn't have known of our games if I hadn't introduced him to shackles and gags."

Lesley coughed and put down the glass. "You turned a straight guy without any knowledge into your sub? Jacklyn, my dear sis in crime, you amaze me. How did you do that?"

Jacklyn ran a finger along the rim of her glass and let the memory show in her words. "On our second night, I tied him up with just a knot around his wrists, and I asked him to trust me. He hesitated at first, but he looked so gorgeous. You can't imagine how he intrigued me."

"Right now, I can."

"I felt his insecurity, and it was sweet, but then—you know I loved him even more because he didn't push me away. He didn't call me crazy or say that he'd leave me at once because I was way too perverted for him."

Lesley cocked an eyebrow, and her lips twisted to a mocking grin. "Really, Jacky-sis, are you telling me he let you have him your way? What kind of guy is he? The brother of the *Monster from the Black Lagoon*? A man so ugly he wouldn't get a girlfriend any other way?" She made a gesture when Jacklyn said *no*. "If he had no experience with kinky games . . . why would he go for it?"

"He's open to new things, and I convinced him that he can trust me, and that I can make him come like no other woman ever could."

Lesley gaped at her. "Wow. Now you've got me. What does he look like?"

Jacklyn pulled out her cell phone and opened the gallery. She had some snapshots of Nicolas in the park running and of him preparing dinner in shirt and shorts. She had taken one picture while he was asleep. She liked it most because of his completely relaxed expression.

"He looks much younger than your other friends. How come?"

Jacklyn shrugged. "I don't know. When I look at him, I wonder why I went for older guys all the time. He's great."

"Okay, so he's a fine guy . . . very manly features, built like a builder without pumped-up muscles. I'm impressed. You don't have any pics of him being tied up? I'd really like to see your work."

Jacklyn heard eagerness out of her husky words. "No, you just want to see whether he's well endowed. Yes, he is." She bit her lip as she put down the cell phone. "I've got something even better than pics of him in bondage."

"You filmed him? Naughty girl." Lesley chuckled and settled back comfortably. She pulled up her long legs. "Bring it on."

Jacklyn hadn't shown the tapes to anyone. She had told Nicolas she'd destroyed all the evidence of their weekend in the woods, but in a moment of weakness, she had exchanged Harry's USB stick with an empty one. Nicolas wouldn't approve of her keeping the films, but Lesley was her soul sister, and she trusted her.

Jacklyn opened up her notebook and opened the first file. Lesley was captivated by the show of submissive and mistress. She curled her lips to a knowing smile that lasted throughout the game Jacklyn and Nicolas played.

"The chains are a turn-on, no doubt." Lesley whistled through her teeth and emptied another glass of wine. "You kept most of the stuff from that dungeon in Philly, right? It's like coming home." She laughed and clapped her hands. "Oh, Jacky, you could make thousands of dollars with this movie!"

"Stop talking like that." Jacklyn cringed on the couch. She looked at the apartment door as if Nicolas would walk through any minute. "Nick doesn't know I still have them. He's not a guy who'd brag about his sexuality. He wants to keep this private."

"Hmm, I understand, but it's a pity, don't you think?" Lesley lifted the empty bottle. "Do you have another one? I can't remember when I last drank such a good vintage."

"Sure." Jacklyn got up to fetch a bottle from the cooler, and when she sat down, Lesley had switched to the second movie. "He's great, don't you think?"

"He's a temptation on two legs—with a lot hanging between them. Would you mind me watching you play?"

Jacklyn's laugh was breathless. "Oh, he would mind! Les, please, don't misunderstand me. I wouldn't mind you in our bedroom, which I turned into a small version of a playroom, but he couldn't stand your presence."

"You think he wouldn't get a boner while a stranger enjoys the view? What a pity." Lesley reclined with her glass in one hand and watched the scene evolve. "You trained him well. He's eager, he's flexible, and he's got stamina. He's got a great cock, too—not that big but straight—though he isn't circumcised."

"You list this up like it's a sports game."

Lesley raised a perfectly formed eyebrow. "You lost your distance, hmm? When we worked together, you didn't mind these jokes."

"Love makes a difference." Jacklyn sighed and sipped wine. "Nick had a real outburst of strength yesterday. I swear I got so wet I was dripping. He fought the restraints with all he had. He needed to vent, and pulling the restraints was the best thing that day. That's what he said. I watched the show of force and stopped breathing. He was amazing. He was a force of nature, and for a second, I wondered if the restraints would hold."

"A pity you don't have that on tape." Lesley frowned.

"You could put up a camera for your sessions. Save the best hours of your games for another viewing. No, don't misunderstand me. I don't want you to show it at birthday parties, but it could be fun to watch it again as a couple. And the way I see it, you keep him blindfolded on many occasions." She chuckled when Jacklyn shook her head. "Come on, you could show him how splendid he looks. And he does look great, don't you think?"

Jacklyn blushed and shook her head when she took her wine glass. "Les, he's a great guy. I won't ruin his trust in me. I won't go further than he's comfortable with."

"Ah, I hear you want to go further, but he doesn't?"

"Not yet." Jacklyn pondered. "I'm granting him time. I want his cooperation, and I want him to be comfortable with my kinky way. In the beginning, I spent evenings with explanations instead of swinging a crop."

Lesley burst out laughing and couldn't stop.

Jacklyn raised her brows. "What's so damn funny?"

"You. Listening to you. You were the toughest mistress ever. You bashed the guys until they screamed for mercy."

"I played it safe."

"You dished out beatings as if the devil had hired you to serve him on earth. If you ask me—you did a great job for him. He's probably sitting on his throne now and wondering where you've gone."

"I told you I wouldn't work in the dungeon for the rest of my life. It was fun, though. I don't deny that."

"How could you? Some of the guys were addicted to you, stronger than to any drug they used. Well, if they used drugs at all." Les pointed at Jacklyn. "You served them well." She put down her empty glass and stood. "May I use your bathroom? I think I should change my panties."

"If you want me to . . . I can get you a spanking bench."

Lesley looked over her shoulder with a sexy grin. She twitched her brows. "I've got some in stock. Leather-covered bench, leather cuffs combined with dark brown wood. Looks spiffy."

"I'd need some room for it, and as you can see, there's little room here." Jacklyn sighed. "Right before you came, I tried to convince Richard to help me buy a house, but he refused. I suppose he thinks Harry Fuller's trying to betray me."

"Richard and Harry are here in DC?"

"Harry's got some real estate and a club in DC. He's a big businessman now. Richard still lives in Philly."

"He was the lawyer you bashed, right?" Lesley smacked her lips, frowning. "He was the rather feisty guy who couldn't get enough. Whatever you dished out—he wanted more." Lesley slumped on the bed. "Do I have it right? You want to buy a house? Does your beloved sub know of that?"

"Of course Nicolas knows."

"I hear what you're not saying. He doesn't want to move, right? He likes the apartment. He doesn't want any changes and—"

"And he rejects the idea of moving into a house Harry Fuller owns. Correct."

"But it's not his call. He's your sub. He goes where you go."

Jacklyn sat down beside her. Her voice was soft. "You don't understand. Nicolas is not my twenty-four-seven sub. He doesn't take orders from me or runs around naked to serve my needs. It's a bedtime arrangement. Not the lifestyle variety."

"Yeah, I wondered where he is."

Jacklyn lowered her chin, smiling. "He's with the FBI."

"No shit!" She frowned. "You aren't saying he's in custody, right? Ah, okay. He's a special agent? A federal officer?"

"Yep."

"But how does this fit?" She made a face as if the idea of an agent being a sub was unthinkable. "I mean he has to make a thousand decisions a day, right? He has to be strong and brave. He fights bad guys on the streets and is allowed to shoot criminals. How can he give up all that while he's with you?"

"That's the million dollar question, isn't it?" Jacklyn leaned back against the pillory. "He likes to give up control. He says it's great to give up responsibility, too. And I convinced him that pain leads to outstanding arousal and great sex."

"Ah, I see where this is going." Lesley pointed at her, smacking her lips. "You satisfy him. Every time, I suppose?"

Jacklyn nodded.

"Well, that's only fifty percent of what you could get. Do you keep him chastised?"

"I don't have to."

"He doesn't allow it."

"That, too."

Lesley rolled her eyes. "Come on, Jacky, you could have it all if you insisted." She got up and paced the bedroom, using her hands while she spoke. "You could have much more if you wanted to. Isn't that right?"

Jacklyn gazed at her girlfriend and searched for words. Though she had thought the same way years ago, she realized Nicolas had changed her. "You don't understand the way our relationship works. I have control over him because it's what he likes and what he permits. Okay, I introduced him to my kinky way of sex, and you can say that I kind of pushed him, but that doesn't mean I can exaggerate it."

Lesley stopped pacing to frown. She opened her mouth but didn't say a word.

"Does the word *arrangement* sound too strange for you?" Jacklyn smiled tentatively. "You think this can't work?"

"I think it's not enough. I think you give yourself away below value."

"Don't mix the club dungeon actions with a relationship, Les. Nicolas is an independent character. He's strong and lives in the real world. There's a clear line between the real life we lead and the fantasies we live here in the bedroom. We respect each other, and I won't do anything he's not comfortable with."

"Collars, hmm?"

"You're a good observer."

Lesley chuckled and pulled a strand of hair around her finger. "That's part of the job." She slumped on the bed again. "Tell me, why can't you use collars on him?"

"He was a kidnap victim, and the kidnapper used a control collar on him. As you can imagine, that ruined his trust in any collar. Even fastening the top button of his dress shirt or wearing a tie was difficult for him for some time."

Lesley whistled through her teeth. "What a fucked-up situation. It's astonishing he was up for the games after that."

Jacklyn lowered her chin. "Yeah, it was a tough time. We went without ropes and cuffs for several months. His nightmares were bad enough."

"And still you got him back to this . . . pillory and shackles included. How?"

"The wonders of love." Jacklyn laughed when Lesley snorted in pretended annoyance. "Nicolas trusts me, and he loves sex. He even urges me to do new things with him."

"Fine. That's a free ticket to do what you want. It's your sex life fantasy after all."

"He's outstanding."

"I saw that on tape." Lesley lay down and rested her head on her hand. "Tell me more about this gem you got in your bed."

Matthew heard the rubbing of the lab coat material when

Miller reached the desk.

"Agent Hayes, I've got something I need to tell you."

Nicolas lifted his gaze from the report he was reading. "Yes?"

Miller took a deep breath and put a sheet of paper in front of Nicolas, smiling broadly. "That's the incendiary composition the robbers used in Minneapolis. Obviously, they were into that MO right from the start, yes? It's clear local police hadn't connected the two incidents, but when I asked them—you see here the composition is the same as the one found in the van at the Federal Triangle. And I narrowed the providers."

"You know who sold the stuff?"

"Even better." Miller beamed with delight. "The man's in custody for arson in Minneapolis. He's being interrogated as we speak." He moved his head left and right. "I took the liberty to send agents to the penitentiary right after I found out about his involvement."

"That's very helpful. Thank you." Nicolas smiled. "You did a really good job."

Miller appeared to grow two inches and forgot about pushing back a loose strand of hair from his forehead. Blushing, he nodded vigorously. "Thank you. You're welcome. Results will be sent to you. I told the agents you were the agent in charge."

"Very well."

Miller released his breath. "I'll look at the other stuff I got . . . from Chicago, I mean." He turned and strode back through the aisle.

Matthew raised his brows as far as they would get. "You're the agent in charge. They'll report directly to you." He nodded at Nicolas' irritated expression. "He's got a crush on you."

"That's BS."

"Nope, I don't think so. I was non-existent for him, while you appeared like a star. Did he ask you out for a coffee or anything else? Dinner, maybe?"

"You're imaging things." Nicolas lowered his gaze to the report. "And I'm truly not a men's man."

"Well, I know men who swing both ways. Hey, wait, don't kill me with that look!" Matthew laughed. "I don't think you look gay. At least, I don't feel attracted to you."

"Thanks a lot."

"After my experience with women, I might try men for a change."

Nicolas wiped his face. "In both robberies close to Chicago, the escape van was involved in small accidents. First, the van bumped against a fire hydrant, and second, it hit another car and pushed it against a shop window. Both times, the vans sped on and escaped." Nicolas looked up. "After that, the robberies in the Chicago area stopped and started over in the DC area again half a year later."

"You think they got another driver?" Matthew nodded, contemplating. "There've been no accidents here on their escape routes."

"I saw the man drive. He was excellent. He swerved around hindrances like a pro. You don't learn that within a few weeks."

"But that's not good news . . . the group members changed."

"Or they added. The fourth man's not confirmed for the robberies close to Minneapolis and Chicago. It's possible they found a new member."

"And have to divide the loot through four instead of three? An unusual act."

"But we know two men are brothers, possibly twins. The other one could be a close friend. After all, they've been robbing banks for some time. The way I see it—they met this guy with a reputation for excellent driving. Why should they not ask him?" His fingers hovered over the keyboard. "The question is . . . how can I narrow a search for an escape van driver in the Chicago area without any further details?"

Nicolas heard laughter through the door. It was the high and exuberant giggling he associated with teenagers. He stopped at the living room and forced a blank expression as he would do at any given crime scene. On the couch sat a woman in stunning black clothes, giving him the eye so openly he turned away. She looked like a model stepped out of a club magazine, an enticing twitch of lips included. She scanned his body up and down, and Nicolas bet his salary that the women had been talking about him until the moment he'd put the key in its lock.

Jacklyn rose from the place beside her. Her cheeks were flushing red, and her smile suggested bedroom secrets. The top buttons of her blouse were open, and under different circumstances, he would've swept her off the floor to kiss and cuddle. He stood rooted.

"Hello, my wonderful lover." She kissed him sensuously.

Nicolas moved backward, out of reach, smiling in spite of his insecurity. He tasted wine on his tongue. "Jacky, don't you think you should introduce me?"

"Hmm, do I have to?" Jacklyn pointed toward the couch. Her voice betrayed she was tipsy. "This is Lesley Gilbert, one of my best friends, coming directly from Philadelphia."

"Via Amsterdam and Berlin." Lesley lifted her glass toward him. "It's nice meeting you."

"Yes, you, too." Nicolas took off his jacket and stopped opening the knot of his tie, realizing Lesley was staring at him. "I'm gonna freshen up and go visit Jason."

Lesley blinked at him, twitched her eyebrows, and ran her

tongue across her lips. Her smile indicated more than just friendly interest.

Nicolas held his breath as his insecurity grew. He didn't know where to look or what to do. He knew if she got up and ripped the shirt off his body, he wouldn't protest. The feeling turned awkward within seconds, and he sweated.

"You won't join us for dinner?" Jacklyn pouted. She put a finger around his belt and pulled without effect. "It's not fair to come home so late and run away again."

"Jason asked me to stop by two days ago. I put it off, but can't do that for long. And in my defense, I didn't know you expected a visitor."

"Aunts and best friends don't have to call ahead." Jacklyn beamed at him and stretched to kiss his chin. She let go of his belt. "So, okay, hurry up and join us later."

Nicolas nodded toward Lesley, feeling as if he'd taken off much more than his jacket.

Nicolas felt better the moment he left the apartment, and his mood lifted seeing Jason's happiness about his visit half an hour later.

"Long time no see!" Jason invited him with a wide move of his arm to sit down in the comfortable armchair close to the large window in the living room. "How are you? You look kinda stressed."

"Another day, another case."

With a dazzling smile, Elaine delivered a cup of tea. She stressed that the cookies were homemade.

"Thank you, that's kind." In spite of his grumbling stomach, he turned down Elaine's offer to join them for dinner. She pouted but didn't insist and left with the duster she'd picked up from the table.

"Yeah, another case." Jason nodded, quietly chuckling. "Come on, pal, don't try to fool me. What's troubling you? I like you being here, don't get me wrong, but last time you told me you wouldn't stop by for another week."

Nicolas waited until Elaine had closed the door. "Jacky's got a visitor . . . Lesley. They know each other from Philadelphia, which means—"

Jason laughed. "She's another very fierce lady in tight pants and lots of leather with a roar instead of a laugh."

"Exactly."

Jason's face sobered. "Really? I thought I was blurting out my fantasies."

"Nope." Nicolas put down the cup and munched on a cookie. "I don't know how to describe it. She looked hungry. I bet they'd discussed a *lot* before I came home."

"And you were afraid of detailed questions about your crown jewels?"

"They were beyond that. The way Lesley checked me out told me she wanted much more than a friendly conversation."

Jason held his tongue until his face reddened.

"Make fun of me. Thanks a lot." Nicolas exhaled, frustrated. He put the rest of the cookie in his mouth. "Maybe I'm overreacting."

"They had plans to undress and shackle you and then have their way with you until you screamed uncle. Are you shivering?"

"It's more like a shudder. Thanks for firing up my imagination. Now I can't get rid of that picture."

"I bet you had this all played out on the way here. Do you want something stronger than tea? And do you plan to stay overnight? I can tell Elaine—"

"No, thank you. I'll tell Jacky there won't be any playtime with another partner involved." He frowned. "She was quite tipsy already. They'll probably be asleep when I come home."

"Wishful thinking. So, your lady has lady friends from her times as a mistress. That's interesting. It's not unusual, I'd say.

You could learn a lot about her if you asked her friend."

"The way Lesley looked at me, she had something different in mind than chatting about Jacky." Nicolas emptied the cup and put it down gently. "I guess I'll go for a whiskey or whatever else you have."

"All right." Jason made it to his feet and limped toward the shelf on the other side of the room.

"How's your therapy? Are you making progress?"

"Well, I walk without crutches, so, yes, I'm making progress. But there's still that dull pain, and the doc says he can't do anything about it. It'll get better, but slowly." Jason returned with two glasses. "I don't know if the proposed six weeks of therapy will be enough. What I wanted to know—did you have a tendency to combine sex with pain before you met Jacklyn?"

"Don't you think that's too intimate a question?"

Jason shrugged and sat down carefully. He put up his leg on a stool. "I thought you'd be in confessing mode and wanted to take the advantage. And this time you can't deny that you started the subject."

Nicolas sipped the alcohol and stared at the flower arrangement on the dining table. He liked the simple and yet tasteful decor Elaine had chosen for her home. The furniture, the books, and many plants made the room cozy.

"I can't tell whether I had a tendency because the situation never occurred. Sex was always gentle from both sides." He shook his head. "What should I say? Jacky knows which buttons to press. She taught me that a crop and handcuffs make a great difference in satisfaction. And I—"

Jason lifted his hand. "Okay, I get it. Don't get my mouth watering."

"You're a sissy. You still can't walk straight, and Jacky said you'd better exercise every day instead of complaining. Please, don't tell me you'd go for pain when having sex."

"You're mean. You tell me you're my friend, but slap my face the next moment."

"Sorry, pal, but especially today, I'm at odds with Jacky's behavior." Nicolas shook his head again. "My apologies. I didn't mean to be rude."

"Maybe you're at odds with yourself. While on the one hand, you want her to surprise you with new toys, on the other hand, you want to control her and know in advance what she'll be doing. That doesn't fit."

"I don't want to know exactly what she'll be doing. I want to know whether she's doing it for my sake, for our sake, or because she's manipulating me that way. If I interpret Lesley's visit correctly, Jacky will present me with more ideas in the next few days."

"I see. She'll train you with cookies until you completely forget about meat?" Jason chuckled. "Don't lose your balls on the way, Nick."

"You can pick them up for me."

"Nope. I won't. I'll crush them. I'm your official ball crusher." He pointed at Nicolas' wrists. "Don't tell me your privy parts look the same as your arms."

"No, certainly not."

"But she's getting fiercer. You can't hide those welts anymore."

"Matt saw them, too."

"Hmm, how's the guy?"

Nicolas summed up Matthew's revelation about his ex-wife and the circumstances leading toward his transfer. Jason's eyes widened, and Nicolas was glad to distract him from the subject of Jacklyn's behavior.

"He won't say a word about your kind of relationship." Jason emptied his glass and nodded toward him. "He's guilty of closing his eyes. No, don't say you believe every word he said. He could've known if he wanted to. His wife betrayed him with more than one guy. How could he not see it?"

"Because he loved her. And if you ask me—he still loves her. He's divorced, but it didn't mean the end of his feelings for her."

"Now you're the expert for extraordinary relationships?"

"I'm no expert, but I understand him. And if the bureau declared him innocent, I won't hold anything against him. I wasn't involved. He's only an interim partner for me." Nicolas got up and took both glasses to the shelf. "Do you want another?"

"Yes, please. How's the case evolving?"

Nicolas brought Jason up to date. They emptied two more glasses of whiskey, munched the sandwiches Elaine delivered in between, and forgot about the time.

"You know what most intrigues me?" Jason wiped his lips with a napkin. "The criminals adapt to the circumstances. They don't change their MO but their surroundings. They're local, but as soon as the police get too close, they leave and find another district, another city to commit the same kinds of crime."

"And they hope to get away unnoticed by the FBI for the longest time."

"They were under investigation, but it ended when they left Illinois and stayed quiet for half a year. If you consider the sum of money—they had to live chastely."

"Or they committed crimes we don't know of."

"Like robbing jewelers or supermarkets. You can't consider every kind of crime and bring them together. That would only work if you had identified at least one of the robbers."

"But you're right . . . they don't risk the police stepping on their toes. They prefer fresh grounds and hope to go undetected."

"Well, if they'd change states after every crime it would be even harder to find them. Right now, you've got a group of four who'll plan for another robbery. Bank or armored car. They could widen their range, but they'll stay around DC until your investigation gets too close to them."

"That's your professional opinion?"

"That's my gut feeling. They've got away so far. Even the van at the Federal Triangle didn't hold enough evidence to nail one of the men. You only just found out they might be brothers. They escaped without a car, which means they knew about the DC metro and its schedule correctly to the dot." He nodded, still in thought. "They're confident they can get away with another robbery before their MO gets risky."

Nicolas sat down with his glass and a deep frown. "I want this case over, but without more clues, we'll be running in the dark and only find witnesses after another robbery. They're damn clever and careful."

"And they're having fun with what they do . . . masquerades included."

"Matt said there might be a mastermind behind them."

"That's a great idea." Jason reclined more comfortably, grimacing. "It fits my point of view. The robbers are young and having fun, but the evaluation and the timing must be done by someone clever, experienced, and clear-headed. Remember, they drove to Federal Triangle because that was their plan B from the beginning. They didn't choose the route by chance. Someone tells them where to go and when. Then the mastermind leans back and enjoys the show."

"I thought about that, too, but we couldn't determine a car or van reappearing at the crime scene at the time of the robbery. I assume the mastermind either doesn't show up or changes cars every time . . . if there's such a person at all. Maybe the shooter is the clever planner. He's determined enough to shoot and kill if necessary."

"Maybe the arsonist will confess who he sold his stuff to."

Jason cocked his head when Elaine peeped through the slit at the door. "Pal, I guess you'd better decide if you want to stay or leave. My lovely girlfriend wants my attention."

"I'll leave." Nicolas stood and pulled Jason up. "Thanks for your time and insight."

"Oh, don't get mushy on me. Believe me, I'd prefer running around with you over limping the whole day. It's fun for a week, but no longer."

"I'll be glad to have you back."

"I bet. It's totally boring without me. I know that."

CHAPTER THIRTEEN

Matthew could tell by the tightness of Nicolas' shoulders that—again—the morning hadn't been as amicable as it should've been between lovers. While Nicolas took off his coat and put it on a hanger, Matthew fetched him a cup of coffee.

"Thanks." Nicolas sat down and switched on the computer.

"You're welcome. CSU-Miller aka *wanna be your lover* showed up recently to deliver the results of the interrogation in Minneapolis. Read about Jefferson Palmetti, the arsonist." He nodded toward the sheet of paper in front of him. "I guess Miller wanted praise, but I wasn't the right one to pet him."

Nicolas narrowed his eyes, then looked at the report.

"You need a wedding ring to show you're taken." Matthew sipped coffee and leaned back. "How's it going between Miss Beautiful and you?"

"Too personal." Nicolas read the first page.

"Was she too personal with you, or are you referring to my question?"

Once more, Nicolas looked at him, irritated. "We're searching for a bearded blond guy named Manny, broad as a truck and with an accent somewhere from Illinois. He didn't know much about the stuff but threatened him into selling the best he had. Palmetti took the threat for real that Manny would break his bones if he didn't deliver. A bruiser, a shooter, probably a killer. We knew that before."

"No. The best is yet to come. It's a page-turner."

"You're a fountain of good mood this morning." Nicolas turned the page. "Reasons?"

"I expected praise for showing up sober."

Nicolas twitched his brows. "I expect my partner to be sober."

Matthew tried hard not to laugh. "Do you practice that threatening glare in front of the mirror? Oh, come on!" He swung the chair back. "I hope you don't play poker. I could sense your uneasiness the moment you entered the office. I know something's bothering you. Just spill it and feel better."

"Palmetti told Manny where to find a driver. That's interesting."

"Unfortunately, Palmetti doesn't know the name or whether Manny made contact at all. At least, that's what he says. I bet he wants a deal. Then he'll talk."

"The agents in Minneapolis will find the driver, and once we got a face and a name, the robbers will try to escape."

"They did that before." Matthew shook his head. "We shouldn't search publicly once the man's name is known. The robbers are clever enough to either change their hunting grounds or drop the driver. I bet Manny won't hesitate to get rid of him if he thinks the others are in danger."

"Brothers, yes." Nicolas read the report again. "Call it a hunch, but I can't imagine these guys just found each other by chance and decided to rob banks."

"The mastermind—"

"No, not the person in the background. We know the shooter on the roof is the brother of one of the robbers at the bank." He looked up. "What if they're all brothers?"

"Except one . . . the driver."

"Yes. He's the last one on the list. You're right—if we involve the media, the brothers will sacrifice the driver and run." He put the report to the side and checked the emails. "No news on any assault in the DC area. That means they're still doing research." Nicolas leaned back and wiped the bridge of his nose. "We know their preferences. Do we have a list with possible targets?"

"It's still too large to have men positioned at each one of them. I'm working on details and comparing the banks to the surroundings—like buildings on the opposite side of the street. Agent Spring sent out a global alert to all the bank managers, but they said security's already tight, and they couldn't do more even if they wanted. Security companies have been alerted, too, to report any unusual observers. I bet the gang spies on the bank in several disguises."

"But this man named Manny can't hide how tall and wide he is." Nicolas started typing. "It's a shot in the dark, but the bank guards should watch out for men matching the description."

Jacklyn hastened to pick up the phone, recognizing Richard's office number. "Hi, how are you doing?"

"Sit down in case you're standing."

Jacklyn sat on the edge of the couch. "Okay, that doesn't sound like you've got good news. Spill the beans."

Richard cleared his throat. "I know you want that house. Your rudeness made that very clear, but I think you should reconsider."

Jacklyn rolled her eyes and cursed.

"Yes, Jacky-darling, sometimes things aren't what they appear. In plain words . . . the legal position concerning the property of the neighboring premises is unsettled. This means that either a concrete company or a painter's shop owns the property. There's also another legal argument about approximately a hundred acres pending." Richard breathed deeply. "Please, don't cry, Jacky. I know it's hard to let go, but—"

"I can't believe Harry lied to me."

"Technically, he didn't lie. He owns the premises with the house and is free to sell it. There's no debate about that. But he didn't tell you that the neighborhood will change next year. The plain meadow behind the houses will be exchanged with some industrial buildings."

"The area will be destroyed by industry?"

"As a result—yes."

"That's why owners are selling their houses and moving away." Jacklyn sank into the cushions. "They already know."

"It's good you told me about it."

"With another intention, but, yes. Thank you for keeping me from doing something foolish."

"Oh, my pleasure. You could pay me with some extraordinary treatment. I heard there's a new dungeon opening in DC in December, and if I'm not mistaken you know the owner. Advertisements are all over the papers. Invite me, and I'll be your *Lawyer of the Year* for the next decade."

Jacklyn laughed amid tears about his suppliant tone. "How can I say *no* to such a challenge? Yes, all right! Don't faint because—"

"I'm not fainting. I'm getting a hard-on and trying to conceal it. My office . . . well, let's say it's not empty, and this will be really embarrassing the moment I have to get up."

Jacklyn laughed out loud. "You're kidding me."

"I'm not. Who'd dare kid a mistress as fierce as you? But before you give yourself completely to hilarity, let's find a date and quick. I won't let you out of this conversation without a fixed appointment."

Jacklyn took out her pocket planner. "What about Harry? Should I invite him, too?"

Richard inhaled sharply. "You're a naughty mistress! By God, this is turning into a revival festivity! What a splendid prospect!"

"So, this is a *yes*."

"Yes to everything you can dish out. You have enough practice, so I understand, with your beautiful hunk. Are you still an *item*, as the young people say?"

"We're still a couple, and I love him, Richard. I'll do you a favor, but this is a *one-time-only* arrangement. Do you understand that? It'll be hard explaining my decision to Nick, so don't expect me to repeat it."

"Oh, I don't!" Excitement was in his voice. "I'll look forward to our meeting and savor every . . . strike."

They decided on a date, and Jacklyn put down the receiver. Her mood had lifted immensely, and she was grateful.

Jacklyn phoned Lesley to share the good news.

Matthew leaned back on his chair, his gaze directed at the whiteboard where Nicolas had pinned every detail of the crimes with post-it notes and a timeline. The team had spent hours checking incoming clues from other offices, now that they had enlarged the radius of the investigation and tried to determine crimes that might or might not be listed on the bank robbers' agenda. The inquiries were devastating—there were too many similar crimes to nail them to Manny and his gang. Nicolas had pointed out that the FBI couldn't be certain about the number of the gang given the mastermind who acted in the background.

"You were generous not to demand a new partner. Why?"

Nicolas looked up from the screen and waited to answer until Agent Spring was gone. "When I was transferred to DC, Jason was fresh from the academy . . . a divorced freshman who didn't have his mind on the cases. He made mistakes. He was unfocused. No one wanted to work with him."

Matthew raised his brows and swung back on his chair. "If I have this right, you were new, too, and they put you together? That's unusual."

Nicolas broke eye contact and cleared his throat.

Matthew chuckled. "Ah, you were the smart-aleck student with the intention of improving the FBI working rules in his first year. I see. They didn't like you, either."

"Unfair, but yes. We stumbled over our feet in more than one way and would've run ourselves into the ground if our old senior agent hadn't interfered. He coached us for months."

"Generous. How come you appointed yourself as leader of this office?"

"I didn't."

"Agent Spring was close to jumping to attention reporting to you."

"No, he wasn't. I try to give my best, and that's what my colleagues do, too. I don't order people around."

Matthew made a sound of contradiction, and as expected Nicolas' anger flared.

"I had to sort you out, because you were endangering both of us. It wasn't my intention to browbeat you, but you left me no choice."

"I could've done without you ramming my back against your car."

"Point taken." His gaze flicked back to the screen. "The FBI bureau in Minneapolis reports the arsonist made another statement. I wonder what they offered him in return. We're searching for a man called *Slithery Tom*. No last name, no decent description beyond *tall, muscled, about twenty-five to thirty years old*. Palmetti says he was a Joliet resident. His present location is unknown."

"Will they ask around in Joliet?"

"They're on it, searching for a man who might've been a criminal driver in his youth." Nicolas frowned. "I wonder whether his meeting with the robbers was coincidental."

"You mean because one of the robberies took place in

Joliet? That doesn't fit the time frame. Tom didn't drive the escape car in Joliet."

"He might've recommended himself after he got the news of the miserable driver." Nicolas looked up at the whiteboard. "I'm still at odds with this gang. Usually, robbers start their career close to home. They loot local drugstores and gas stations. Most of them get caught several times in their youth and start over years later."

"And your point is?"

"We found DNA in the van they left at the Federal Triangle, but the evidence revealed that the robbers had no criminal past. With the butts you found on the roof, CSU could at least determine that two of them are siblings, possibly twins. Still, they don't have any criminal record. How's that possible?"

"Because they were clever? Because their juvenile record was sealed?"

"That would need a court ruling." Nicolas leaned back, deeply frowning, and playing with a pen. "Is it possible they knew from the beginning that they had to wear gloves and keep their hair short or under a hoodie? Did they watch TV about crime lab techniques?" He shook his head and stood. "I don't know about you, but I need to be out of here to think."

"That's fine with me."

Jacklyn surprised Nicolas with an outstanding dinner and was happy about his appetite, concluding that a pleasantly filled stomach would improve his mood. When they settled in the living room, Jacklyn brought two glasses of red wine, set them on the table, and sat on Nicolas' lap with a cat smile.

"In a cuddling mood?" Nicolas kissed her neck and caressed her arm with affection. "I like that."

Jacklyn considered him a devilishly good-looking man

with that fine stubble and slightly tousled hair. His mischievous smile would make him a perfect cover model. She saw his anticipation of love and wanted to lean against him and have his big hands all over her body. The more she enjoyed his affection, the more her prepared words stuck in her mouth. She kissed him to gain time and rephrase.

"Nick, there's something we need to talk about."

"Concerning a house? Is that why you nailed me down with your weight?"

"It's about a house and then not."

He frowned deeper, and Jacklyn's heartbeat accelerated.

She looked in his eyes and hoped he'd understand. "Harry was about to sell a house to me that would be close to an industrial area in one or two years."

"I knew he was a crook. I told you so before." Nicolas exhaled angrily. "And? Did you tell him to go to hell for good?"

"So, you were right. He wanted to frame me. Happy?"

"No, this wasn't about being right. I would've wished—"

"Yes, it was. But I'll repay Harry—with interest. He'll suffer for his lies."

"What do you mean?"

"Well . . ." Jacklyn made sure her look was apologetic. She put a hand on his cheek. "Richard researched the background, and you know he doesn't need money. When the conversation turned around to payment for his help with me not being framed by Harry, he wanted a spanking at Lesley's new dungeon."

Nicolas frowned. His tone was incredulous. "And you agreed?"

"I agreed. After all, he's to be praised for keeping me from acting foolish. Don't you agree?"

Nicolas dropped his hand and moved his head away from her fingers. "Where's Harry in this plan?"

"I'll invite him, too, and let him feel how I deal with

cheaters." Jacklyn narrowed her eyes. "He'll think he's invited for a night of fun, but when—"

"I don't want you to do this." Nicolas shook his head and gently but decisively pushed her off his lap so that she sat beside him on the couch. "Jacky, you left Philadelphia behind. You told me you don't want to spend your life as a dominatrix. You told me you opened the physiotherapy office for a reason." He put his elbows on his knees and opened his hands. "Why would you want to spank Richard? That doesn't fit."

"Oh, but it does." Jacklyn's heart raced, seeing his disappointment. "And I told Richard it'll be a one-time-only invite. Just to say thank you."

"With a crop in your hand. That's quite a way of thanking someone."

Jacklyn laughed without merriment. "Chocolates wouldn't do. Please, Nick, don't think I love you less or that I'll return to my old job. I'll fulfill Richard's request and will take revenge on Harry my way. That's all."

Jacklyn saw the tightness around Nicolas' eyes and mouth. He breathed heavily and got up to stand a step away from the couch, hands in his pants pockets and his shoulders drawn up.

"I'm jealous. Right now, I'm freaking jealous, and I don't know how to handle this."

Jacklyn wavered whether it would be right insisting on her decision and making her lover angry. "I don't love you less when I do this. Please, Nick, consider this an arrangement like special treatment for a patient. You aren't jealous of all the male patients I treat at my office, right? Don't look at Richard or Harry as competitors. They aren't. This is a business. My heart's not in it."

"It's hard to believe, don't you think? You're friends with both men. From what I learned, Richard has always been a very special client." He looked at her intensely. "Are you sure you can keep this a single event? I think you'll like it."

"I'll certainly like it, but I won't repeat it, that's all."

His lips twitched. "I don't want to share you. Not with a friend, not with any other man."

Jacklyn bit her lower lip to keep from smiling. She was puzzled by his strong opposition. "You're telling me you want to be the only man in my life I'm allowed to spank?"

He opened his hands, frowning, and searching for words. He looked young, like a teenager learning about his girlfriend having mature ideas. "We're in a relationship, Jacky. Of course I don't want you to go anywhere to spank other men. I don't want you to dress up for them and perform whatever twists you make to turn them on. And this is about sex, no matter the name tag."

Jacklyn hesitated to get up and embrace her lover. She wanted to be close to him, but he looked agitated, on the border of being angry. A voice in her head told her she should've seen this coming. He was—as she realized with a hint of despair—six years younger and less experienced than her. So far, she hadn't perceived he was fixated on her so much. This was another misjudgment on her list. She wrung her hands in her lap. She didn't want to lose him over such a trivial event.

"Nicolas, you put more into this single evening than I do. I was a professional dominatrix. You know that. Believe me, I can clearly keep business apart from private life."

"But it's not like spending overtime at your office." Nicolas hung his head, and his words were quiet. "But I know I can't talk you out of it anyway. Right?"

Jacklyn pursed her lips. Their gazes met. "No, you can't. I won't make excuses to Richard, and I don't see any further obligation. He's a man of honor."

"With a very unique taste for rewards."

"Even so. Nick, you sound like a man from the last century.

Please, understand that there's a difference between job and relationship, even if this sounds odd to you. Can you do that?"

"You'll have it your way no matter what I say." Nodding without agreeing, he left the living room.

Jacklyn granted him time. She had learned from former relationships that both partners were better off thinking alone for a while before they tried for a compromise. She wasn't surprised to see Nicolas return in a much better mood after a run. Upon her inviting glance, he kissed her chastely.

"Hmm, I like that stubble," she whispered and kissed him again.

"I like every inch of you."

Jacklyn chortled. "And are there inches you like more than others?"

"Nope." He washed his face at the sink and reached for a towel. "Do you know why men love leather and rubber on a woman so much? Because that reminds them of a new car."

"Did you come up with that while you were running?"

"No. Two colleagues at the office tell jokes throughout the day. I guess Matt laughed until he got home."

Jacklyn put away the last dishes and closed the cupboards. She felt Nicolas behind her.

His voice was soft. "I don't want us to go to bed angry."

She leaned back in his embrace. "That's a good idea. I'm with you."

He kissed her hair, exhaling. "I'm still jealous."

"I know." She made up her mind studying his face. "Let's make a new game. I'll blindfold you and put a chain around your balls. You can try everything you want to please me, but instead of telling you off, I'll tug the chain when I don't want you to go on."

"Ah, you'll yank my chain."

Jacklyn laughed. "Quite literally." She lifted her chin to look him in the eyes. "Will you do that for me?"

Frowning and obviously thinking hard what to decide, Nicolas caressed her face. "You made me love what you love. And now I'm addicted to you. What more shall I say?"

His honest look caused goosebumps on her arms. The thought of him being addicted to her was both thrilling and frightening. She gathered her wits. "It's more like . . . I opened a new book for you, but now you want to be the only one reading it."

His tentative smile and his caressing hands warmed her heart. "It's a rare book. I want the privilege to be the only reader."

"The only reader, yes. But there are others who might look at the book and yearn to read it."

"You're telling me—"

His look was that of a lost boy. She kissed him as if trying to make it all good. "I'm telling you you're still the one privileged reader, no matter how many men look at the book."

CHAPTER FOURTEEN

Herman looked around and made sure they were alone before he pulled Katherine into the training room. "Police are looking for Tom in Joliet." He opened his eyes wide. "Do you know what that means? Do you?"

"You're bruising my arm, Manny."

He let go, gathering his wits. Katherine leaned against the wall and drank from her water bottle. He thought she was the most stubborn woman he'd ever met. He swore he'd choose a lover with fewer sophisticated airs and graces if he had the chance and the time.

"What do you want me to do?"

Herman flexed his fists and failed to control his anger. Since he'd heard the news, he couldn't stop thinking they were in danger, no matter the distance. He despised Katherine's display of coolness. "I don't know how they got to Joliet or what kind of clues the police have, but I don't want to wait any longer. Hurry with the preps for our last robbery. Please, before anyone talks about Tom or what he's done for us."

"No one knows that you hired him, right? Who'd be able to tell details about you and Tom?"

"I don't know. But I don't like the police knowing about one of our team. It would be the same if they came up with Theo and Ben being twins. I mean that they're searching for twins. Or what they look like. I couldn't stand that." He ran a hand through his sweaty hair. He already missed his easy-going life. "If the police knew about that—"

"I warned them to never show up together in public. If they

violated my rules, it's not my business." Katherine screwed the bottle cap on and turned to leave. "If you're worried so much, why don't you get rid of Tom?"

"You know damn well that we need him! He's the best fucking driver we've ever had!" Herman held her back once more but dropped his hand when she glared at him. "If they got a face to the name, they might find our hideout. Do you want that?"

"Tell Tom to stay home until we strike. That's the only thing you can do right now."

"And you? Will you be ready in time?"

"*In time* means I won't rush through the preps, okay?" Her voice was void of emotion. "If you can't wait any longer, take your money and leave." She stared at him narrowing her eyes. "I told you before I wanted to stop, but you wanted more—for Ben and Theo. Don't make me regret my decision, okay?"

"Stop bitching, Kate! How often will you slap my face, huh? Until we pull through the robbery? Until we part and walk separate ways?" He propped his hands on his hips to keep them from grabbing his sister. He was burning with energy without a vent. "I just wanted you to know that the circumstances have changed."

"How do you know about the police snooping around?"

"I've got a friend in Joliet. He told me."

Katherine lifted her brows and snorted. "To keep an eye on the family property?"

"I bet it was sold long ago. No, Kate, please, do what you can to speed this up."

"I don't want to strike this week. There'll be much more money closer to Christmas."

"But security will be tighter, then."

"And you'll be a good shot and keep them off, won't you?"

Herman hung his head, grimacing. "Yeah, I'll do what

needs to be done."

"The Christmas party's tomorrow night." Nicolas swung back on his chair, raising his brows. "Will you come?"

"Why should I?" Matthew threw his pen across the desk and watched as it slowly rolled toward the edge and fell. He sighed. "I don't know a soul, and I don't have a date. And before you start—I'm not interested in some bureau one-night stand that'll ruin both our reputations." He claimed the fallen pen. "And I wasn't talking about making a move on you."

"I wouldn't recommend a love affair at the job."

Matthew chuckled. "Thank you. Anyway, I'm not fond of parties."

Nicolas sat up straight, put his hands on the desk, and nodded with his chin toward Sullivan's office. "Listen, I understand your reluctance. I don't want to be there, either, but—and here it comes—Sullivan's a nut when it comes to his Christmas speech. It's the same every year, and we all know it by heart, but he'll check the numbers. If you don't show up, it'll look bad, especially because you're the new guy." He waved a hand. "Just sayin' . . ."

"I hate superiors with an attitude."

"Don't tell me that's news to you."

"Nope. Still, I'd hoped it would be different here." Matthew glanced at Sullivan's office. "He'll show up with his usual question, right?"

"We are slow, Matt. There's no question about it. We've interrogated every man and his mouse about the robberies, and Miller's working his ass off to feed us with information. However, we aren't closer to them than we were a week ago. The evidence shows the gang is careful, doesn't stumble over their asses, and searches for a perfect goal."

"I hate to say it, but it looks like we'll have to wait and be prepared for their next robbery." Matthew looked at the icon of an incoming email. "Now look here . . . our colleagues in Joliet are reporting about Tom Pinnock, a former race car driver. That explains a lot." He nodded toward Nicolas. "And yet you were able to corner him so that he left the van at the Federal Triangle. Kudos."

Nicolas shook his head. "They'd planned to change transportation."

"In case of an emergency. And you were very close, Nick. Very close."

"The report says Pinnock had a race car career but vanished all of a sudden. Friends and family don't know where he is or what happened to him. At least we've got his fingerprints now."

"And a face." Matthew raised his brows. "Do you want to share the information?"

Nicolas was about to say *no* when Senior Agent Sullivan appeared to perform the daily ritual of collecting recent information about the different cases his agents worked on. He didn't trust emails, and the men and women knew it was easier for him to deliver his browbeating face to face. No matter Nicolas' hesitation, Sullivan rejected keeping the information within the FBI, stressing the bureau's duty to speed the investigation by public support.

"You can't deny that you need all the help you can get, Special Agent Hayes, even from amateurs. And that's it." Sullivan pointed at Nicolas' monitor. "Send the email to me, and I'll prepare the press release."

"Yes, sir." Nicolas chewed on his argument until Sullivan left to ask other agents about revelations. His mood had dropped beyond the basement.

"You need all the help you can get," Matthew mimicked Sullivan in mock seriousness and broke down laughing.

Nicolas watched his superior's back, clenching his fists. "If the gang sees this—"

"They either shoot Tom or change states." Matthew's expression sobered. "I heard your words in my head."

"Now you feature mind-reading, too? You're a man of many talents."

"Yep, that's me. I could even train dogs." Matthew stood. "I went through the list of possible targets once more and came up with ten, which I consider highly rated. Will you have a look?"

"Will you show up at the party?"

Matthew sighed even deeper this time. "Yeah. I'll be there."

After another tasteless dinner he'd warmed up in the microwave, Matthew switched on the TV and settled on the couch with a glass of whiskey and the phone. He felt lonelier the longer he was away from Chicago, though he'd never considered he might be homesick. In his younger years, the idea of traveling the country for the FBI had been appealing, and he'd dreamed of being successful and getting promoted with every solved case. After meeting Nerina and marrying her, his focus had changed. Living and working in Chicago had been perfect for him and his loving wife. Every day, he had looked forward to coming home to her, chitchatting about his job, and listening to her family stories. He liked Nerina's parents, and they had shown him how fond they were of their son-in-law in many ways. After he'd taken Bouncer for a walk, they had eaten dinner together. Later in the evening, they had watched movies and competed for the best quotes.

Watching an episode of *Buffy* didn't do him any good. Nerina had loved Spike and would've given the dog that name if Matthew hadn't strongly objected. She had laughed then, and they had compromised on naming the Shepherd *Bouncer*.

Matthew still saw her flushed face and how affectionately she had caressed the dog behind its big ears. The dog had missed her every time she left for downtown at night without telling Matthew where she went or when she would return. Both man and dog had paced the house, worrying whether anything had happened to her. As a police officer, Matthew thought of a list of terrible scenarios. Upon her return, he'd taken her to task about why she hadn't answered her phone. Her tipsy explanations that she had been to town with friends had soothed him. Nerina had kissed and made up with him, and they ended in bed together, so he forgot about his doubts.

Looking back, Matthew realized how cunning Nerina had been. During her trial, Nerina's lawyer had frequently implied Matthew's complicity and that it had been impossible for Nerina to commit the crimes alone. Though the accusation didn't suffice to convince the jury, Matthew admitted in private that he'd been completely blinded by love for his Italian beauty.

Sobbing, Matthew emptied the glass and refilled it before he dialed Bert's number. He reached for a Kleenex when his friend growled his name. They exchanged the usual banter before Matthew made up his mind.

"Can you come to DC? Take a few days off from your hard work?"

Bert whined in his throat. "Monty, you know I would, but I've got this thing with big cities, with the government by and large, and so many people in one place—"

"Bert, I want my dog back, and I want you to drive him to DC. I can't ask for two days off because we're in the middle of an investigation, but—"

"You don't want that, Monty, believe me."

"But I'm fucking lonely."

"Yeah, I got that from the sniffling in between, but it would be terribly unfair for Gladys and Umberto, and you know that."

Matthew lit a cigarette and remained silent.

Bert sighed. "Really, Matt, I know you love him, but I won't tear him away. The dog stays with the new owners, okay? It's better for him and for you. If you want a dog, buy a new one. Believe me, Bouncer would bring back a lot of memories."

"That's the idea."

"But it's a bad one. You'd constantly think of Nerina, and I bet you do that often enough, right? It'll be easier to get over her without daily reminders. Take consolation that Bouncer is okay. Get a dog from a shelter, if you really want one. Bring home a buddy just for you."

"I hadn't thought I'd be this lonely. DC is so different from Chicago. It's both awesome and terrible. I don't know a freaking soul. And I have to show up for the Christmas party at the bureau. That's fucking gruesome! I don't wanna go."

"But you will?"

"Sure. I can't risk being on the blacklist of my boss."

Bert laughed a full belly laugh. "I see. That's why I work for myself and only for myself."

"What about your online dating idea?"

"Ah, well . . . let's say it didn't work out as planned."

"I assume you met with a woman, and she emptied her wine glass directly into your face?"

"It was more like she delivered a blow to my face."

"Fuck me sideways!" Matthew sat up straight. "How are you?"

"My ego is so bruised it won't leave the house."

"Oh. And I thought I could convince you to come to DC and have a beer with me. I mean, it was just an idea, and you don't have to come immediately."

"Stop babbling, you whiny old moron! I already decided to come before you chewed my ear off."

"Really?"

"Yeah, I'll find a flight and come. Don't hold your breath! I've got some things to do before I leave my cozy home."

"Sure. Let me know when you'll be here, and I'll fetch you from the airport."

"Your address will do. I'll get a rental car anyway. And I want your word you'll take me to some grand restaurant and make an evening for me I won't forget. You got that?"

Matthew smiled. "I got that."

Chapter Fifteen

Upon coming home the next day, Matthew had a chat with Lawrence on the stairs and told him about his obligation. Stroking Bingo behind the ears and listening to Lawrence's friendly words about Christmas parties and funny anecdotes lifted his mood immensely, and he was ready to face the party and endure whatever his boss dished out.

The dress code in the DC office was the same as in Chicago. The agents were ordered to wear a formal suit and a white dress shirt along with shined shoes and a polite demeanor. In front of the mirror, Matthew fumbled with the bow tie, repeating his mantra. He would stay until after Sullivan's speech and head home as soon as no one was looking. If the bar served decent drinks, he might feel obliged to stay for another hour.

"See, Nerina, I can do that alone. I'm the invincible master of my fucking universe." He lifted his clean-shaven chin to adjust the lapels, put on his winter coat, and added his wallet and keys to his service pistol and ID. Sighing, he looked back to the interior of his apartment. "And I'll be a lonely cowboy far away from my home that's not here." He locked the door and took the stairs to the garage.

His dark blue sedan looked different than before. Matthew hit the button to open the doors but stopped a step away seeing the car had two flat tires.

"Fuck this! That's just impossible!" He slammed the hood as he walked around the car, detecting that all tires had been cut. No other car close by had taken any damage. "I can't believe this." He ran a hand through his hair and fumbled for his cell phone the moment he heard movement behind him.

In a split-second, Matthew dropped the phone, pulled his service pistol, and took cover behind his car. The black man with the ski mask sidestepped to get out of the line of fire.

"Freeze! FBI! Come into the light where I can see you! Put your hands up!"

Before the man hid behind a column, Matthew fired two rounds but had no time to find out whether he'd wounded him. He sensed another thug approaching and barely evaded a knockout blow to his head. The club hit his left shoulder, and Matthew dropped the gun, screaming with pain. He turned and rammed his right elbow against the attacker's masked face. The club clattered to the floor. The lanky black man stumbled, shook his head, and came back. Matthew couldn't shield his face quick enough and was hit on the jawbone. His eyes teared as he crashed against the car, lifting his arms in time to deflect the next swing. Instinctively, he kicked the man's groin as hard as he could, aware he had only a second until the companion reappeared. Matthew lashed out with his injured right hand, aiming for the man's nose. Dazed and spilling curses as much as blood, the thug doubled over and fell against a concrete column, hands on his genitals.

Matthew slipped along the side of the car, hoping he could get inside and lock the door. He groped for the handle when the second attacker grabbed his shoulder, turned him around, and punched his stomach right below the sternum with a fist large and hard as a baseball. Matthew's knees buckled, and he went down, unable to breathe. The attacker reached inside Matthew's jacket pocket for his badge and ID, ignoring Matthew's feeble attempts at fighting him. He looked up and saw a small golden ring in the man's eyebrow, half-hidden by the black wool. Writhing in pain, Matthew watched the gangster pick up his gun before he helped his minion stand. The lanky man wiped his bleeding nose with the back of his hand, then pulled out a pair of handcuffs to tie Matthew's wrists around the lowest metal bar of the railing in front of the car. Matthew realized he was hidden from view by other people walking the aisle.

The lanky gangster slapped Matthew's temple with the back of his hand, then picked up his club. "Now you're fucked-up, motherfucker!"

"Why? What for?"

"You got what you deserve, asshole!" He shook his head and turned to his companion. "This should've been easier, damn it!"

Matthew heard one of the thugs crack his phone on the concrete as they were heading out of the garage.

Grimacing, he pulled up his legs, fighting to stay conscious, fighting to breathe against the pain. He swore he'd identify the hoodlums and repay them the same way. The more rational part of his mind wondered what the gangsters would do with his weapon and badge.

Jacklyn leaned back in the passenger seat and sighed. She took a mint drop out of her clutch and put the second one in Nicolas' mouth. "Is it okay to say your boss is boring beyond comparison?"

"I agree with that." Nicolas lifted his right hand. He smiled and put the key in the ignition. "I owe you my deepest gratitude for your company and good jokes and how you kept the party going." He steered the car onto the street. "On the other hand, my dear lady, I don't want you to be close to my male colleagues again. You turned their heads in no time."

Now it was her turn to lift a hand. Her smile was sweet and lacked innocence. "I take the fifth."

Nicolas laughed. "I knew you'd say that." He kissed her

once he stopped the car at a red light. "Not to mention, you were the best-looking woman. Every man was jealous that you'd go home with me."

"Oh, you're exaggerating." Her look was full of love. "Jason, for example, kept his eyes strictly on his lady."

"And he should." Nicolas hit the gas pedal. "Elaine would behead and quarter him if he acted differently."

"Before or after she would've shot him?" Jacklyn giggled.

He loved her for that moment of girlish hilarity so unfitting her age and classy outfit. "Right after. There wouldn't be enough left of him to fit in a plastic bag."

"Uhh, that sounds awful. Where was your new partner? Matt, right? I didn't see him."

"Me neither. But the worst is—Sullivan noticed his absence, too. No matter the excuse, our boss will—"

"Behead and quarter poor Matt?"

Nicolas burst out laughing. "Now who's in an aggressive mood here, huh? Are you?"

"Are you implying you want something special before we go to bed?" She loosened her hairdo and twisted a lock around her finger. "I don't know what you think—and sometimes I don't want to—but I liked the new game we played. What about repetition?"

Nicolas took a deep breath and—with an effort—kept his hands on the wheel. "Yeah, I guess I would like that."

Matthew regained consciousness once he heard steps on the concrete. He raised his voice as best he could. "Help! Over here!" The pain below his ribcage made him cringe against the railing. His hands were numb.

The steps clattered closer, accompanied by paws scratching the floor. "Wait, Bingo! I'm coming! You don't have to—" Lawrence Binkley stopped in his tracks. His eyes opened wide, and he gasped as he put his free hand on his heart. "Matt! Good Lord in Heaven, what happened to you?" He knelt and looked Matthew up and down. "Are you hurt? Well, forget that. I see it. Were you mugged?" He looked around in haste.

"In a way . . . yes. The key . . ." Matthew nodded toward his pants pocket, and Lawrence quickly retrieved the handcuff key to open the lock. He helped Matthew stand. "There were two." He doubled over in pain, and only Lawrence's strong hands kept him from falling. Breathing was hard, and he stuttered. "I grazed one of them, I think, and the other one lost some blood, too, in the fight. I have to—"

"Yes, I'll call the police, but first I'll take you to the hospital. You look awful."

Matthew stopped and made an effort to speak. "I can't leave the crime scene."

"I can't leave you here like this. You look like you're gonna collapse any moment. Come on." Lawrence pulled Matthew's arm around his shoulder and escorted him down the aisle.

"No! Seriously, I have to wait. The gangsters took my badge and gun, and I don't know what'll happen. The sooner—" Matthew felt a wave of nausea and weakness wash over him. He held tight to Lawrence's shoulder, strangely touched by his neighbor's altruism. Bingo jumped beside them as if urging its owner to hurry.

"I know what you mean." Lawrence sighed. "Okay, you win. Sit down in my car, and I'll call the police and an ambulance right away."

"Okay." Matthew suffered through five more steps and slumped on the passenger seat of a new *Honda*. He fingered for his phone and cursed, remembering that it was lost. Lawrence dialed the emergency line and told the police sergeant about the robbery and that an FBI agent was involved. "Police and an ambulance will be here in a few minutes."

He was about to put away the phone when Matthew held out his hand. "May I use your phone? I've got to call the FBI and tell them what happened."

"Are you sure this is a good idea? I mean, your boss will be less than thrilled, right?"

"I can't change that." Matthew dialed Nicolas' number. "If I don't report it right away, it'll be worse." He listened to the ringing, but his partner didn't take the call. Quietly cursing, Matthew left a message and reported the robbery to the agent in charge of the night shift. He handed back the phone. "Thanks. If the beating wasn't the worst, my boss would add another bashing." He slumped against the seat, weary and unable to focus.

He heard Lawrence talk to Bingo but couldn't make out words. When the dog put his muzzle under his hand, Matthew passed out.

Every time they played, Jacklyn took delight in undressing her lover. The simple actions of pushing the jacket across his shoulders and taking off his bow tie aroused her. He smiled at her as she unbuttoned his shirt.

"You got the hang of seeing me naked?" He bit her earlobe gently. "May I return the favor?"

"You may." Jacklyn dropped his dress shirt and let Nicolas open the zipper of her dress. She felt his hands tremble along her ribs and stopped his scouting expedition when he was about to unclasp her bra. "But you may not go too far."

"Aww . . ." Her long dress dropped to the floor.

"My turn." She didn't protest him kissing her. She didn't protest when his kisses became wild and demanding while she relieved him of his pants and boxers. The undershirt was next, and both had a good laugh as he raised his toes, indicating the socks were still on his feet. "You may keep them and not get cold feet."

"I don't think I will." Nicolas kissed her throat and décolleté at the laced rim of her bra. "I want you, my Belle, I so want you."

"Not so eager, my wonderful Beast." Jacklyn giggled when his stubbly chin touched her belly. "I'd prefer you to follow me to the bedroom."

"You've got something on your mind?" Nicolas took off his socks on the way and waited beside the bed.

She opened a drawer and turned around, thinking about so many kinky toys she would've loved to add. She got horny imagining him with collars and chains, with muzzles and hoods. There were so many role-play games they hadn't tried so far. "More than you imagine." She flipped him the blindfold and held a thin chain in her hand. "I guess I'll help you with that."

Nicolas knelt on the bed, playing with the piece of cloth. She fastened the chain around his scrotum and was even more aroused than when she shackled his hands and feet. Nicolas' low moans were in her ears as she caressed and kissed his limp penis.

Jacklyn looked up to him. "I consider this a reward for both of us after the boring evening. Put it on!" She pressed the blindfold against his chest, smiling invitingly. "Come on, or the first thing I do is pull that chain." She tugged the end playfully.

"I wanted to see that hint of glee in your eyes before I yield to you." Nicolas adjusted the soft blindfold. "And now don't dare move too much. I won't be able to chase you through the room."

"Would be fun to watch," she whispered in his ear. At the same time, she guided his hand between her legs. "But not tonight. Try your best, Beast, or bear the consequences."

Matthew was treated in the ambulance. A glimpse at his watch shocked him. He had lost three hours lying unconscious in the garage. In spite of the increasing pain, Matthew refused to be taken to a hospital. The medic released him with the advice to take it slow the next few days. Matthew was glad to learn he had no ruptures or broken ribs, only bad bruising of his shoulder and below his sternum that would hamper moving and breathing. When the painkillers kicked in, two FBI colleagues were already in the garage, and Matthew reported the robbers and the missing gun and badge. He spent an hour with a notebook looking through the database pictures of known muggers in DC and identified the attackers. In a moment of stunning clarity, he realized these were the same men who had assaulted him close to the liquor store eight days ago. Hardy Snyder and Terence Wilks were known for armed robbery and other offenses in the greater DC area. Matthew filled out online forms concerning the theft and the criminals and sent them to Sullivan. He expected a browbeating like a volcano eruption but had no energy to worry.

When the FBI colleagues left, four policemen were still securing evidence, and Matthew leaned against the closest column for support when Lawrence walked down the slope from the street.

"I'm surprised to see you here." He kept Bingo on a short leash, but still, the dog wanted to jump Matthew's legs. "You don't look . . . snazzy."

"Say I look like shit and you nail it." Matthew held a hand across his belly. "I've had better days. Did the police question you, too?"

"They asked a lot of questions." Lawrence shrugged. "But nothing out of the ordinary."

Matthew frowned. A sudden distrust evolved, but he was unable to put it into words. "Were you out for a walk the whole time?"

"Oh, no, I was in my apartment in between but came down again. I thought I should look out for you. Well, I admit I had hoped you'd ride with the medics, but—as I see—you weren't open to reason." Lawrence nodded a few times toward the policemen. "I answered all of their questions, and I guess you did that, too. Why wait?"

Matthew's head throbbed too much to think further than his wish to go to bed. "You're right. I'll talk with the sergeant in charge and ask if he still needs me."

"Okay. I'll wait and take you to your apartment."

"No, thank you. I'll make it."

"If you think so. But you'd better see the bunk, pal. If you need anything, don't hesitate to give me a call."

"Thank you. For everything you did tonight. I'll pay you back somehow."

Lawrence laughed briefly. "Affirmative." He gave a sloppy salute and turned with Bingo at his side.

Matthew watched him leave toward the stairway and turned to a haggard old sergeant with a chubby face and a high brow. His hat sat haphazardly close to the back of his head, and while he spoke, he tried to fix it.

"Are you all right, sir?"

"In a way." Matthew glanced at his ruined car. "The two men you're looking for are Hardy Snyder and Terence Wilks, known for armed robbery and other crimes. They're in the database. Hardy's the one with the rings through his nose and eyebrow."

"I see." The sergeant frowned as he took down notes. "I assume the FBI is on it?"

"Concerning the theft of my badge and pistol—yes."

The sergeant's look was full of sympathy. "Was anything else stolen? Your wallet? Cell phone?"

"No. They smashed the phone, but only to keep me from

alerting the police, I suppose. Though I wonder how I would've got there." Matthew had pondered how the crime had evolved and understood the sergeant's doubtful glance. "They must've known I'm an agent and are possibly out to commit a crime under my name and with my gun." He scratched his sweaty forehead and avoided touching the bruise on his jawbone at the last moment. His hands shook, and his knees were weak. "Sergeant, please, launch the search. I'm convinced this robbery was committed for the single purpose to get the possession of my equipment. If you don't have any further questions—"

"You've got an apartment in this building?"

"Yes."

"We'll get back to you." The sergeant nodded curtly and left.

Matthew waited for a minute, watched the lab technicians work, and tried to grab hold of an idea he couldn't name or describe through the fog in his mind. Weary and close to collapsing, he walked back to his apartment.

Nicolas massaged Jacklyn's slender back, listening to her soft moans of contentment and trying to determine how he'd please her best. While he spent time with her in bed, he forgot about everything else—the case he was working on, his partner, his various obligations. He enjoyed their game so much that he wished the night would last until the weekend and continue with breakfast in bed, followed by another day of lovemaking. If ever possible, he'd have stopped working for a month just to enjoy time with his lover.

Jacklyn knelt in front of him and held the chain short enough to indicate she wanted him to stay close. That was fine with him. He reached around to cup her breasts while his hard-on fit between her butt cheeks. With growing arousal, he kneaded her breasts with more vigor, relishing her firm body as well as her seductive moans. The sudden pull on his scrotum was a welcome addition to his desire, and he doubled his efforts to get into the rhythm. Jacklyn pulled harder and moved forward simultaneously, out of his reach, out of the warmth of his hands. Nicolas felt betrayed and left in pain. Next, her foot rested on his chest, inching higher.

"I shall caress Belle's sweet little toes?" Nicolas chuckled. The chain tinkled and was let loose again. "More service to the lady before—ouch! Okay, I'll do it." Devotedly, he sucked on her toes, massaged her feet, and worked along her calves and thighs until he reached the triangle of her pubic hair. Dedicated like an explorer on recently detected land, he satisfied her with his tongue and fingers, getting off on her moans and moves. She spread for him and rested her hands on the back of his head. He held her legs when she came, and the tip of his tongue on her vulva caused another half-suppressed scream of pleasure. Nicolas lifted his head and smiled while Jacklyn panted. He felt her ribcage rise and fall in the afterglow as he caressed her sides. He couldn't think of any happier moment.

"My wonderful Belle is satisfied?"

She rolled to the side and out of his reach without a word. He stretched out his hand in confusion, wondering what she had in mind when she pulled the chain between his legs and tightened it at a loop.

"On your back. Spread your legs."

Nicolas did as ordered and wasn't surprised when she shackled his ankles to the rings left and right of the built-in pillory. Pleasantly tied up and expecting more, Nicolas groaned with bliss as her lower body touched his eager cock. Cautiously, he rested his hands on her hips, and when she didn't protest, he placed her above his member. Jacklyn ran her hands along his arms and after brief contact with his glans moved up again, giggling like a girl.

"My Belle, you aren't playing fair."

She kissed him sensuously. "I'm a woman. I'm not meant to play fair."

He heard her leave the bed and return with something tingling in her hands.

"You aren't about to add your earrings to the game, right? I don't want you to pierce my nipples if you don't mind."

Jacklyn chuckled and gently touched him. "I could play hoop-la with your cock. It's waving at me right now."

"Don't even!"

Laughing out loud, she stopped his attempt at taking off the blindfold. "Not yet!"

Jacklyn fitted a ring around the base of his cock, pulled back the foreskin and placed the second one around his glans, effectively cutting off Nicolas' witty reply. The tightness hardened his sex like never before. He didn't know whether the restriction was pain or pleasure and wriggled on the sheet.

"Now, my Beast, this will be a long ride with me as the rider."

"You're trying to tame the Beast?" He chuckled. "Seriously?"

Jacklyn flicked her tongue across his glans, and he inhaled sharply because of the thrill rushing through his body.

"I'm teaching the Beast some new tricks."

Chapter Sixteen

Nicolas poured coffee and handed Jacklyn the cup across the table. "It crossed my mind . . . you didn't look at Agent Addleton throughout the evening."

"Right." She drank and put down the cup to dip a piece of croissant. "He got so much attention, he didn't deserve mine. He's a prig, but a harmless one. His annoyance with women, in general, is a show. Men want admiration, the praise of the crowd, people who abase themselves at their feet. They indulge in every word or gesture of appreciation. He's just like any other guy who needs the boost to feel good."

"The women will hate you for the praise you poured on the other men."

Jacklyn waved with the rest of the croissant. "Women can learn these tricks and use them effectively . . . with their men or against other women. A woman can have every man she desires. She needs to know how they tick and then—" She snapped her fingers.

Nicolas nodded as he reached for the jam. "Manipulation."

"That sounds so negative. Women manipulate, but they also pull the strings in the background and remain clear-headed in a crisis—more often than men."

Nicolas paused for a moment, jar and knife in hand. "You're saying . . ."

"Given some time, I could've manipulated a good part of your group against one or two members and made them do what I want. And they would've cooperated."

"How?"

"The trick is simple. I've got to be convincing. I've to look through them and find the weak spots."

"In all of them? That takes time." He put jam on his croissant.

"Just the leader. If you have control of the leader, you have control of the group."

"You wouldn't convince Sullivan of anything. He's too conservative for that."

Jacklyn went on eating. "Sullivan's the boss, but clearly not the leader. He lacks the support of the group. If he didn't start a conversation, he wasn't in it. While he stood at the table with drinks, the others walked away or waited until he'd turned around. He didn't have a good joke at hand to fraternize with his staff. And he's certainly not a man to motivate his agents by example. Shall I continue?"

"Then who's the leader in your eyes?"

"You. And the older agent with the gray hair and a preference for redheads. I think his name's Clarington. He was surrounded by agents and their wives the entire evening. They had a good laugh now and then, even when he was getting drunk. But then many were getting drunk quite quickly."

"I don't fit for a leader." Nicolas smiled. "Maybe you should apply for the job."

"Too much female influence isn't good in an office like yours. Yes, I'm a woman who votes for equality, but at the same time, I understand the dynamics in a mixed group. A woman is only accepted as a boss if she's more a man than a man and thinks like a man. That's not healthy." She frowned. "By the way, have you heard from your new partner?"

"Not a word. Maybe he couldn't leave his friend Jack Daniels behind."

"That's a pity. I wanted to get to know him."

"To turn his head?"

"Nope. I had to be careful around Jason. That was

enough."

"Elaine would've stabbed you with a butter knife if you had made a questionable move."

"Hey, I made good-natured banter, and Jason thought every word I said had a double meaning. That's not my fault."

Nicolas laughed out loud. "He was pulling your leg."

"Elaine didn't think so."

"Elaine's a very kind and loving person, but she doesn't understand quips."

"That's why I stopped. I hope Jason doesn't think I considered him boring."

"He'll live." Nicolas wiped his mouth with a napkin and stood to check his cell phone. He listened to the message and cursed. "Matt was quite sober last night." He put away the phone. "He was mugged in the garage of his apartment. I've got to go."

"Nice of you to drop by!" Matthew's smile couldn't cover his uneasiness. "I thought you wouldn't check your phone this week."

"I'm sorry, really." Nicolas grimaced looking at Matthew's bruised face. "I was off duty last night and—"

"Please, spare me the details. I hoped you'd at least check your phone somewhere in between . . . the action."

"I do. Usually. I should've done it." Nicolas took off his coat and went for the coffeemaker. "You should've reported in sick. You don't look fit for duty."

"I checked the video surveillance of the ten banks I shortlisted and found several tall and broad-shouldered men matching the description at three different banks. Then I called the guards and asked whether they remembered tall men like trunks visiting frequently over the last couple of weeks, most probably in different clothes. They couldn't nail a person, claiming there were so many customers each day it was impossible to remember any of them. I thought these guys were trained to watch carefully. If by chance they remember anything, I left my number." Matthew sighed and took the coffee cup. "Thanks."

"Jacklyn gave me the idea of a woman standing behind the men we're searching for."

"A woman?" Matthew cleared his throat and took a swig. "In between sheets? You've quite interesting conversations while—"

"We had the conversation this morning. She pointed out that women manipulate men the way they want them to be."

"I don't doubt that," Matthew mumbled into his cup.

"Take into consideration we probably have three brothers and the driver. They're young and reckless, and she's the one directing their moves."

"You call that a hunch, don't you?" Matthew put down the cup when his hand trembled.

"You invented the idea of a mastermind behind the group."

"I've never mentioned a woman. What kind of guy allows a woman to tell him where to go and what to do?" He stopped with his mouth open. "Okay, don't take that personally. How can I rephrase so that you won't slap me?"

"The woman has to have a special connection with them—either a lover or family member."

"Now that's gross! We're already considering three of the men to be brothers. Now you come with a sister or even their mother? What are they? The Osmonds?"

"Just for once—try to wrap your mind around this. The brothers commit the crimes, but since we assume there's too much yardage between their goal posts, there's someone directing their moves."

Matthew nodded. Even the small movement sent waves of

pain through his body. "It's back to checking the surveillance tapes then. What kind of woman are we looking for?"

"Probably tall and trained." Nicolas drained his cup and put it down. "She'll also wear different clothes and costumes. I propose to check the tapes with the tall guys you already found."

"On the same dates? Yes, I'll go for that."

"And again, I'm sorry I didn't check my phone. I would've come to your place. Do you have any idea why those gangsters wanted your badge and gun?"

Matthew was touched by Nicolas' open sympathy. "I guess they want it to commit a crime with my fingerprints all over the scene. I don't know how or why they chose me, but there's trouble ahead." He turned upon the clapping of the door. "And Sullivan's just in yelling distance."

Herman checked the magazine of his *AAC Honey Badger PDW* for the fifth time in an hour. He hadn't been nervous on any other robbery Kate had planned, and he was shocked he had nerves. He hadn't eaten breakfast, and the thought of food made him gag. While cleaning and assembling the weapon, he had turned his back to his brothers. On the other side of the room, they were throwing quips about the large sum of money they would get and how they intended to spend it. Herman knew he should tell them to save some of the money for later, since there would be no fresh supplies, but he knew the conversation would be useless, anyway.

Though Kate had demonstrated she'd planned the robbery as meticulously as the others, Herman was convinced there was a snag in it and that he'd be blamed if anything went wrong. If luck turned against them—he was sure of that—they wouldn't make it out alive. He wondered whether Kate would ever look back, or if she'd cry over a failure. During the days of preparing the assault, she'd made it clear this was a job she did more reluctantly than the others. Herman wondered whether her anger went so far as to let the brothers run into a police trap, but then he dismissed the idea. Kate worried for all of them to get out alive. She had said so several times.

Theo laughed out loud and slapped Ben's shoulder. Herman wanted them out of harm's way. He wanted the robbery over and hoped they would be back to divide the loot that night. He didn't want to persuade Kate to commit another robbery—and then he realized with a start that the end of their joint crimes meant the end of their lives together. The group would split, and every member would seek a safe hideout to start a new life. At least, he hoped he'd be able to invest money and live unburdened by prosecution. Though he didn't know Kate's intentions, he was jealous that she had precise plans and would execute them regardless of the day's events.

Theo looked up when Herman glanced across his shoulder.

"All set, bro. We can roll, run, and shoot whoever crosses us."

"Yeah . . . you just be careful, okay? No risks. I mean it." Herman stowed the weapon in a bag, closed the zipper, and walked toward the stolen van Theo and Ben had modified for their needs. The closer he came to departure, the more he doubted the success of their plan. He sat on the passenger seat and stared at the wheel.

"Worried?"

Herman looked into Kate's smiling face. "No. I'm not worried."

"You look worried, like hell. Don't you trust me anymore?"

"I thought about—" He lowered his voice when Tom left the house. "I thought about the investigation and how much the FBI knows. They've launched a manhunt for Tom, and

God knows how much more they already know. It's high time that we pull this through and leave."

"They know diddly-squat. If they had anything, any lead, any clue pointing toward us, they would've stormed our house. Rest assured, my dearest brother, the FBI is far behind us."

"Yeah, pushing us."

The smile stayed glued on her face, and though she tried for a convincing tone, there was something in her voice that made his skin crawl. Herman noticed she'd applied her make-up carefully, with more eyeliner and a darker lipstick than usual. She looked lovely and five years older, suiting her classy two-piece suit. He didn't dare ask what she had in mind with her share of the loot or where she'd go. The pain of getting separated grew with the hour. Since their miserable childhood, the siblings hadn't been separated for more than a few days. Once they parted after the robbery, it would be for a much longer time. Herman saw in Kate's eyes that she was counting the hours until she was allowed to leave for good.

"Have you forgotten? As long as the police don't know our faces—"

"We'll vanish in the crowd. Yes, I know."

"Still, you sit here with sweaty hands like a teenager close to his first date." Kate stretched to kiss Herman's cheek. "You'll make it. I know it. And then—" She shrugged and went to her new *Oldsmobile* Theo had modified. Should the police catch up to them, that car would outmatch the entire fleet. Turning, she waved at him. "I'm counting on you, Manny!"

Herman leaned back, stared at the ceiling, and went through the plan once more. He didn't say a word when Tom took the driver's seat, and he refrained from joking with his brothers. His throat was constricted as thoughts tumbled through his mind like snowflakes. There were so many things that could go wrong.

Sullivan cocked his head and raised his brows as far as they would go. He opened his hands as if hoping for an epiphany. Matthew kept his face emotionless in spite of his bad premonition. He had a list of places where he wished to be rather than in his superior's office, including a dark garage with hoodlums. His head throbbed as well as his bruised shoulder.

"First, you tell me mentioning Tom Pinnock's name to the press would scare the robbers away." Sullivan directed his attention at Nicolas. "Second, you tell me you want armed SWAT teams at three different banks in three different counties because you assume one of them might or might not be the next target." He shook his head as he leaned back in his armchair. "I won't deploy personnel because of some hunches you got."

Matthew broke eye contact and looked at the desk rim. He didn't dare glance at Nicolas standing next to him, assuming he'd be angry as well.

Sullivan tapped the desk with the form Matthew had filled out. "I'm especially skeptical to believe an agent who's unable to protect his weapon against thieves. It's an unheard-of event, and you'll have a lot to explain, Agent Montagna. Such reckless behavior might be acceptable in the Windy City but certainly not in DC. Though the police caught the robbers quickly doesn't mean you're exonerated. We'll talk about that later. Dismissed."

Nicolas made a growling sound in his throat before he spoke. "Sir, you could at least have a SWAT team ready to strike. The gangsters plan their robberies to the last detail. The three banks we took into consideration correlate with the others they attacked – location, size, easy access, and clear escape routes. You demanded progress in the investigation, so why won't you trust our clues?"

Sullivan slipped the form into a file. "There were about four weeks between their robberies at least. I assume they'll strike close to Christmas for a larger loot."

Nicolas opened his mouth, then shook his head to speak up a moment later. "The biggest loot was never their intention. They choose a time no one expects and forego a bigger result for the benefit of fewer guards at the location."

"Agent, your statements contradict. Are the robbers on the run? Have they killed Pinnock and moved on? Or are they still exploring a target or more, if I follow your description? You must make up your minds, gentlemen. Leave my office. I've got work to do."

Facing the floor in front of him, Matthew followed Nicolas to their desks, unable to find words of mollification. Wearily, he slumped on his chair and wiped his eyes. He doubted his decision to stay on duty. There was no way to gain Sullivan's praise or at least forgiveness, and as long as their boss despised Matthew, he despised Nicolas as well, a stupid behavior but no less true. Matthew wanted to slip into a hole like Mickey Mouse and vanish until Christmas, ten days of uninterrupted sleep included.

The telephone rang, and Nicolas took the call. "Are you sure it was the same man?" He listened for a minute. "And he went to the counter and stumbled against another customer on purpose? Okay, you escorted him out. Anything else?"

Nicolas put down the receiver.

Matthew was about to burst with curiosity. "Do we have more than a hunch?"

"A guard of the *Woodrow Bank* in Frederick said he recognized the same tall, broad-shouldered man he'd seen the week before."

"When?"

"Yesterday. And he said it's possible the man entered the

bank twice. They're checking the tapes right now."

"The bank's on the long list but still on the list." Matthew reached for the phone, wincing with pain. "I'm alerting the Frederick County Sheriff."

"Do it from the car. It's an hour drive, and I want to be there now." Nicolas took his coat and swung it around his shoulders on the way through the office.

Compared to Nicolas' sheer elegance, Matthew moved like a drunkard on a slope as he tried to put on his jacket without howling in pain. He was bathed in sweat when they reached the garage.

Nicolas started the car. "You okay?"

Matthew nodded as he dialed the number in Frederick and explained to the sheriff that the *Woodrow Bank* in the northern district was about to become the next target of the bank robbers. The sheriff started a discussion about the necessity to deploy his people without distinct clues but yielded when Matthew insisted that the FBI ordered him to support the investigation and possible arrest of four robbers.

"He'll alert his men and will be on his way shortly." Matthew dropped the phone into his lap and reached for the painkillers Lawrence had deposited at his door without asking. He washed down two pills with a swig of water from a bottle.

"Shall I drop you off and drive alone?"

"Shut up and don't ask dumb questions. Period."

Nicolas nodded and sped the service car toward the interstate leading out of town. "There's no shame in—"

Matthew snorted as he pushed the bottle back into his coat pocket. "There's enough shame in losing the gun to those assholes, thank you. Dropping out now would end my career within the bureau in a week."

"That's BS, and you know it."

Matthew's voice dropped. "I invested too much to get a second chance. If I blow this—who'd want to work with me?"

"Did you get your gun replaced?"

"Yep, after some haggling and a mountain of forms. And I got a phone, as you see, with the same number. I know what you're thinking of."

"Again?"

Matthew chuckled quietly. "We might get into a shootout, and you wonder whether you can trust me to cover you. Yes, you can. My right hand's much better, and the medic said my left shoulder's only bruised."

"Comforting."

"A hit to my head would've been worse."

"Still no idea why the thugs wanted your gun and badge?"

"The two crooks are for hire. Agents *Batman and Robin*—sorry, I can't remember their names—interrogated them. They said they handed the gun and badge to a client, but so far haven't revealed his name."

"It's Agent Sevigny and Agent Setton." Nicolas shook his head. "But *Batman and Robin* fits much better." He burst out laughing. "Sevigny looks like a mantis without antennae. Imagine him in a black suit with a cape! And Setton is at least twice as old as Robin and twice as broad. Thanks for the picture you put in my head."

"You're welcome."

Nicolas glanced at him. "I'll buy you breakfast if we nail those buggers today."

"Strong coffee and more painkillers will do. Yeah, that'll be fine with me."

Disregarding the speed limit, Nicolas made it to the north side of Frederick in less than fifty minutes. He parked in an alley out of sight of the bank to meet with Sheriff Dacosta. They shook hands at the introduction.

The sheriff nodded toward the main street. His tone

indicated he could drop personal feelings for his profession. "I've got patrol and traffic units positioned at the possible exit routes, disguised as workers. They can erect police barriers within seconds. Additional service cars are waiting to move in if necessary." He cocked his head, pursing his lips. "If you don't mind my curiosity—how come you expect them to hit this bank?"

"Call it a hunch," Matthew mumbled in his deepest voice.

Nicolas frowned and summed up their investigation briefly. "The reappearance of the same man indicates they were casing the bank as a possible target. We assume the men take turns and enter the banks as customers in various disguises."

"Okay. So, we sit and wait?"

"Until the armored car shows up, yes."

"How do you know it'll be today?"

Nicolas exchanged glances with Matthew and faced the sheriff again. "We assume the robbers are reacting to the identification of their driver, Tom Pinnock. Either they've dropped him dead somewhere or are using him for one last hit. Either way, we think they want to pull through the last robbery and leave the state."

The elderly sheriff glanced up and down the street as if calculating the possible damage. "They won't go inside the bank?"

Nicolas hesitated. "That was their method before. The last robberies took place right in front of the banks. They took the money sacks from the guards and escaped in a van."

The sheriff took off his hat and smoothed his gray hair. "Fine. The transporter's due at sixteen hundred. We've got another hour to kill." His phone rang, and his eyes widened, listening to the news. "The gangsters are in Frederick. But not at the *Woodrow Bank*. It's the *Federal Trust Bank*! Police were alarmed a minute ago. They're on the run!"

"We're on our way!" Nicolas ran toward the car and put it in gear before Matthew had closed the door. He made a U-turn and hit the gas so that the car fishtailed close to the corner.

"You were a stunt driver in your first life?" Matthew asked, fumbling with the seat belt.

"Best in class. Hold on!" Nicolas hit the wheel with his palm. "They framed us! They knew we'd watch possible targets, and I went for it! Damn it!"

Matthew turned on the siren and blue lights, and with some difficulty, programmed the navigation system with the address of the Federal Trust Bank. "There were so many possible targets and —"

"Sullivan will kill us over this misjudgment."

"I bet he wouldn't have done any better."

"And since when does that matter? He was up a blind alley last time and still got out without a scratch. He knows how to put the blame on everyone else." Nicolas took the corner as fast as he could without sliding and headed for Highway 15, chasing vehicles. He overtook a truck that was about to switch lanes and evaded toward the shoulder to avoid a crash. "Fuck this!"

Matthew clung to the handle and the seat. "Dunno. I prefer living till the end of the day, if you don't mind."

"Too late to get off. I want those buggers arrested today. They've fucked with us for the longest time!"

Matthew turned up the volume of the police radio frequency. Patrol units were on their way, but because of the FBI's request to guard the *Woodrow Bank*, the service cars were just now redirected and wouldn't arrive in time. Traffic units were ordered to build up roadblocks to the west. According to the sheriff's gruff order, this would be the most likely escape route.

Nicolas overtook two camper vans and left the highway at

the same speed. He was angry and drove that way. He disregarded the red traffic lights, sped around corners, and missed a parked pick-up truck by inches. The driver was lucky that he heard the siren and stopped. Nicolas didn't heed other pedestrians and realized Matthew had been quiet for minutes. He had no time to check on his partner. Nicolas' concentration remained on the thick traffic and how to find the street the robbers would take with their loot.

An excited voice blurted on the radio. "It's a gray van without logos, heading south-east!"

"South-east?" Matthew changed the screen detail of the navigation system to show the highway exits and the area of southern Frederick. "Where the hell are they going?"

"Time to find out." Nicolas braked at the intersection in a traffic jam, and no siren, blue lights, or honking cleared the way. Two trucks had collided minutes earlier and blocked two lanes. Other trucks and cars were struggling to pass by. "This isn't happening!" Nicolas rocked the car while trying and failing to speed on. Finally, he put up with scratching another car's fender and used the sidewalk until they reached the next intersection. The car bumped back on the street. "Don't say a word!"

"It'd stick in my throat." Instead, Matthew asked the police forces for updates.

"We're giving chase at Brigadoon. They're heading for Centergate." The officer sounded excited. "We're closing in!"

"Gimme directions!" Nicolas barked.

Matthew told him in clipped words where to turn, and Nicolas sped the car to its limits whenever possible. His hands on the wheel were sweaty. A voice in his head warned him that the robbers would disappear if they couldn't nail them today. According to the officer's report, they left the Old National Pike toward Washington National Pike, still heading south-east.

"We lost them!" The police officer stuttered the last location of the robbers' van. "The van caused a car crash, now the Pike's blocked and the van's gone. They must be close to Crestwood Boulevard. We're continuing our search. Assistance is needed."

"Where could they go?" Nicolas glanced at the screen but had to concentrate on the road ahead. Because of the police chase, many cars had stopped and blocked the road. He slowed down to find a way between the vehicles without losing focus on the next exit.

"They'll lose the van somewhere and—if I was in their shoes—I'd try to blend in." Matthew pointed at the screen. "There's a theater and a shopping mall with a large parking lot."

"Fuck! If they get there, we'll lose them. Tell the police—"

"I'm on it." Matthew informed the police forces of the possible destination and ordered patrol cars to search for a van left at the curb or in an adjacent alley. He warned them of getting too close, since other vehicles had been blown up after the robbers had left them.

"Order the police to lock up the mall and the theater."

"Seriously? You want to lock up a mall crammed with shoppers in the afternoon? Maybe it's just me, but I'd hate you for keeping me inside when I wanted to leave with my kids. Not to mention you might cause a kidnapping if you push the gangsters into a corner."

"Then how will we find them?"

"We don't know if they're heading for the mall. Even if they go there, they could vanish with a stolen car, escape through emergency exits or dress up like a customer or service assistant. How do you want to determine their identity?"

"They'll carry large bags with money." Nicolas smiled briefly. "Or do you think they'll abandon their loot?"

Matthew took the mic again and pressed the button.

"Officer, what about casualties? Do you know anything about the amount taken?"

"Two guards were severely wounded and are in a life-threatening condition. The robbers shot at once. Three people were slightly wounded. The robbers took the money and were off in forty seconds." The officer took a deep breath. "A customer close to the bank was also shot. Medics say he won't make it." After another silence, he said, "Four sacks with money, makes about a hundred thousand dollars in cash."

"Roger that."

Nicolas nodded. "They'll have to divide the money fast while driving, then leave the van and head for a hideout—"

"Or for another car they parked yesterday." Matthew glanced at the surroundings. "They were even faster and more reckless than before. You were right. They knew we were closing in on them."

"Most certainly."

"Tom Pinnock."

"Yep. But now I'm no longer certain that Sullivan compromised our investigation." Nicolas hit the brakes to avoid colliding with an old lady at the crosswalk, who had obviously neither heard nor seen the FBI car. "And we're taking the blame." He drove on according to Matthew's directions, looking left and right for the gray van.

Two minutes later, they received information that the van had been found burning in a parking lot next to a theater without a trace of the robbers. The officer concluded that even if cameras had filmed them, the resolution wouldn't suffice for clear identification. However, the video might show the escape car. Officers were about to retrieve the tapes.

Nicolas looked at the screen and drove toward the theater. He didn't want to admit defeat, neither to Sullivan nor to himself. He didn't heed Matthew's words. His thoughts circled the possible escape routes and how the robbers had shaken off the police so fast.

A column of smoke indicated the crime scene. Two police cars secured the street and the rest of the parking lot. As before, the robbers had chosen a remote location to blow up the van. Nicolas stopped the car and got out. He wanted to smash the robbers' faces and yet stood beside the burning van, frustrated so deeply he had no words.

Chapter Seventeen

Herman checked the side mirror frequently. His heart raced at the speed of their escape car, and he anticipated the police would show up any second.

"Slow down!" he barked.

Tom took his foot off the gas pedal. "Okay, cool down. We made it. I'm not speeding, Manny. And there's no one behind us. The accident slowed them down."

Herman scratched his head and checked the mirror once more. "That was clever, really."

Tom's smile was smug. "Thanks."

Herman tried and failed to look relieved. Behind him, Theo and Ben were cheering on top of their lungs, and their only complaint concerned the missing booze to celebrate the victory. Herman felt like throwing up.

"Did you see 'em go down? Chop, chop! And off they went to Neverland!" Theo exchanged a high-five with his brother. "Manny, you did just fucking great! Bang! I thought you'd gun down everyone around! What a show!" He whooped exuberantly and slapped Herman's shoulder. "You were fucking awesome!"

Herman knew nothing he could say would dim his brothers' mood and bring them back to reality. He relived the minute of the shootout—the two guards dropping to the pavement and the man in the blue suit who had happened to exit the bank the same time as the guards. His eyes had been wide as saucers, and he'd lifted his hands in a futile act of defense. Herman had pulled the trigger instantly, thinking of his brother and how he could protect him while he collected the bags. He didn't give a damn about the money. Ben had let off several rounds into the armored car and scared away pedestrians. Others had run screaming down the street, adding to the confusion, and keeping other armed forces away. Herman had counted on more guards and probably police assistance and decided to shoot first and be on the safe side.

"Where's Kate?" Herman asked while Tom steered the car out of town, still monitoring traffic and checking for pursuers. "Ben? Where did she go? She's no longer in front of us."

"She told me to drive with you. That's all." Ben slapped Herman's shoulder. "She'll show up at home, I'm sure."

Herman was glad they couldn't see his face. Tom glanced at him, and Herman was convinced he was angry, but for the life of him, he couldn't tell why. And right now, he didn't care.

The camera of the theater's parking lot surveying the western part was so old the video consisted of dancing snowflakes with weird silhouettes. The flames were bright and blocked the view of the robbers' escape.

Matthew pushed off the police car's door and ran a hand through his hair. "There's more to see in a fucking mouse hole at night! I can't believe it!" He turned around to a police officer. "Are there more cameras around? Would you, please, try and find one that worked properly?"

Nicolas watched the firemen extinguish the last flames. Matthew heard him curse that CSU wouldn't find anything useful for identification. "How could they escape so fast?"

"The accident on the Washington National Pike was a fucking brilliant maneuver, slowing down the pursuers, and granting them a clear getaway once they'd changed cars." Matthew glanced at the sheriff arriving at the parking lot. He made an effort to calm down. "The second clever move was to avoid the most likely escape route as if they knew we'd go for that." He straightened to face the much older man. "What made you so sure they'd turn west?"

"It's much closer to the highway, easier to access, and a lot easier to drive." The sheriff shook his head, looking at the remnants of the van in the hindmost corner of the parking lot. "Their driver must be a pro. I just checked the accident site. He slipped between two cars and then grazed one of them. That driver overreacted and rammed the car to his left—bang! The cars turned on their axles, and the WNP was blocked." He shrugged. "Without that stunt, my men would've gotten to them. I'm sure of that."

"Thank you for your help," Nicolas said nonchalantly and shook hands with the sheriff. "The FBI will take over the investigation. We'll talk to witnesses and secure the evidence."

"Sure." Sheriff Dacosta tipped his hat and turned around to tell his men to prepare for departure.

Matthew thought the sheriff was glad he was rid of the responsibility. He followed Nicolas to their service car but stopped when the young officer returned, smiling. "What have you got?"

"What you wanted." The officer opened a notebook and a file. "That's the camera at the exit. The quality's not high-end but better than the other."

Matthew and Nicolas watched intently. There were two dark sedans stopping side by side. The passenger door of one of them opened. A tall man with a large *Nike* sports bag slipped out and ran toward the second car, threw the bag in the trunk, and got in. Both cars left the parking lot fifteen seconds later and filtered into traffic smoothly.

"Enhance the video, get the license plates, and inform your colleagues immediately to search for the cars. Here's my card. Get the information to us ASAP." Matthew fingered for a cigarette and the lighter. "Check the traffic cameras in the time frame. Maybe they sped away from the theater and got caught by a speed camera. Maybe they were scared or reckless. There must be a way to follow them to their hideout."

"They made a mistake." Nicolas shook his head. "I bet they thought the camera wasn't working."

"Bad for them. Good for us." Matthew lit the cigarette and blew out smoke. "What about a late breakfast? I'll pay."

Nicolas didn't reply but got in the car where he sat and pretended to be impatient.

For the first time in their investigation, Matthew had hope that they could catch the robbers and not look dumb again.

Jacklyn brought the second bottle of wine and refilled Lesley's glass. With a sound of contentment, she slumped on the chair and stretched her legs across the armrest. "I like your dungeon a lot. I think it's the perfect mix of sexiness and terror to intimidate the subs."

Lesley toasted, drank, and licked her lips. "Yep, it's the way I like it. My interior designer thought I'm mad, but I knew exactly what I wanted." She cocked her head. "You were really tough today."

"The guys got what they deserved. Richard was so exuberant, I think he'll skip work all next week and enjoy all his aches."

"Harry's face was priceless."

"Oh, yes, it was the moment he realized he wasn't in for a free session but had to wait until the secretary told him that he was free to watch a movie. He stormed off with curses that made everyone blush. He won't frame me again."

"Nope, he certainly won't." Lesley slapped Jacklyn's upper arm with the back of her hand. "And the best is . . . he wasn't satisfied!"

They laughed themselves to death, and Lesley spilled wine on the table when she tried and failed to set down the glass. "Oops, sorry! I bet I shouldn't try anything today that demands fine-tuning with my hands! My co . . . coordinate . . . my fingers don't function anymore. I guess I swung the whip too hard."

"Or too often." Jacklyn burst out laughing once again. "I haven't had that much fun for a long time!"

"You had fun taking revenge, my sister-in-crime." Lesley wiggled a finger at her. "Nothing else. Harry was in a murderous mood when he left."

"I want a picture of that face." Jacklyn put down her empty glass. "Just to remind me of my victory over his attempt at betrayal."

"You take that personally, huh?"

"His son's on trial for murder, but when Nick said that his father might've been in league with his son, I refused the mere possibility. I claimed Harry was an honest businessman. Now I know better."

"And you're pissed you were wrong." Lesley's brows twitched. "I know that feeling."

"Ask me about feelings." Jacklyn raised her chin when a key was turned in the lock. She exchanged glances with Lesley. "I think my hormones are starting to dance."

"May I join?" Lesley licked her lips, watching Nicolas enter the apartment. She sounded breathless. "I so want to join."

Matthew checked the incoming emails. The search for the two escape cars was still on. Police cars in the area were on high alert, and the airport staff was ordered to look out for Tom Pinnock, probably with an armed escort.

Batman and Robin aka Agent Sevigny and Agent Setton told Matthew on the phone the robbers had sold his weapon and badge to a portly man in Arlington. They hadn't seen his face but stated he had a Chicago area accent. Worse news was that the weapon had been used to kill Private Detective Tim Corty, a fifty-five-year-old Chicago resident, currently on vacation in Washington, DC. Two hours ago, his body had been found in his motel room after a friend had reported to the police that he couldn't reach him. The coroner estimated the murder had happened the night before, fitting the time frame Matthew had spent locked at the railing in the garage.

Though it was good news Matthew couldn't be the killer, he was still stunned by the ruthless murder and possible consequences. Sevigny added that Matthew's badge had been found in a garbage can close to the motel.

Matthew reached for a water bottle. "Do you know why Corty was the target?"

"Close to leaving for DC, he'd investigated in two cases of pending divorces. You know, the ones in which the husband wants to know whether his wife betrayed him." Sevigny paused. "The only possible connection I see—" He cleared his throat. "You know that I had to look into your personal file, don't you? Well, Corty might've been on the heels of another woman belonging to the Chicago mob, married to a police officer."

"You're telling me, this was pre-meditated," Matthew said bleakly.

"Yes. Tim was also a crook who blackmailed several clients over the years. It's possible he stepped on someone's toes too often. That's all I can tell you right now. We're still trying to find the client Snyder described."

Matthew wiped his face carefully, aware of the bruises and scratches. He felt old and useless thinking of the trouble ahead. The bank robbers were still on the loose, and the only task that kept him on his feet was to find a way and nail the gang before they left the state.

Nicolas closed the door and got the picture of the untamed Jacklyn Hollander, a woman born to be a mistress, even though she sat like a girl on one of the armchairs with one leg swinging free. She was dressed in black leather hot pants, a tight bra, and pantyhose with an intricate pattern. Beside her sat her girlfriend, no less impressive. Lesley wore a leather costume of more stripes and laces than fabric, revealing a firm body and endless legs. The leggings ended at her ankles so that he saw her naked feet with dark red toenails.

Nicolas stood like a boy gaping through a peephole. His heart beat in his throat as images ran free, none of them G-rated. Two mistresses in one apartment—it was an overdose of sexiness and a challenge to his good manners. He dropped the keys on the sideboard and added his gun and badge. His mouth was too dry to speak, which was all right, since his mind was too numb to form a coherent thought. All he could do was stare and decide whether to challenge them with a sound bite or wait for their decision. While his body was tired from the long day, the equipment between his legs was close to a rebellion if nothing good happened.

Jacklyn got up and pointed at him. "Drop your bag and lose your clothes."

Nicolas lifted his hand, gazing at Lesley, who sat like the incarnation of a sex goddess on the couch. She wasn't moving, but her smoldering glance told him of intentions that caused him goosebumps and increased the number of images of how the evening could evolve.

Jacklyn spread her legs and cocked her head. Her look and voice were stern. "I won't say it again."

He dropped the bag and wiped his mouth. "Jacky . . ." A crop materialized in front of his chest, cutting off his argument. He shut his mouth without another word.

Lesley unfolded her legs with a purring sound, her gaze still set on Nicolas' face.

He broke into a sweat when Jacklyn snapped the crop against his chest with every word. "Out of the clothes!"

Nicolas didn't know whether he wanted to break her thrall. The fight took place in his mind while he dropped his coat and jacket. A part of him knew Jacklyn was performing to show her girlfriend how much power she held, and he thought about resisting her dominance. Another and at this time, more influential part wanted to abase itself at her feet and do whatever she demanded. Haltingly, Nicolas took off shoes and pants and—upon another harsh slap against his chest—added shirt and socks to the pile.

The crop slipped toward the waistband of his boxers, where Nicolas' anticipation was clearly visible. Jacklyn kept eye contact. He was insecure about whether she was giving him a chance to skip the evening entertainment or not. When she narrowed her eyes, he understood.

"Out of it. Go, take a shower. We'll join you . . . soon."

Nicolas obeyed, his mind in a swirl of emotions. He made it to the bathroom without stumbling.

"She's not coming back." Herman slumped on the couch and buried his face in his hands. "My God, I knew it. She's not coming back."

Theo flipped the remote control onto the coffee table. It bounced off and clattered on the floor, resting in good company with socks and a sweater. "What the fuck are you talking about? I bet she's celebrating somewhere. Maybe she found a shop and she's buying fancy clothes. Women are like that. Why wouldn't she come back? After all, we got rid of the car, got away, and we're here with all the money, more than we thought. It's a blast!"

Herman raised his head, torn between sadness and anger. "Because she'd planned to leave long ago, you moron. Because she knew this morning she wouldn't return." He sobbed. "She didn't want this last job, okay? She did this for us. For both of you! I should've thought of it when she came out all dressed-up like a model."

"Yeah, she looked fucking great. Like some rich lady from a palace." Ben slumped on the couch and spilled the popcorn. "I'm with Theo. She's taking a tour, loses the car somewhere, and then comes back with the new one." He smiled broadly and threw popcorn at Herman. "Didn't I tell you? I stole one for her—a new *Audi A6*. Was a hard piece of work, you know, but I made it."

"You stole a car just for her?" Tom gaped at Ben. "And you didn't think she'd use it to get away? How dumb are you? Where did you park it?"

Ben threw popcorn at him. "Don't talk to me like that! I'm not stupid!"

Tom bent forward inhaling sharply. Spittle flew from his lips with every word. "You're stupid as shit! You've always been stupid as shit! Without our help, you'd have ended up in prison or dead long ago. Now, where did you park it?"

"Why should I tell you?" Blushing, Ben put the popcorn bowl aside and got up. "Why should I tell you pieces of shit anything? She's my sister, and I did this because she asked me to!"

"Yeah, but I'm her fucking lover, you halfwit!" Tom pushed Ben at the shoulders. "Get out of my sight. I can't stand your babbling anyway."

"If she loves you so much, why didn't she tell you where she went, huh?" Ben pushed Tom's chest, and he grunted. "You're only some fuck horse for her, good enough to drive the car but for nothin' else." Ben swung wide, but Tom evaded the punch to his temple. "She deserves better than some fucking race car driver!"

Tom dished out three hard blows to Ben's face and stomach and watched the younger man collapse, coughing. He slapped the back of Ben's head.

"Never call me that again!"

"Take your money and leave." Herman was on his feet while Theo took care of his brother. "Go ahead! Take the bag and leave our house! We don't need you anymore. And you'd better hurry before I wipe the floor with your face."

"I'm better off without you anyway!" Retreating, Tom pointed at Herman. "It's only a question of time until you'll get caught. Without Kate, you're but a bunch of fucktards!" He smoothed his hair, grabbed one of the black bags from the table, and rushed out.

The door thunked shut.

"Why do you say she's not coming back?" Theo asked when they helped Ben sit on the couch. He sounded desperate. "Kate can't leave us. We need her."

Herman looked from Theo to Ben. "We need her, but she doesn't need us."

Jacklyn licked her lips. Her heart raced, and she couldn't wait for Nicolas to turn off the water. Lesley twitched her brows, and her smile indicated her typical wickedness when it came to submissive customers. Jacklyn knew what she was about to say before she opened her mouth.

"He didn't say *no*, did he? He took off his clothes. This means he's game." Lesley cocked her head and played with a strand of hair as she strolled toward the bathroom door. "Shall we surprise him?"

Jacklyn laughter was breathless. She slapped the crop against her thigh. "I suppose I surprised him enough already. I'm not sure if I—"

"He's your sub," Lesley hissed. "I still don't understand—why do you have second thoughts?"

"Because I love him. If I push him too far, he won't trust me again."

"But think of him chained to the bed, blindfolded, and collared. Okay, no collar for him, but handcuffs and a gag—a black rubber bit gag, it's the manliest. Doesn't that stir your juices?"

"I haven't thought of anything else since the moment he came home. I admit I'm wet beyond belief." Jacklyn laughed but wasn't truly happy with her longing. "If I—"

Lesley lifted a finger to her lips. "No *ifs*. For once in your life, do exactly what you want to do. The moment he doesn't follow your order, you know he doesn't want what you do. I think he's strong enough to say *no*, right?"

"I'm more afraid he doesn't want you to join."

"Then I don't join. I can look smug and keep my hands to myself."

Jacklyn snorted, but couldn't remain serious. "You cannot keep your hands off my man if I don't fight you. I know that damn well."

Lesley rolled her eyes and turned around, throwing her hands in the air. "Come on, we're born ladies who prefer a spanking over a candlelight dinner! What shall I say?" She struck a pose. "I'm Washington's new *leading dominatrix*. Did I tell you? I'll be on the cover of DC's city magazine next month."

"You told me about twenty times. Yes, I'm proud of you. But we're talking about my boyfriend, not some paying customer in your dungeon. Do you—" She stopped when the bathroom door opened.

"You know that I can hear you?" Nicolas asked and threw the small towel back inside he had used to dry his hair. "Do you also know that I made up my mind the moment I dropped the keys?"

Lesley's jaw dropped, and Jacklyn was rendered speechless.

Nicolas put his hands on the rim of the towel he'd wound around his hips. "So much for the fierce mistresses you pretend to be." He smiled broadly. "That ruins your appearance, don't you think?"

"You . . ."

Nicolas gently cupped Jacklyn's cheeks and kissed her. "I want to make you happy." He glanced at Lesley. "And, no, I'm not kissing you."

Matthew knew he was acting foolishly, but he checked the dark desolated place behind the liquor store and was relieved it was empty. He bought two bottles of his favorite brand and hurried home, looking back over his shoulder frequently even though the movement was awkward.

Bert had told him he'd be on his way to the airport the next afternoon, and Matthew toasted the TV screen with a happy smile. He ended the call when his cell phone rang. The agent in charge told him one of the escape cars had been found empty, parked in a suburb close to Frederick. Because there were no traffic cameras, the FBI still didn't know where the bank robbers had gone, but at least CSU had a car to examine for evidence. Grateful for small successes, Matthew emptied another glass. He lost count on how much he'd drunk as he slipped onto the couch, pleasantly numbed.

The smell of cranberry-flavored breath mints was in his nose. Fatsy strangulated him relentlessly and only let go once someone outside called his name. Matt didn't understand the words. Lying on the tiles in the entrance of his house, fighting pain, he was happy to be alive.

Matthew woke with a start, wheezing and bathed in sweat. He suppressed the scream that wanted out. With the next move, he tumbled off the couch, barely missing the table rim. He was nauseous and trembled as he rested on all fours. The TV was still on, spreading flickering lights through the living room. Though it was impossible, Matthew smelled cranberries. He got up awkwardly, made it to the bathroom, and threw up.

Weary and swearing he'd stay away from whiskey and alcohol in general, Matthew shuffled back to the living room that smelled like a bar in the morning. He detested the nightmares. He detested waking up at night and walking through his apartment like a restless ghost searching for something that would release him. The distance between Chicago and DC was obviously not great enough for his mind to make a fresh start and be happy that he still had his job.

During the investigation against Nerina and her family, Matthew had expected he'd get fired. The senior agent had demoted him to a desk job and—close to the trial—urged him to take some days off, but he'd never mentioned he preferred getting rid of him. Nevertheless, the threat of losing his job in addition to losing his wife and home had pressed him like a vise.

Some nights, he hadn't just lived through nightmares but had been unable to breathe. His psychiatrist had helped him the best he could. Yet the nightmares remained, and he woke up several times at night with images of his enemies inside and outside the FBI gathering to kill him in cold blood.

Matthew sat on the couch, glancing at the bottle of whiskey and the pack of cigarettes. He wished both gone if that meant his life would take a turn for the better.

CHAPTER EIGHTEEN

While Jacklyn appeared flabbergasted, Lesley gathered her wits much faster. Her voice was as stern as her pose.

"You think you'll get away with this—eavesdropping? With two mistresses ready to discipline you?" She swung the flogger against his chest.

The slap woke Jacklyn from her state of shock, and for a second Lesley pondered whether she had gone too far.

"I'll tell you what we do with scum like you—shackle and punish." She took a step aside, looking up into Nicolas' gorgeous face and hoping he'd be fun in bed. "Go! And don't dare make a move against us! You'd regret it."

Nicolas glanced at Jacklyn, but Lesley smacked the flogger against his neck, hard enough that he twitched in surprise.

"Off you go!"

Nicolas made a step forward. With a wicked smile, Jacklyn ripped away the towel and used the crop on Nicolas' well-trained ass.

"Hurry! Don't make us wait!"

Lesley knew she should step aside and let the couple play the way they wanted. She could have fun the next day in the dungeon. The list of customers was long, and her reputation from Philadelphia served her well. However, the dynamics between the couple intrigued her. Nicolas wasn't the typical sub, a man looking for a dominant woman in his life to guide him. She tried to wrap her mind around the situation—while he was a hero in his job, he was an obedient subordinate at home. She wondered whether he made breakfast for his mistress wearing an apron and nothing else.

"On the bed on all fours!" Jacklyn threw Nicolas a blindfold.

With a last glance at Lesley, he put it on, then rested on his hands and knees. His lips parted when Jacklyn let the crop travel from his shoulders to his buttocks. Obviously, she knew how to get him into the mood. She knew how to speed his pulse and increase his anticipation that arousal was nothing she worried about.

Lesley made eye contact, requesting permission to join, for she knew she'd die if she didn't try. Jacklyn mouthed she wouldn't allow Lesley to kiss or fuck him, but for everything else she was welcome.

Lesley bit her lower lip and knew she was in for an unforgettable night.

Miller walked with swinging steps through the aisle, waving a piece of paper. Matthew assumed the CSU lab technician needed something in his hand while visiting the agents, for he could've sent the information via email. As usual, Miller's expression darkened once he didn't find Agent Hayes at his desk.

"You've got something for us?" Matthew asked, sitting down with a fresh cup of coffee.

Miller blushed and closed his mouth without saying a word.

Matthew held his tongue to neither smile nor point out that Special Agent Hayes would be absent for another hour, training at the FBI gym in the basement. He wondered whether Miller would run downstairs and watch Nicolas sweat in shirt and shorts.

"As requested, the examination of the bank robbers' car was given priority. We found the same DNA samples and a new one. Again, there's a similarity, so it's correct to assume there's a third brother involved."

Matthew whistled through his teeth.

Miller pushed back a strand of hair. His smile came and went. "The car was reported stolen three weeks ago, so I checked all stolen cars in the area within the last four weeks. There were five more sedans and limousines, one of them a black *Audi A6,* only four months old. Nice, don't you think?" He handed Matthew three sheets of paper. "The license plate didn't belong to the car, but that could be expected."

"Thank you. Good work."

"The search warrant has already been issued. Police patrols have the description of the cars." Miller cleared his throat, and his small smile lost its shine. "You know it's only fishing in the dark, yes? Hundreds of cars are reported stolen each day. There's no guarantee that the bank robbers are using these cars to escape. They could've rented cars under false names or taken a helicopter tour to another state."

"I'm aware we aren't closing in on them fast, but it's a clue more than we had yesterday. Thank you, Miller."

The lab technician left the office, and upon arrival, Matthew told Nicolas of the findings. He also told him he'd been right to assume the second camera at the theater parking lot had been replaced a day ago—a circumstance the robbers hadn't anticipated. As Nicolas opened the button of his jacket and sat down at the desk, Matthew noticed that his partner was more relaxed than on previous days. Curious as a cat in a Christmas tree, he looked for new abrasions and bruises and regretted he'd been unable to join his colleague for a closer look at the gym. It had been difficult enough to get out of bed.

"It's easier when you ask," Nicolas said quietly after checking his emails.

"I thought it'd be kind not to mention you look like the poor kid bruised on the way to school."

Nicolas laughed but stifled it when other colleagues turned their heads.

"Let's say I had an outstanding night."

"I assume there were instruments of various forms and purpose in use, some of them with the intention to keep a man from jumping and running?"

Once more, Nicolas appeared on the verge of breaking down with laughter.

"You assume correctly. You're an outstanding special agent."

Matthew toasted him with his coffee cup. "Thank you. It was hard work." The phone rang, and a young police officer told him that Tom Pinnock had been sighted in Arlington, driving like a maniac after a police patrol had identified him. "Good work. Keep track of him. We're on our way." He smiled at Nicolas as he put on his jacket. "Tom's out of his rat hole."

Tom Pinnock sat in the FBI interrogation room, shackled to the table. Officers had taken his jacket, emptied his pockets, and collected a sample of his hair for a comparison to the hair found in the stolen car. Officers had also found a bag with cash, stolen from the last bank robbery. The former race car driver looked grumpy and angry the longer the agents let him wait.

Nicolas watched him getting restless until he rattled the chains on the metal table and screamed that he needed something to drink. With a can of coke in his hand, Nicolas entered the windowless room, ready for long hours of curses and accusations followed by stoic silence.

"I assume you want something to drink?" Nicolas sat down.

"I assume you want information." Tom met his gaze,

protruding his chin. "What do I get when I talk?"

Nicolas didn't buy his arrogant demeanor. The man stank of sweat, and his hands shook. "What do you have to offer?" He pushed the can across the table, and Tom drank greedily. "Is it worth more than a coke, or are you going to waste my time?"

"I want a prison of my choice and *mit . . . mit-something*. Less years in jail, I mean."

"And for your mitigation of punishment—what will I get?"

Tom crushed the empty can with a vengeance. His look was smug, paired with malevolence. "Three fucktards with a lot of cash."

Nicolas leaned back on the uncomfortable chair and lifted a hand invitingly. "Talk."

Matthew raised his brows, handing his partner a cup of coffee in the morning. Nicolas took off his coat and sat down at his desk, smiling so broadly that Matthew expected him to whistle any second. His good mood was eerie and a counterpoint to the miserable night Matthew had spent trying to stay away from alcohol which—as a bitter consequence—had led to hours of nightmares. He felt wretched.

"Okay, I get it." Matthew rolled his eyes and opened his hands wide. "Come on, you look like my dog waiting for his favorite treat, close to wagging his tail. What did the judge say? Does he agree? Does Pinnock get a deal?"

"You compare me to a dog?"

Matthew couldn't turn away fast enough to cloak his consternation. "Sorry. That came out all wrong."

Nicolas laughed. "Today I'll let that slip. Try it again, and you'll pay for breakfast the whole next year." He tapped the envelope on the table. "Yeah, the judge agreed. Let's talk to Pinnock and get those buggers arrested."

Tom Pinnock kept his word. His counsel for the defense confirmed significant mitigation and left the choice of prison to his client. After signing the papers, Tom delivered the address and a detailed description of the three brothers, including their favorite disguises.

Police forces raided the house at the dead end of a suburban street outside of Germantown. They found clues for the men's presence, but the brothers were already gone. Two cars were parked in the garage side by side with a brand new motorcycle. All vehicles were reported stolen. A CSU unit took over the investigation to find clues to their current whereabouts.

Matthew felt the heat of excitement get to him. He accompanied Nicolas to their superior's office, knowing he'd have no part in the conversation. Nicolas stood up against Senior Agent Sullivan to keep the arrest and cooperation of Tom Pinnock a secret by arguing that the brothers would hurry to leave the state and change their appearance quicker than the search warrants were printed. Sullivan grudgingly acknowledged the course of action, though Matthew doubted their boss was acting in the best interest of the investigation. If he had it right, Sullivan decided it would be easier to collect the mayor's praise after the hoodlums' arrests than being branded for a poor decision.

The men's descriptions and last whereabouts were handed to all patrolmen, warning them to call for assistance.

To his surprise, the warning was heeded. The phone rang around noon, and the sergeant told him that one of the brothers was taking a stroll through the *Springfield Town Center*. Matthew ordered the policeman to follow him but to stay out of sight.

Nicolas stood and grabbed his coat before Matthew hung

up. "Where?"

"*Springfield Town Center.*" Matthew checked his weapon and cell phone and put his jacket across his arm. He thought about a bottle of painkillers but remembered he'd be riding with *Nick the Maniac*. If he tried taking a pill, he'd probably choke to death.

"He's shopping in a mall? That's damn bold!"

Nicolas strode so fast Matthew thought about jogging to catch up, but his midsection hurt too much to try.

"Remember, the brothers still think we don't know their faces. They don't know about Tom's arrest, and I bet my monthly salary they split up after the last robbery." Matthew thanked the goddess for parking garages and shortcuts as he slumped on the passenger seat, out of breath.

Nicolas hit the gas the moment the car was in gear. This time, Matthew wasn't afraid of his partner's aggressive driving. He wanted to catch the bank robbers as much as Nicolas did. His attitude changed when Nicolas crossed a large intersection without braking. Involuntarily, Matthew stopped breathing while he clung to the handhold.

"At least one of the brothers thinks it's safe to spend money." Nicolas shook his head. "Why doesn't he go into hiding? At least for a few weeks? It's damn risky! The money could be registered."

Matthew had his theory about that, but the words stuck when Nicolas overtook a truck that changed lanes without heeding the sirens and blue lights. Somehow, Nicolas evaded, and they sped on without accident. Matthew preferred closing his eyes and praying for a safe way.

"Did you say something?" Nicolas asked when they reached Springfield.

Matthew released his breath. "My heart's in my throat, and my thoughts are tumbling behind somewhere."

"Any theory?"

"About my heart? Yes, it'll stop beating if you crash the car."

"You should know by now I won't." He glanced at him. "Don't replace Jason like that. Trust me. I know what I'm doing."

Matthew contacted the patrolmen. "They're certain it's one of the bank robbers. He's still inside the mall, right now strolling toward the food court." He switched off the siren and blue lights before Nicolas turned toward the large parking lot. There wasn't much traffic, and when Matthew received directions, Nicolas parked the car. They entered the mall next to a clothes store.

"Can you do this?" Nicolas asked glancing Matthew up and down.

"It's too late to ask, don't you think?"

"You could stay here and keep him from escaping." Nicolas moved on, vigilant and self-confident, sidestepping customers carrying boxes and bags as if passing an obstacle course.

Bracing for the pain that wouldn't leave, Matthew stayed on the right side of the aisle while Nicolas took a left. They pretended to be shoppers, but Matthew knew from experience that a criminal paid attention to details even if he appeared relaxed. In his fifteen years of service, he'd been on many observations, and only a few hoodlums had been overwhelmed because of sloppiness. The more intelligent beings were aware of policemen in plain clothes. Given the list of victims, Matthew didn't expect the bank robber to give up.

His hands sweated. The bad feeling of being vulnerable because of his restricted agility settled in his belly. He didn't want to become the target of a cornered robber. Once more, the voice in his head told him he should've called in sick.

Nicolas' look indicated he'd spied the target. The gangster was munching on fries and burger at a table. He was no older than twenty-five, tall and wide in the shoulders. A full blond beard covered his face. He wore a green hoodie and a matching baseball cap. Matthew didn't buy the bored demeanor, and he got nervous when the young man checked his watch before he got up and put the tray back on the rack close to the burger shop. He didn't look over his shoulder while he strolled along the row of shops and picked food out of his teeth.

Nicolas rolled his shoulders and walked on, glancing at Matthew. They had a wordless understanding they'd seize the man before he reached an exit. They gained on him, but when Nicolas drew his gun, a stranger at the next aisle shouted, "Watch out! Behind you!"

Matthew had his gun out and shot the robber in the shoulder. The young man crashed against a garbage can, knocked it over, and fell hard on the tiles, screaming in pain. In a fluent motion, the enemy who yelled on the other side of the aisle pulled a gun from under his leather jacket and opened fire. Matthew crouched and searched cover behind one of the tables. He squinted, praying he'd be able to get up again. Nicolas was somewhere to his left, waiting for a clear line of fire.

Customers fled the food court screaming in terror. From the other side, patrolmen were moving in, weapons drawn and ready. They shouted for civilians to take cover. The young robber shot again. The bullets destroyed a table decoration and the backrests of chairs. Shreds rained down on Matthew, and he blinked away splinters. He returned fire, and the policemen did the same. He stopped once the hoodlum turned tail and followed the people who were searching for safety outside.

"Hold fire!" Nicolas hollered. He was on his feet and running faster than the patrolmen left their positions.

Matthew dealt with the ringing in his ears, forced his battered body to move on, and ignored the increasing pain.

"Arrest this one!" he shouted at a young officer and pointed toward the robber cringing on the floor. "Secure his weapon!"

He followed the escapee and his partner as fast as he could. A large group of people pressed through the doors, and the crook was somewhere in between, pushing customers left and right, and elbowing his way out. In front of the mall, cars stopped and honked as the panicked mass spilled onto the sidewalk.

A young woman was hit and stumbled on the pavement, forcing the following men to evade or jump. Others turned left and right quickly to get out of the line of fire while the bank robber ran toward the first row of parked cars, calling someone's name. Matthew stopped when a blond man, taller and wider in the shoulders than the other two, emerged from a pick-up truck, an *MP5* in his hands. He aimed across the trunk of the car parked next to him.

"Over here, Theo! Quick!"

"*MP*!" Matthew shouted. "Get down!" He evaded to the right, watching Nicolas take a stand and shoot the escaping robber in his thigh.

The young man stumbled and fell on his knees, shrieking. "Manny! Help me!"

"I'm coming! Hold on!" The *MP* muzzle turned to Nicolas the same instant.

"No, no, no!" Matthew had his gun up without thinking and fired four times. The *MP* muzzle flashed in a fiery red as bullets hammered through glass and metal, increasing the mayhem. More cars came to a screeching stop. Nicolas took cover behind the hood of one of them. People dropped prone on the ground. The young robber screamed while Manny fell backward against the pick-up truck and slid down, out of sight.

Matthew looked left and right, afraid there could be another gangster ready to join the fight. When he was certain the threat was over, he gave up his fighting stance. His heartbeat throbbed in his throat, but he gathered his wits and hurried to his partner.

He touched Nicolas' shoulder, searching for injuries. "Are you okay?"

"Yeah." Nicolas' eyes were wide, and his breathing labored. He made it to his feet. "Gotta check—"

"I'm on it." Matthew stayed in a crouch and kept his weapon leveled as he secured the young robber's gun. He flinched, seeing the gunshot wounds in the second man's head and chest.

There was no doubt Manny was dead.

"Time to wrap up." Nicolas looked tired and weary to his bones, yet his mood was exuberant. "Thanks to you, Matt, we're all still in one piece, and two of the gangsters are arrested."

They shook hands, and Matthew couldn't stop smiling. "Thanks for the praise, but *you* stood there fearless and stopped the young dude."

Nicolas shook his head. "Manny was ready to kill us all to save his brother. He was some bad asshole." His face sobered when Senior Agent Sullivan made his entrance, as stern as ever. "Sir, the case is solved. You'll have our report this evening."

"Prepare a short version. There'll be a press conference in an hour, and I've got to explain why four customers suffered bullet wounds while you were on-scene and tasked to stop the killers." With a sharp nonverbal reproof, Sullivan turned on his heels and headed back to his office.

"He's jealous," Matthew whispered, smirking. "We solved the case, and he's pissed we didn't do it yesterday."

"You've learned a lot in the short time you've been here.

I'll invite you for breakfast tomorrow."

"To celebrate? I'm in. But only if you promise to treat me gently."

"I thought about throwing you against the car first."

"You won't be able to do that a second time."

"Do you wanna bet?"

"Do you wanna lose once more?"

Matthew bought an expensive bottle of *Bushmills Black Bush Whiskey,* took a long shower, and decided to surprise his neighbor and celebrate the breakthrough in the bank robber case. As expected, Sullivan had kept the laudatory speech general and avoided the names of the agents in charge completely. Nevertheless, Nicolas and Matthew had parted in a good mood, joking about their different evening expectations.

Matthew heard Bingo bark upon knocking on Lawrence's door. He looked at his watch. Bert would arrive in DC in two and a half hours. Naturally, he'd check in at his four-star-hotel first, but that was fine with Matthew. He needed some time to tidy up the apartment and prepare the outstanding dinner Bert demanded. Smiling, he thought of the reservation he'd made for the following evening. His friend would get exactly what he wanted as a sign of gratefulness.

Lawrence opened, dressed in light gray pants and a white dress shirt. "Hello, Matt." His smile appeared forced, and Matthew understood when Bingo pressed through the door slit to wag his tail and jump at Matthew's leg. "Wow! What's that?"

Matthew handed Lawrence the bottle. "I wanted to say thank you for your support. You were the only one not browbeating me that night." He laughed but briefly and bent to pet the dog. "I just wanted to give you this. So . . . have a good evening and I—"

"No, please, don't go! I've got time. No problem." Lawrence opened the door wide and called back the dog. "Do come in."

Matthew left his shoes on the rack. There was a pair of dark brown leather shoes in a much larger size than Lawrence wore. "Do you have company?" He looked around, but the living room was empty.

"No." Lawrence put the bottle on the table. Still, his smile wasn't convincing. "No, I don't. Let me fetch glasses."

Petting the dog, Matthew watched him walk toward the kitchen. There was a faint smell in the air, different from the prominent cleaning agent and leather polish. Instinct told him to check his back and leave quickly, but his curiosity won. "What I was thinking about—why did you come into the garage? I mean you were about to walk Bingo, right?"

Lawrence opened the bottle and poured two glasses. "I wanted to fetch the last bag with groceries from the trunk. Here you go." He handed him a glass and put napkins on the table.

"Ah, I see." Matthew loved the scent of old whiskey and sighed. He toasted and sipped. There was a fresh water-stain of another glass on the tabletop. Shrugging, he looked at Lawrence again. "But you didn't take it when you left."

Lawrence smacked his lips, looking at Matthew like a lenient teacher correcting a stubborn pupil. "Now, really, Matt, is that something you want to discuss over a really great glass of whiskey?"

"Did you serve in the army?"

"What? No. I told you I was a salesman. But that was a long time ago."

"Yes, you told me, but then you used some words, mostly army personnel use."

"You're imagining things." He narrowed his eyes. "Even if I did—what does it mean? That I picked up some words from a movie. I thought it was funny." Lawrence sighed, putting down the glass on the napkin. "I had a long day. Don't ruin my evening, Matt."

"You also said you've lived here for three years, but your apartment's freshly painted and you've got new windows—a remodeling that's only done for renters who'd moved in recently."

Lawrence snorted and shook his head. "Did you come here to interrogate me, G-man? I'm not a suspect, and I won't answer any of your dumb questions."

"I'm not interrogating you, but . . ." Matthew set down the glass and turned around, suddenly alerted. The smell grew stronger. "Cranberries." He saw the door to the adjacent room open and couldn't believe his eyes. "Fatsy."

"Hey, Monty." Fatsy Gandolfo strolled through the room, a complacent smile on his face. Even in casual clothes and socks, he was an impressive man of roughly two-hundred and thirty pounds. His stout appearance was often mistaken for slowness, but Matthew knew from experience that the Italian born FBI agent could move fast and fight hard.

"What're you doin' here?" Matthew made a step back to keep both Lawrence and Fatsy in view. He regretted he'd come without his gun. Feverishly, he sought a way out while his heart raced and his weariness took a time-out. "You're in league with each other? What's happening here?"

Lawrence pulled a .38 pistol from behind his back and aimed at Matthew's chest. "You should've stuck by Nerina and not given her away like any damn crook."

"Both of you work for the Acardi family? Who are you? A friend of the boss?"

Lawrence grimaced. "I'm his man in the background, you miserable bugger. I'm the man he trusts when it gets bad."

Matthew retreated toward the door, panting as if he'd run. His voice failed him. "I can't believe it."

Fatsy opened his arms wide and made a face as if saying Matthew should've known before.

"Why're you doing this, Fatsy? I thought you were pissed with me because—"

"I convinced you I'd nothing to do with the family, right? My colleagues believed me, too, and I could give you a farewell you'll never forget." He got closer when Matthew had almost reached the door. He swirled a thick roll of duct tape around his finger. "You stay here, Monty, there's nowhere to run."

Lawrence changed position and nodded toward Fatsy.

Matthew broke into a sweat as fear surged through his body. "Why now? Lawrence? Why are you doing this now?"

Lawrence nodded without letting Matthew out of sight. "Marcello told me to keep an eye on you." His smile bore a threat. "He also told me to take action the moment Nerina died."

"She's dead?" Matthew felt like hit in the guts. "Nerina is dead?" A part of him broke down and wanted to cry. The other part kicked his ass telling him he shouldn't worry about his ex-wife but fight to stay alive. "How?" He choked on the word. "How did she die?"

Lawrence's words were cutting. "Killed in a prison uproar. Stabbed in the side and left bleeding. When help came, she was already dead."

Matthew inhaled, realizing Fatsy had invaded his space but at the same time stepped into Lawrence's line of fire. He punched Fatsy's nose as hard as he could, stepped back, and aimed for his enemy's midsection, hoping he'd reach the door and escape into the hallway. Fatsy grunted like a boar, ignored the dripping blood, and delivered a blow to Matthew's stomach. His large fist forced all air out of Matthew's lungs, breaking his resistance immediately. He crashed against the door and slipped down to the floor, coughing and fighting to breathe. White dots danced in front of his eyes, and he threw up the little he'd eaten. Fatsy wiped the blood off his nose, then grabbed Matthew's shoulders to thrust him prone on the floor. Matthew was about to lose consciousness. He tried in vain to pull up his legs to ease the pain in his stomach.

Fatsy knelt on Matthew's thigh. "You've never won against me, asshole. You didn't expect this would change, right?"

"Hurry!" Lawrence stepped closer. "Shut his mouth before he's able to scream."

"Yeah, yeah, don't hassle me. I know what I'm doing." Fatsy bound Matthew's wrists with tape. "He's in no condition to do more than whine."

Matthew groaned in pain and spat. "The assaults . . . the muggers? That was you?"

Fatsy slapped the back of Matthew's head. "Did you think Marcello would let you out of sight? You should've known he'd come after you sooner rather than later. The thugs were stupid like piss. They fucked up the first time." He tore off another strip. "They fucked up the second time when they tied you up instead of bashing you unconscious."

"Why my badge and gun?"

"He wanted you in trouble, done the best way with a murder on your hands. That dick was a nuisance, anyway. And I admit—I wanted you out of the FBI. You don't deserve the badge."

Fatsy used the last strip across Matthew's mouth, cutting off another question.

Lawrence put away the pistol to help Fatsy pull Matthew toward the bedroom. He tried to thwart them as best he could, even kicked out against the table in the vain hope of tumbling glasses and making enough noise for the neighbors to hear.

Lawrence laughed. "Did you forget? You've got the apartment below mine! Idiot! You haven't seen through this, huh? You thought I was the friendly but stupid neighbor with the good heart. You're so easy to see through. I bought a dog and knew you'd be my best friend in a week." Lawrence used the duct tape to tie Matthew to a chair in the corner of the room. The hate in his eyes was raw. "Nerina was a wonderful woman. You could've used your influence to keep her out of harm's way, but instead, you let her die." He looked up. "How much time?"

Fatsy wiped his nose again and checked his watch. "Five hours max."

Matthew raised his brows, and Lawrence bent toward him. "Luigi and the boys took off the moment they learned of her death. And you bet they're in a bad mood. You don't think you're gonna die with a bullet between your eyes, do you?" His laugh was bitter. "Marcello wouldn't send his son for such a simple killing."

Fatsy strolled back through the room. "I heard the fucker brought you good whiskey. Let's have a drink and kill some time."

Lawrence pulled the door shut and left Matthew shivering with pain and hopelessness. He remembered *Luigi the Executor* from pictures. He was associated with thirty-three killings over the last ten years but had never been convicted.

Matthew had five hours to get away.

CHAPTER NINETEEN

When the phone rang, Nicolas turned toward the nightstand grumpily. The dispatcher at the FBI headquarters connected him with a man by the name of Bert Hanson. Nicolas was wide awake once he understood this was about Matthew Montagna and his current whereabouts. He left for the kitchen.

"I'm Nicolas Hayes, Matt's partner. What happened?"

Hanson sounded unhappy and regretful. "I'm really sorry to bother you, sir, and I know it's in the middle of the night, but you see, I had an appointment with Monty tonight, but I can't reach him. I mean, he's not answering the phone. The nice man . . . *agent* at the FBI told me he isn't at the office and suggested that you—"

"Sir, where are you calling from?"

"Marriott Hotel. I'm in the lobby."

"He knew you were coming tonight?"

"Yes. I told him I'd check in and meet him for dinner."

Nicolas tried to imagine Matthew in the kitchen cooking dinner, but he stowed the image for later. "How long have you tried to reach him?"

"About two hours, maybe longer. Even if he's taking a shower, he should be done by now."

Nicolas nodded, though Hanson couldn't see him. "All right. Sir, I'll locate the phone and get back to you. Give me your number." He scribbled Hanson's number and called the FBI once more to search for the signal of Matthew's cell phone. He dressed while he waited and was surprised that the technician located the phone at his partner's home.

While he put on pants and shoes, Jacklyn appeared in the hallway, squinting in the light. Nicolas explained the situation in clipped words and left to tell Hanson on the way to his car they would meet at Matthew's home. There was a chance Matthew hadn't recharged the cell phone, but Hanson replied that he'd tried the home phone, too, without success.

Nicolas parked his car behind a black *Oldsmobile* at the curb. Mr. Hanson's nervousness was plainly visible when they introduced each other briefly.

"I'm glad you came." Mr. Hanson moved his portly body toward the entrance. "It's totally unlike him, really. He wouldn't forget our appointment, and I called him in the morning to tell him about the flight I was taking. I'm sorry I'm babbling, sir, but this is . . ." He shook his head, grimacing. "I'm just worried, you know."

"We'll check his apartment. He wasn't feeling well the last few days."

"*Not feeling well*?" Mr. Hanson snorted as he tried to keep up with Nicolas' pace. "He'd been roughed up and beaten and didn't dare call in sick because of his new job!"

They took the elevator to the third floor.

Mr. Hanson threw his hands in the air. He was out of breath. "I told him the first time he was mugged he should stay home, but, hey, did he listen to me? No, he didn't!"

Under different circumstances, Nicolas would've quipped about the G-men's born dedication to the job. He might've told Mr. Hanson that quitting in the middle of an investigation was unheard of. Now he moved toward Matthew's door with growing uneasiness. One floor up, a dog was barking loudly.

Mr. Hanson knocked on the door. "Monty? Are you there? Come on! It's no longer funny! Open up!"

"He's not there or can't answer." Nicolas pulled his set of skeleton keys and opened the door within two minutes.

"You're a clever G-man," Mr. Hanson said and was about to enter.

"Wait. Let me go first." Nicolas pulled his gun.

Mr. Hanson stepped aside and lifted his hands as if to deflect danger. He paled. "Sure."

The lights were on in the hallway and in the living room. Nicolas saw Matthew's replacement gun, his wallet, and a cell phone on a small table to the right. He checked—it was working. A brown paper bag lay on the top beside the kitchen sink. The table was set for two, and the scent of fresh bread was in the air. When Nicolas gave his okay, Mr. Hanson passed him by to have a look into the other rooms.

He looked devastated upon his return. "He's not here. But his stuff's here. He wouldn't leave without it, would he? I mean—his gun, his phone? Isn't it the rule with you guys to keep your stuff on you all the time?"

"He hasn't gone far." Nicolas put away his gun and looked around as if it was a crime scene. "Can he be around? With a neighbor, maybe?"

"Sure!" Bert slapped his forehead with his palm. "Oh, my God, I'm so stupid! The dog!"

"The dog?" Nicolas thought Mr. Hanson was rattled by the situation. "What about a dog?"

"The neighbor upstairs! He's got a dog, and Monty's obsessed with dogs! I bet he's with him and he's forgotten about the time!"

He was out of the apartment and up the stairs quicker than Nicolas had anticipated, but he followed. One floor up, a suppressed conversation between three men was taking place. There was hissing and mumbled curses in a different language. One man grunted, then there was a thud on the floor as if something heavy collapsed. More curses and a hearty slap followed. A man swore under his breath.

"Sir, wait a moment." Nicolas had his gun in his hand and told Mr. Hanson to keep quiet.

Mr. Hanson paled even more and ducked his massive frame on the stairs while Nicolas continued his way up cautiously. The dog barked again before the door closed. Nicolas understood the urgency in the men's conversation. One of them hit the button for the elevator. At this range, Nicolas identified the language as Italian. His hand around the gun was sweaty. He moved forward to have a look.

Four men were waiting for the elevator, holding their guns close to their bodies, out of sight but ready to draw. Matthew was being kept upright by two thugs. His eyes were out of focus, and his movements slow. Blood crusted the left side of his face.

Nicolas moved around the corner without giving up his cover and shot the man standing at the elevator doors. The gangster went down with a wound to his chest, screaming. The others turned, pulled their guns, and shot simultaneously. Matthew hung between them like a puppet that would drop the moment they let go. The elevator stopped. The doors opened. Nicolas pulled the trigger and hit the second man in the shoulder, forcing him back against the apartment door. The dog barked again.

The remaining gangsters pushed Matthew into the elevator. When Nicolas assumed they were inside, he swiveled around the corner to shoot again only to look into a muzzle. He had a split-second to duck to the side while aiming at the man behind the gun. He heard a scream, then the doors closed.

Nicolas turned around fast enough to see the thug with the shoulder wound raise his gun. Nicolas shot him in the chest and turned to run downstairs. Mr. Hanson crouched down in a corner, whimpering and folding his arms around his head.

"Stay here!" Nicolas barked and was down two steps at a time, afraid the gangsters had reinforcements waiting. He dropped the thought about calling for assistance. There was no time.

Panting, he made it to the first floor and came to a skittering stop as he made out a stranger in the poorly lit entrance. The man dropped his cigarette the moment he saw Nicolas' gun, moved sideways, and emptied the magazine in his direction. Nicolas pressed himself against the wall, trying to become a small target. The elevator stopped when he gunned down the enemy. The elevator doors opened, and Nicolas hurried to change magazines.

He took his fighting stance behind a large flower arrangement, waiting for the gangsters to get out. He hoped they'd rely on their partner and that they were in a hurry. Upstairs, loud voices called for the police. Nicolas breathed through his mouth, staring at the light falling from the elevator into the darker hallway. There was movement inside, and a man barked a command. A second later, one person made a step forward, keeping the elevator doors from closing.

Nicolas watched as Matthew stopped on weak legs, looking left and right, breathing loudly through his nose. A tall and massive man had him in a stranglehold and was pushing him with his body one step at a time. The gangster held a gun to Matthew's head. Even in the dim light, Nicolas saw hate in his enemy's eyes.

"Don't try to stop us, G-man! One move and Monty's dead!" He glanced left and right as he pressed his body into Matthew's back and forced him through the hallway. Mathew's eyes were wide with terror.

Nicolas hesitated as long as the second killer stayed in the safety of the elevator. The massive man pushed Matthew again, then spotted his companion on the floor close to the outer doors. Spluttering Italian curses, he doubled his efforts to reach the street. Matthew stumbled and groaned when his enemy pressed the muzzle hard against his temple. The second thug left the elevator, securing both sides. Nicolas ducked behind a large palm leaf and moved to the side carefully, hoping he'd stay invisible.

Two shots hammered into the plants. One missed Nicolas by inches but tore a hole in his jacket sleeve.

"Hurry!" the second thug hollered as he ran. "Get us out of here!"

"Get down!" Nicolas shouted.

He thrust himself to the floor, slithered to the rim of the large flowerpot and shot at the massive man's upper body the same instant Matthew dropped to his knees as if the strength had left him. Matthew fell on his left side, screaming into the gag. His opponent dropped the gun as he stumbled to the side and crashed into the glass door with a deafening noise.

The second gangster shot in Nicolas' direction while running toward the exit, forcing Nicolas to stay down. He was still shooting as he tried to pull Matthew from the floor, but he wasn't strong enough. He cursed viciously upon his retreat. Nicolas pushed around the pot and shot until the magazine clicked empty. The second gangster slumped across Matthew's legs and didn't move anymore.

Slowly, as if time had stopped, Nicolas emerged from his hiding place. He changed the magazine automatically—an action meant to calm his mind and his hands. His ears rang in the sudden silence, and the smell of gunpowder was overwhelming. Nicolas' breathing came in labored hisses. With great effort, he made it to his feet to stumble unbalanced toward his partner. He crouched beside him at the end of his ropes. Matthew struggled to get away from the dead gangster but lacked the strength.

"Wait. I'll help." His voice sounded distant in his ears. He removed the duct tape from Matthew's mouth and pushed the dead gangster to the side when he realized he should check the two other men for weapons.

Both criminals were alive but badly wounded. They were no threat anymore. Nicolas collected their weapons on the way back to his partner.

"How come you were here?" Matthew asked while Nicolas cut away the tape from his wrists. "I hadn't . . ." He hung his head and licked his lips. "I thought I'd be dead in an hour."

"Your friend, Mr. Hanson, called me." Nicolas folded the knife and put it away.

Police sirens were getting louder. Upstairs, residents entered the floor and shouted for help.

"Bert? He's here?" Matthew wheezed trying to sit up. He slipped back, groaning and putting his arms across his belly. "How come he knew?"

"He's clever." Nicolas took off his jacket and folded it to put it under Matthew's head. He stayed at his side, too weak to get up, anyway. "You look even worse than before."

"Thanks to you, I'll live." Matthew touched Nicolas' wrist and dropped it again. "They'd have killed me."

Nicolas looked around, then back to his partner. Though he'd seen a lot in his years at the FBI, his hands were shaking. "Who did I shoot?"

"Chicago mob." Matthew pointed with his chin at the unconscious fat man lying three yards away in the broken door. "May I introduce Fatsy Gandolfo. He should be an honest FBI Special Agent, but in the end, he was only a miserable bugger on the mob's payroll." Their gazes met. "Don't look so astonished. I thought you'd have fun with your daily shootout."

"I could've done without." Nicolas took a deep breath, turned, and steadied himself at the wall to get up. "Police are here."

"Yeah, this will be a long night." Matthew failed to smile and wiped at his eyes. His voice was quiet. "I called Bert to spend an evening with a friend. I hadn't thought it would end like this."

"Well, being friends with you is never boring."

Chapter Twenty

Within twenty minutes, a squadron of police cars arrived. The ambulance parked right in front of the building, and Nicolas took care that Matthew wasn't interrogated by any curious officers or one of the FBI agents who showed up on orders from Senior Agent Sullivan. Nicolas answered the questions as best he could, stressing that he hadn't anticipated enemies at the house and that there had been no time to wait for reinforcements.

Residents were assured that the shootout was over and the criminals arrested. Bert came down the stairs on wobbly legs and with his face bathed in sweat, but he insisted on riding with Matthew to the hospital. Nicolas watched him enter the truck and wondered how the medics dealt with the little space left. The truck sagged as it departed from the curb.

Nicolas spent the rest of the short night coordinating the investigation and ensuring that no detail was missed. Lawrence Bilks' apartment was unlocked and the dog freed before CSU took care of the evidence. The apartment's neat appearance cloaked the hideout of a mafia killer. He had hidden three automatic shotguns and five pistols in compartments in the kitchen and the bedroom. The investigators detected grenades and a large box of ammunition in the bathroom and under a shelf in the living room. Miller appeared exuberant while he and his team took fingerprints and confirmed that even more members of the Chicago mob had visited their comrade. The search warrants were out an hour later, and Nicolas saw eagerness in his colleagues' eyes that a major breakthrough against organized crime was in reach.

The shootout left three men dead and two in critical condition, unfit for an interrogation. Nicolas demanded guards at the hospital, assuming the mob would send reinforcements from Chicago once the failed kidnapping became known. There was no debate about the charges, and the arrested killers would face long sentences.

Nicolas was most surprised by Fatsy Gandolfo's role in the crime. He couldn't believe that an FBI agent supported the mob, no matter the reward. Police and FBI forces secured evidence and left the apartment building in high spirits. Nicolas was lauded by his colleagues for his quick and decisive action. He didn't expect any praise from Senior Agent Sullivan, who didn't show up at the crime scene. However, no one had expected him to get up in the middle of the night.

The sun was already up when Nicolas returned home, on the phone with the hospital nurse who assured him that Matthew Montagna was in a stable condition. Her voice indicated she was close to giggling, and Nicolas thought of Bert and his behavior as a mother hen. He bet the portly man needled every doctor until he answered his questions. The picture made him smile upon entering the apartment.

Jacklyn welcomed him with a kiss that didn't cover her worry. She flinched, seeing the dirty jacket with a hole in the upper sleeve and his deranged look. Tears trickled down her cheeks. He kissed her back with feeling, making up for the hours he'd been in danger.

"It's all right. I'm okay, the bad men are dead, and Matt's been taken to the hospital. He'll mend. No need to worry."

"I shouldn't worry, hmm?" Jacklyn sniffled and tried to smile as she led him toward the table. "I won't worry but celebrate that you're here." She presented him with an opulent breakfast. "I thought you'd be hungry after the long night. I saw the news and—" She wiped away tears. "Nick, I'm really happy you're home."

"And I won't leave today." Nicolas took off his sweater. "If I can help it, I'll be home tomorrow or today. I'll call in sick, okay? We stay in bed and only get up when we're hungry." He took her in his arms, buried his face at her shoulder, and held her fast. "I love you, Jacky. I can't tell you how much."

Jacklyn stroked the back of his head gently. "I love you, too, my tough and wonderful Beast."

"A *diaphragmatic rupture*—that shouldn't be messed with." Bert nodded gravely as he made his way back to Matthew's bedside. He still wore his best suit but had opened the tie and top button of his dress shirt. "You'd better be glad that the surgery went so well. But you have to stay in bed and not move too much. Nurse's order." He sat on the armchair and quickly changed to another one once he couldn't squeeze his backside between the armrests.

Matthew curled his lips to a wry smile. His throat was sore. He had trouble breathing, and the injuries from Fatsy's beating had turned his body into a landscape of cuts and bruises. He preferred to lie still and be grateful that the medication took away the edge of the pain. Bert's presence lifted his mood. He hadn't known how much of a mother Bert had in him, and Matthew was glad to have such a friend.

"You only say that because you like the word." He could only whisper.

Bert handed him a cup with a straw and made him drink the warm tea.

"I could tell you a lot—about your job, your choice of neighborhood, your credulity." Bert frowned as he put the cup back. "In your job . . . shouldn't you be more cautious? Distrustful? Or was it enough that this crook had a dog? I think it was the dog." He nodded when Matthew didn't react.

"I bet Lawrence knew exactly how to draw your attention and make you comfortable. Do any of your colleagues know what he planned?"

Matthew inhaled and fought for composure. "Nerina's dead." He felt battered again with more force than before. Lawrence and Fatsy had taken turns beating him, and in between, they had described the way Nerina had been treated in prison and how the last fight had led to her death. "She was killed in a prison revolt." He wet his lips, staring at the ceiling. When Bert reached out, he took his hand. "It shouldn't bother me so much, but it does. I didn't want her to die, Bert. I never wanted her harmed, and it feels as if I'm responsible. Fatsy and Lawrence were right—I abandoned her."

Bert pursed his lips and put his right hand over Matthew's. "I know. I liked her, too, and you're right—no one wanted her dead." He sighed and hung his head. "Now that's a tough bridge to cross."

"What do you mean?" Matthew looked at his friend's concerned face. "Is there anything I should know?"

"Well, yes. I thought you . . ." He took a deep breath and moved his head left and right. "You know me. I'm a very spontaneous person, and this time I might've gone too far. I don't know how to tell you, but I told the nice lady from the dog shelter she shouldn't dare hand Bingo to anyone but you." He made a face as if expecting a slap. "Was that jumping the gun?"

"No!" Matthew regretted his outburst immediately and cringed when the pain hit him. "No, it's all right. Ouch! Such good news is simply too much." He tried to smile and squeezed Bert's hand. "Thank you. Thank you so much."

"Ah, okay." Bert patted Matthew's hand. "I won't fetch him for you. And I won't live in your apartment and take care of him. In other words—you're welcome."

Returning to the office two days after the shootout, Nicolas felt a twang of sadness looking at the empty desk. Though he longed for Jason to return to the service, he had got acquainted with Matthew. However, both would take up working at the bureau after the New Year. He sat down, remembering Jason's relief when he learned that Elaine had known all the time that he disliked her tear-jerking romance novels. She had confessed how much she loved him for his attention and effort to get to know her better.

Nicolas wrote the final conclusions about the bank robbers and polished his operational report concerning the armed conflict at Matthew's apartment building. Typing, he forgot about time and surroundings and was astonished when Dave Miller stood next to his desk.

"Can I help you?"

"It's more like—I can help you." Miller pushed a strand of hair off his forehead and handed Nicolas two pages of a report. "As I learned, you arrested two young brothers—twins if I'm correct—and killed the third brother at the *Springfield Town Center.*"

"Yes." Nicolas was confused. "This doesn't look like your final summary of the evidence."

"Well, it's not." Miller wiped his mustache and cleared his throat. "As much as I understand you want the case solved, there's something you should know. I found the fifth kind of hair in the house police raided. It belongs to a woman."

"So, one of the men had a girlfriend." Nicolas shrugged but frowned when Miller shook his head.

"No. This hair belongs to the sister of the three brothers."

"Without a doubt?"

"I tested the samples three times. So—without a doubt—there's another sibling involved in the crimes."

"And she's blonde and looks like her brothers," Nicolas

said quietly.

"She might. I can't ascertain that much, but marked similarities are possible, yes."

"Thank you." Nicolas felt a hard knot in his stomach. He took a deep breath and leaned back on his chair. "Seems like we'll have something to do in the new year."

"Well . . ." Miller cocked his head and smiled as if trying to cheer up Nicolas. "You didn't expect me to neglect this clue, did you?"

"No, of course not. You do a great job, Dr. Miller, there's no doubt about that."

"Thank you." Miller blushed and fought with the loose strand of hair again. "I wish you a blessed Christmas."

"The same to you." Nicolas pondered where the sister might spend Christmas and whether she'd read the papers to find out that Manny was dead and the twins were in custody awaiting trial. He wondered whether she'd stay in hiding or develop a plan to help them escape.

Given her cleverness, he hadn't much hope to find her as easily as her brothers unless she left her hideout to take action. "And no good New Year to me."

The End

YOU MAY ALSO ENJOY THE FOLLOWING FROM eXTASY BOOKS INC:

Project Recruitment
Ann Raina

Excerpt

The tall, brown-haired woman with the touchpad had a steady, melodious voice that carried through the hall. She greeted the more than one hundred men who gathered on the chairs and benches in the small town hall. All of them were noicy and most men were agitated, some bragging of their abilities. Most of them had put on their best clothes, though no one could tell in advance what the Olis family wanted or who would be chosen. The young woman with the ponytail scanned the groups out of large blue eyes. On elegant shoes, she carefully walked up and down the small stage as if waiting for a signal. When the noise settled, she pointed to the large screen behind her, smiled at the audience and answered questions before she came to her main presentation.

"Welcome again to the Olis program for local development to improve life conditions. My name is Pilanui, and I will guide you through the main topics. The program calls to all young men no older than thirty Drysilas-moon phases. The program will last for one moon phase and is to be continued if needed. All of you who apply today will sign a contract for one moon phase. The second one is on a free-will basis. The payment is comparable to the income of a medium-corporation owner, which means most of you will earn more money in one season than you might in ten while working in the fields." She smiled and waited for the hooting to end. Many young men could not read and write, but letters and numbers were not necessary if the payment would fit. "The program demands that the members live in a controlled environment all the time. There are no exceptions. If one of you leaves the test area, he will be expelled immediately and will not earn any money."

"What's the program about?" one man shouted from a row behind Sidarra.

The woman lifted her gaze and then put on an even warmer smile before she continued. "We want to test and compare the development of health in young males if they live in a surrounding that hardly changes. We will take all of your personal data as a start, and will follow the development during different test phases. In the end, we will know what kind of environment suits men best and how your health can be improved by living conditions and nutrition. You will work during the moon phase, and all harvests of fruits and vegetables will be distributed to the inhabitants of this area. Some of you will even learn new skills from handymen we'll bring along."

More hooting and some rude offers followed, yet her smile never wavered.

"What kind of tests will you run with us?" another man wanted to know.

The young woman swung around to face him. "We will collect data on your internal organs, blood cells and how your bodily functions change due to work-rest times, nutrition and external stimulation. The test series will be repeated frequently to get a consistent overview."

"Why only men?"

She turned her head, touched the pad and the screen behind her showed the list of test series the program included, illustrated by some short scenes showing men while their blood pressure was taken. Few men even spared it a glance. "This is the first program, young man. Another one will follow."

"Why did you come here with this program? Why did you not do it on your continent?" Sidarra asked.

The woman looked at him with clear eyes, very self-confident, still smiling and helpful in her tone. "The programs released on Telendalan were very successful. The resulting data on more than one thousand men led to changes in living abodes and cultivation. Our people are healthier and live longer due to better nutrition. We want to bring our experience to Ellendalis and help your people share the same improvements."

"Will all men be accepted?"

"The program has its limits. We cannot accept more than fifty persons at this time. But for those who cannot join today, we will make sure that another test area will be equipped to take them up." She lowered her touchpad and looked around. "Are there more questions? If not, I would like to introduce you to Piteroi. He will help you fill out the application form. Please, there is no need to hurry. All applications will be read and evaluated. After all applications have been filed, you will receive an answer. Thank you."

She left, and Piteroi entered the stage and set up a tall table and a computer. "Please, step forward in single file."

Najodai held Sidarra back when he stood to follow the stream down the aisle. The noise level reached a deafening degree, and Najodai had to scream to be heard. "Are you sure you want to do this? She hasn't told you much about what will be done to you."

His friend shook off his hand. "Leave me alone with your permanent distrust. Please, don't you understand? I need the money. And if it's just some tests and blood samples, I can stand that."

"You cannot leave even if you want to, don't forget that."

"Isn't it the same here? I cannot leave this village without any money. And if I want to see Yisnia again, I need some coin. And can I get it anywhere else? Not at all. Right. I know so. I tried."

Najodai took a deep breath and remained on his seat. He looked around and saw some men leave without signing up. He admired them for their courage. Money was always needed, and the village, Ethisan, had no large corporations to offer employment. They had some agriculture, some forests, and some handicraft businesses in this dry and desolate area. Wells were few and water costly. The inhabitants envied the few who made it to the city. However, if you had learned nothing the employers in the city needed, you had no chance to get a job, as Sidarra had experienced. It was a spiral, the snake that bit its tail. From what he knew, there were many homeless and sick people roaming the city streets.

He leaned back, watching the long row of men and his friend in between.

The offer from Olis of Telendalan had hit the village like a hammer. The largest corporation ever known to man was about to set foot into the poor region along the Ethis-swale. First, they had erected tents, then a large area had been cleared for a huge roof that spanned from the rim of the depression to the horizon. And when everything was settled and the rumors had spread wider than the roof, the Olis family had started their advertisement program on the local channels. The show had been teasing, huge, overwhelming. Their offer made the mouths of the young men water. It was a one-time chance to get acknowledged, to become someone beyond being a farmer or handyman and get rich in the meantime.

Sidarra had always wanted to be a trained clerk, someone to work in a large building with other intelligent beings around. On a trip to the big city, he had met Yisnia, and his longing to change his situation had become an obsession.

The woman was the daughter of a rich farm-machine dealer who lived close to the city. They had stumbled into each other, Sidarra had reported. Of course, she had been reading a pad, and he had looked heavenward at the towers and their sparkling ads, though he could not read them. And then, as if they had both felt it, they had smiled at each other and fallen in love.

It wasn't long before she visited him, and she never commented on his small hut or the simple clothes he wore. She had even given up wearing her tight skirts and fancy shoes and had worn simple dresses, boots and blouses. Sidarra had been grateful and intrigued by her. She had talked little about her family, but for an intelligent man like Sidarra, it was not hard to guess that the rich and influential family would never allow their only daughter to be together with a poor, untrained farm helper from Ethisan.

Najodai remembered the days and nights Yisnia had stayed. When Sidarra had left to buy bread, she had secretly told him that her father had already arranged a match with an equally rich son of a high-standing family. She would have preferred to move to the village over getting involved with some rich guy, but family demands were hard to ignore. Najodai had listened with astonishment. Then she had laughed and stroked his cheek, a gesture he cherished as much as her quick smile and her positive view of life. She matched Sidarra with every fiber of her being.

When her vacation was over, Sidarra had accompanied her as far as the outer rim of the valley to say goodbye. Najodai had never seen his friend so sad, and he had not had the heart to tell him that Yisnia might go on with her life without looking back.

The line was getting shorter, and Sidarra was the next to sign up.

Najodai grimaced. He could not lose the strange feeling in his guts that there had to be something wrong. Why should a large corporation offer something for free? In his lifetime, he had seen employers who had ripped people off. Why should Olis be different?

He wiped his eyes, sighing. Sidarra had always had things his way. He was stubborn beyond reason and at the same time warm-hearted and reliable. He was a good friend, someone to talk to and do crazy things with.

It would be a lonely moon phase without him.

About the Author

Ann Raina lives and works in Germany with cats and a horse. Riding and writing are her favorite hobbies. Her latest series, starting with *Twisted Mind,* is about an FBI agent, his demanding lover, and cases of violent crime.

In all her books she combines romance, suspense, and humorous elements, for no thrilling story can stand without a comic relief.

For contact turn to annraina@yahoo.com

On Facebook https://www.facebook.com/ann.raina.7

www.ingramcontent.com/pod-product-compliance
Lightning Source LLC
Chambersburg PA
CBHW071306170626
46809CB00001B/349